Praise for *First Serve*

"*First Serve* is the lyrical, heartwarming, and inspiring story of three women whose friendship and courage help them navigate the challenges of high-stakes professional tennis, racism, physical trauma, and a long-missing father to come out the other side stronger, wiser, and closer than ever."

— Peter Guzzardi
Author of *Emeralds of Oz: Life Lessons From Over the Rainbow* and former editor at Random House, Inc.

∾

"Cynthia Suzanne Sauer writes an engaging novel that captivates. It was enjoyable to read the story from start to finish. I, particularly, loved the many twists and turns and the recognizable parts of the tennis scene—from tournaments to people to clubs. Well done, Cynthia."

— Kim Bastable, MS, USPTA, PTR
Professor of Practice and Director of Professional Tennis Management, University of Florida

∾

"Cynthia Suzanne Sauer takes us on a journey of self-reflection and self-discovery in her novel, *First Serve*. Through the main character's story, we are compelled to question our own moral compass and reflect on the choices that we make that ultimately shape our future. As a high-performance coach for over thirty years, I value the tremendous impact that we have on the lives of those we coach. Cynthia's messaging around friendship, prejudice, tragedy, and redemption exposes the truth about human decency and what it really means to unleash human potential. This is a must-read for not only tennis enthusiasts but for coaches, parents, and teenagers alike because there is hope and a bright future through the connection of sport and friendship for all."

— **Emma Doyle**
International High-Performance Coach, Author, Speaker & Owner of Open Door Coaching USA

First Serve

Acing Life

A Novel

Cynthia Suzanne Sauer

AquaZebra™
Book Publishing
Cathedral City, CA

First paperback edition September, 2023

Book design by AquaZebra

AquaZebra™
Web, Book & Print Design

Cover photo by Ryan Searle on Unsplash

Library of Congress Control Number: 2023941802

ISBN 978-1-954604-09-4 (paperback)
ISBN 978-1-954604-11-7 (hardback)

Published by AquaZebra

AquaZebra™
Book Publishing
35070 Maria Rd
Cathedral City, CA 92234
mark@aquazebra.com

Cynthia Suzanne Sauer
CynthiaSuzanneSauer@gmail.com

Dedication

To My Parents, Theodor and Suzanne Sauer,
Who Inspired Me To Never Give Up.

Chapter 1

Long Island, New York—Early 1960s

I opened the front door of my elementary school and walked in to begin fifth grade. My stomach was in a knot. All I hoped for was some peace and quiet. As I rounded the corner to enter the long hallway to my classroom, I saw them: the same pack of five girls who had made my life miserable in school last year. They were already snickering, and they quickly closed in on me.

Here we go again. My heart began to race in my chest—a familiar feeling. The same pain.

"Look, 'It' came back," the tallest girl said.

I hated when they called me that name—'It'.

"What's taking you so long, 'It'?" another giggled. "Can't you walk faster?"

The tall girl grabbed my wrist and twisted it hard.

"Ow! Let me go." I yanked my arm free but threw myself off-balance and crashed onto the hard floor. A sudden, sharp jab of pain shot from my hip to my lower leg. Tears threatened to humiliate me even more, but I held them back.

"Hey, leave her alone!"

I knew that voice. My best buddy, Joanne, lifted me up. "You okay?" I nodded. She spun, as balanced as a dancer, and got into the girl's face. "Don't do that ever again."

"Oooh . . .who cares about 'It'?"

Joanne leaned so close, the other girl was up against the wall. "I do."

"She's weird. Join us instead," a third girl said.

"No. Why would I do that? She's my friend." Joanne quickly turned toward me and hooked her arm into mine. "Let's go, Lucie."

The bell rang. *Oh boy, late for class.* Joanne took my trembling arm and walked with me all the way to class. I hesitated before entering.

"Come on. It's okay." Joanne smiled, nudged me forward, and helped me to my seat in the back row.

"Thanks, Jo."

I took a deep breath. Joanne Kelsch never cared how I walked. She never asked why my hips sometimes swiveled too far around. She only knew I was different. Many times when I stumbled, Joanne would be right there, patiently waiting while I worked it out myself. Never pushy. She just wanted to help me walk straighter. There was a steadiness about Joanne, as if all the storms on Long Island were only a whispering breeze. I was anything but steady. She was kind, and also clever; perhaps that's what drew people to her. Yet she chose me to be her best friend, and I had no idea why. We met in Brownies, and were inseparable.

Joanne and I met after school at our usual spot. From the tall pine trees overlooking the athletic fields, we'd walk home together. I leaned against one of the trees waiting for her. I tried to forget what happened earlier in the day, but something told me I needed Joanne now more than ever. She arrived a few minutes later and suggested we take the long route down and up a gentle slope. The stand of maple trees looked so pretty with leaves beginning to turn red.

We walked for a while before I said, "I'm getting a little tired, Jo. Can we cut through the woods?"

"Sure." She veered onto the dirt path that offered the fewest trip hazards.

We passed a woman walking her basset hound and stopped to pet the sweet dog. I loved our dog, Stretch, a dachshund. I walked him most days around the neighborhood.

We didn't linger too long with the hound dog because the wind had picked up, and we still needed to reach the open field toward home. Several yards ahead, the path narrowed.

"Well, look who's here!"

The girl from school who'd twisted my wrist leaped out from behind a tree. My heart pounded so fast, I thought I'd faint.

"Hello, 'It' and guard dog," she said.

Two other girls rushed from the other side and pushed Joanne to the ground. They shoved me into the dirt. They ran off through the woods before we could fight back. I looked over at Joanne. I spit out a mouthful of dirt. "You okay?"

"Yeah. You?"

"Yes." I swiped the dirt off my stained skirt and struggled to stand. My feet didn't want to work. "I hate them."

"Me, too. Here, let me help." Joanne tried to pull me up, but we fell over each other and smacked the ground again. We laughed and couldn't stop. She tried again and pulled me up.

"Thanks, Jo," I said.

She looked down at her dirty dress. "Mom's going to kill me; it's brand new."

"Don't worry, Jo. We can change clothes before my mom comes home."

"When's that?"

"About an hour."

"I need to call my mom when we get to your house and tell her I'm with you."

~

After Joanne called her mother, we headed for my bedroom above the garage and plopped down on the bed.

"Luce, I lied to my mother and told her your mom was here."

"Well, at least she didn't ask to speak to her." I rose from my bed to the tall dresser and took out two T-shirts.

"Here, try this Nancy Drew T-shirt on. It's new. I have one just like it, except mine is kind of ratty. See?" I proudly held it up in front of me. "Mom wanted to throw it out, but I kept the T-shirt. It's my favorite."

"Cool! Thanks, Luce. It's so soft."

"That's why I like it so much. Here, try on these shorts; they should fit."

"Thanks. Hey, I got an idea. Since it's Friday night, maybe I can stay over tonight."

I hesitated. Joanne arched her brow. "Or maybe that's a dumb idea."

I couldn't spit out any words.

"Well, never mind," she said with a shrug.

"No, wait," I said. "It's just that . . . I have to tell you something first. A secret."

"Really?" She leaned forward. "I'm ready. What secret?"

"You have to promise not to tell anyone else."

Joanne rolled her eyes. "Duh. I know what a secret is."

"I'm serious. Pinkie swear."

We linked pinkie fingers. "I promise," she said.

I took a deep breath and slipped my hand underneath the bed. The eighteen-inch steel bar was cold. I grabbed the orthopedic, high-top, laced shoes attached to each end of the bar. Proof that I was different. Damaged goods. I had never told a soul. Slowly, I pulled out my shame, the leg brace. My heart pounded so hard I could barely hear my own whisper. I handed her the brace.

Joanne went wide-eyed. "What's that?

"My leg brace. I wear it every night to correct my hip defect."

She stared at the brace, then at me. "Can I try it on?"

"What for?"

"To see what it's like to be you."

I choked back tears.

"Show me how to put them on."

I did.

"How can you sleep with these? They're super stiff. How do you turn over?"

"It's hard. Sometimes I take them off without telling Mom."

"No wonder you're grumpy!" We laughed.

"Lucie, I'm home," Mom called out. She worked at the local college library as a secretary to the director and was often home by three or four o'clock. The college was only ten minutes from our house.

"Be right down, Mom. Jo's here too."

❧

"Hi, Mrs. Sampson."

"Hello, dear. Oh, I see you two have twin shirts on." Mom smiled. "Lucie, have you offered Joanne a snack?

"Uh, no. We've been busy. Mom, do you think Jo can stay over tonight? It's Friday."

"Why, yes, of course. Give your Mom a call, Joanne, to see if it's okay with her. Phone's at the end of the hallway."

Joanne returned a few minutes later happy as a clown. "Mrs. Sampson, my Mom said it would be fine, but I have to be home by 9:00 tomorrow morning. She'll bring over my pj's and toothbrush later."

"Good!" My mom nodded. "We always enjoy your company."

❧

After dinner we returned to my bedroom and Joanne closed the door. We sat opposite each other on the twin beds.

"Luce, my Mom's been acting a little strange lately."

"Strange? How?"

"The other night I overheard Mom and Dad talking. We might . . . might be moving."

My arms fell limp. I looked at her. "You mean, like, to another house?"

"I don't know. They were whispering when I passed their bedroom. The door was closed. Sounded like some big secret. I don't know anything else."

"Oh, gosh," I said with a sigh. "Tell me when you know something."

We played Monopoly on the floor with the property cards and money bills alongside us. It was about eight o'clock when I saw headlights beam through the window as a car pulled up our driveway. "I guess your mom's here, Jo."

"Let's finish this game first; I'm winning. Besides, our moms can chat a bit."

It took us forever to finish Monopoly, and once again, Joanne won. I looked over at the clock on my night table . . . nine o'clock.

We were putting the game away when a knock at the door surprised us. "Come in," I said.

"Hi, girls." Dad smiled at Joanne. "Your father dropped off your toothbrush and things."

"My Dad? That's weird, 'cause he works the late shift on Fridays, till midnight. You talked with him, Mr. Sampson?"

He nodded. "Lights out by ten, girls. Joanne has to be home by nine tomorrow morning."

Chapter 2

On Sunday afternoons, Dad and I raked leaves. He said the exercise would do me good. He was athletic and the most handsome Dad a little girl could ask for. I got my blue eyes from him and his wavy hair. But Dad's smile was all his own, broad and happy. When he spoke, the smile I'd hear in his voice was relaxed. "Autumn days fall by as quickly as the leaves from the trees. Enjoy them while you can." And so I did.

I loved shuffling through the leaves and feeling them crunch beneath my feet. The leaves danced from branch to ground while I walked three short blocks to Joanne's house. It was Joanne's eleventh birthday, and I was excited to give her a homemade gift, a four-inch, wooden duck that Dad helped me carve in his basement workshop. The duck felt smooth in my hands when I carved the wood.

The skies darkened. A few cold sprinkles of rain touched my neck. I shivered, hurrying around the corner to Joanne's street. I ran up to Joanne's front door.

A neighbor's voice from over the hedge startled me. "That family moved away."

I never knew a heart could stop beating, but mine did at that very moment. I mumbled, "Where to?"

The neighbor shrugged his shoulders. "I don't know."

"Do you know the town?"

"Sorry. They cleared out yesterday morning."

Tears slipped down my cheek. A blister on my thumb from raking leaves throbbed along with my heart.

The walk home took forever. *Why didn't Jo call me? What happened? Didn't her father like me? Our mothers get along just fine—maybe because of their French heritage. Joanne's mother was always kind to me.* My thoughts raced as my heart cried out for understanding.

For the last two summers, she'd invited me to spend one week with them at their bungalow in Long Beach, New York. Joanne and I spent hours swimming close to the water's edge and riding our bikes on the boardwalk. On rainy days, we acted out Nancy Drew mysteries and short skits that Joanne wrote, or we pitched in with chores around the bungalow. I remember the day Joanne rode too close to the curb and fell off her bike. She'd needed six stitches on her right cheek. Every once in a while, she'd touch her cheek to see if the little scar had disappeared. It hadn't. When my right hip ached, we'd sit under the shade of tall pine trees tracing pictures in the dusty dirt with fallen tree branches.

I stumbled home and collapsed into my mother's arms. "Mom, she's gone. She left without telling me where she was going. I never got to say goodbye."

Mom rubbed my back. "I'm so sorry."

Joanne was funny, sporty, full of life. How was I going to live without the dimpled smile that brightened everyone around her? Her lessons on listening to seagulls and walking straighter. Or, how to spread peanut butter on toast so it could melt in your mouth. How could I live without my best friend, the one who would help me when I stumbled through life?

I burst into tears.

"What happened?" Dad asked as he entered the living room.

"Joanne and her family moved away," Mom said.

He scratched the back of his head. "Oh, I see."

"Charles, are you all right?" my mom asked.

"Yes . . . fine, dear. I'm so sorry, Lucie."

I fully expected Dad's arms to wrap around me because he was a world-class hugger. I remember the way he fidgeted with his watch—and the color that had drained from his face.

Two weeks had passed since Joanne moved away; the light was extinguished from our walks home together. I tried to walk straight without swiveling my hips too much, but I felt unsteady. I shook, knowing I was on my own.

"Hey, Mom." I took off my sweater, threw it on the kitchen chair and pushed up my blouse sleeves to wash my hands.

"Lucie, what's that bruise on your arm?" Mom asked. "Did you fall, sweetie?"

I loved her beautiful face and kindly smile, but I knew she ruled the house.

"No, not really."

"What then?" she asked, studying my arm.

"It's nothing."

"It surely isn't nothing."

"It's nothing, really." I started to walk away.

"Don't walk away from me, young lady. What happened? Come sit and let me have a closer look."

"A girl pushed me into my locker, that's all."

"What! Who did it? Why would she do such a thing?" Mom pulled up a chair next to me at the kitchen table and softly touched my bruised arm.

"She likes calling me 'It'."

"'It'? Good God, how awful."

"I try to ignore the name, but today—well, I just couldn't. I stiffened and headed toward her." Like Joanne would have done.

"That's when she pushed me."

"Is this the first time she called you that?"

My voice quivered. "No. Other kids call me 'It' too. Started in fourth grade. They talk about me in whispers. Like they're telling secrets, but loud enough for me to hear. When they call me that, I walk away."

"I'm going to speak to the principal about this. It's not right."

"Please, don't," I begged.

"I will make an appointment to see him. That's final."

I stomped out of the kitchen, yelling. "Thanks a lot, Mom! Just what I need!"

The next evening, when I took the steps up to my second-floor bedroom, I overheard Mom and Dad talking in their room. The door was closed, but Mom's raised voice made it clear she was angry. She told Dad she met with the principal that morning, who believed it was just kids being kids. He promised to monitor my classmates' behavior and keep a watch over me.

Hearing that, I wanted to dissolve into a little pile of dust in each of my shoes.

"We need to find a way to protect her, or else she'll retreat into her bedroom and withdraw from her classmates," Mom said. "She already spends too much time in her bedroom."

"It's hard to protect her entirely, dear. You know that." Dad's voice was softer than Mom's.

"At least lessen her pain then," she said. "I think I know a way."

"Which is?" Dad asked.

Their voices faded, so I entered my room and closed the door. I changed into my flannel pj's, climbed into bed, and strapped on the leg brace. I hardly slept that night as the cinching of the straps sent pain through my hips and down my bony legs.

Chapter 3

Thanksgiving became my favorite holiday that year. Not because I loved turkey or because I had so much to be grateful for, but because I had four blessed days of relief from school. But right after the Thanksgiving holiday, Mom mentioned an article she'd read in the local newspaper.

"*The Town Beacon* announced it's looking for young people to help with a project raising money for the local March of Dimes chapter. You go door to door and ask neighbors on the weekends if they would like to buy Christmas napkins. It's for a good cause, helping people who have orthopedic difficulties. Would you like to do that?"

"Not really," I grumbled.

"Well, it might take your mind off those 'It' comments. Dr. Fetner said to walk as much as possible. Did you know that the March of Dimes helped pay for your leg braces?"

Her voice was too bright, in that way it always was when she was trying to pull something over on me. Only then did I remember hearing her through the closed bedroom door, saying to Dad a while back that she might know a way to "lessen her pain."

Bingo.

March of Dimes, Dr. Fetner, helping people with problems like mine—wow, she'd covered all the bases. And she'd gotten it in the paper, too. I'd be a real heel to say no.

"Why not give it a try? Might cheer you up a bit.
"Do I have to?"
"Yes."

～

I started the following Saturday. I dragged our Radio Flyer garden wagon from door to door, ringing our neighbors' doorbells in the hope that a neighbor would buy napkins for a good cause.

Each napkin had a different Christmas carol printed on the front and back in red and green: *Joy to the World, Go Tell It on the Mountain,* and *Angels We Have Heard on High.* Most neighbors bought at least two packages.

I stopped short of the house at the end of the block. The front yard looked like one big weed patch, and the two tall maple trees kept the entrance dark, even when it was sunny outside. The roof had tiles missing and the chipped window shutters were closed. The kids on the block never went close to that house, especially at Halloween. No way was I going to knock on that door.

I returned home, cold and a bit hungry. "I'm done. Did the whole block."

"Did everyone buy some?" Mom asked enthusiastically.

"Everyone I asked." The kitchen smelled of sweet gingerbread, my favorite snack my mom made.

"Who wasn't home?" she asked.

"I never knocked at the house at the end of the street."

"Why?"

"It's creepy. She probably can't afford fancy napkins anyway. No way I'm going near it."

I reached for the gingerbread. Mom swatted my hand away.

"You most certainly *are* going there. Just because the front yard isn't all that nice doesn't mean the person inside isn't nice. You of all people shouldn't judge on appearances. Now go on back to that house, knock on the front door, and introduce yourself. Still plenty of light outside."

I stomped my foot and left the kitchen. I paced by the front door trying to think of how I could avoid this, but the lack of gingerbread in my future was a powerful motivator.

I stuffed two napkin packages in my winter coat, pulled my woolen beanie over my ears, braved the bitter cold, and made my way to the end of the block. I tripped over some branches on the way and wanted to hightail it back home, but I took a quick breath and rang the doorbell. Nothing happened. Rang it again. Nothing. I knocked on the door one last time and heard footsteps inside. The door partially opened.

"Yes?" Her eyes searched mine. "Do I know you?" Her eyebrows knitted, but she half-smiled at me.

"Hello, ma'am. My name is Lucie Sampson. I live at the other end of the block." I pointed in the direction. "I'm selling Christmas napkins for the March of Dimes." I took out the two packages and showed the woman both sides. "Fifty cents a package. Would you like to buy one?"

It was then when she fully opened the door that I realized she was old—terribly old. A little bent over, wrinkles everywhere on her face, and wavy gray hair. She wore a green and black plaid housedress with a frayed green shawl.

"Of course," she said cheerfully. "Wait here, I'll get my purse." She left me shivering there a long time, and when she returned with a small, green change purse, her knobby fingers found it hard to twist open the gold clasp. She tossed her hair out of her face and tried again. Success. "Here's two quarters for one package." Her warm smile brightened my spirits. "What did you say your name was again?"

"Lucie Sampson. I live at the end of this block."

"How nice of you to knock on my door. And nice what you are doing for the March of Dimes." She tried to straighten her back, but couldn't.

"Thank you, ma'am." I reached into my jacket pocket, grabbed the second package and handed it to her. "For you. Merry Christmas," I smiled broadly.

"Well, thank you, Lucie. Merry Christmas to you, too."

I walked down the path and turned to wave goodbye before heading home.

Once I was back home, I couldn't wait to tell Mom. "She wasn't crabby at all. She was really nice."

"Yes, she is."

"You know her?" I tilted my head, confused. "Why didn't you tell me before?"

"Her name is Mrs. Bezdek. Her husband passed away six months ago. She's a lovely lady. Her grandson has difficulty walking."

"Like me?"

"Well, he has to wear braces during the day. He can't walk without them."

"Oh no."

She handed me a mug of hot chocolate. I eyed the gingerbread. "After dinner."

Chapter 4

Throughout the winter months, my walking hadn't improved very much, and my legs and hip still ached. Dr. Fetner explained the problem. I had hip dysplasia that made me severely pigeon-toed. I thought my toes were the best part of my wonky legs, frankly, but he said it just meant that the front part of my feet turned inward. My hip socket and thigh bone were not properly aligned, and my hip socket was shallow. Dr. Fetner recommended physical therapy to improve my range of motion in the hip and strengthen the muscles that stabilized the joint. Unfortunately, he ordered me to continue wearing the night brace for another year. I dreamed of the day when I could throw away the brace with its punishing screw heads.

Going to physical therapy twice a week for forty-five minutes after school was tedious and felt like torture except when the physical therapist started with gentle hip circle stretches. After a few minutes, the exercise routine began.

"First, the Abduction Lift. Lie on your side," Jacob said. "You need to lift your top leg twelve inches from your bottom leg, then lower it. Don't let your legs touch." I gave it a try. "Stop. Your legs are touching. Do it again." I tried again with more success. "There you go. Keep doing them for eight repetitions." I followed his instruction. "Nice job. Rest."

"Can I rest a little longer I'm tired."

"No. Turn over on your other side and do the same exercise." I obeyed. "That's it. Good technique. Eight reps like before." I did the lifts. "Now you can rest, Lucie."

"Thanks."

"Next exercise is Abduction Lifts with Internal Rotation. Repeat what you just did, but turn in your top knee and foot. Got it?" Jacob asked.

"I think so."

"Do eight reps." I pushed through the moves. "Good, looking good. Okay, stop. Now rest."

"Phew. This isn't easy."

"Get used to it, Lucie, if you want to get stronger. Now, flip over and do the same exercise." I rolled over. "Don't slouch your shoulders. That's it. Nice." I relaxed. "The last exercise is called the Fire Hydrant Bent Knee Abduction Lift. This one will be harder for you. We'll take it slow. Lift your leg up without rolling your hips back. Start and end with your top leg parallel to the floor. Let me demonstrate."

I stared at him, my eyes bulging. "How am I going to do that?" I asked with total disbelief.

"I'll hold you until you're steady. You'll be just fine," he said in his most encouraging voice.

I felt reassured, like Joanne's spirit was returning.

"Good, you got it," he affirmed. "Repeat. Nope, try again and keep your leg parallel to the floor. Try again," he said. I struggled. "Slow down; let your muscles work." I slowed down and focused. "You got it now. Do eight reps." These were a major challenge. "There you go! Rest for a minute. Turn over and do the same thing. You're doing just fine, but you got to keep at it," he explained.

∿

As the months progressed into spring, I felt better, a bit stronger and steadier. Sort of like an athlete. Dad must have noticed my improvement because one morning in May he asked me if I wanted to go to the tennis club and watch him play with a friend.

"Sure, why not."

The sun warmed my shoulders as I sat on the hill to get a better view. Blades of grass tickled my ankles, and the idea of what I was about to see tickled my insides: my very first tennis match.

Dad looked up and waved from the red clay court, where he was about to play against his old college buddy. I tracked the ball as they hit it back and forth with their wooden racquets. Up to the net for a short ball. Backwards to hit a deep one. Calves flexing as they moved side to side, corner to corner. Dusty red clay sprinkled his white socks when he slid to reach a ball. Dad was lightning-fast as he chased that ball. Sometimes he'd hit it right back to his buddy; other times, he'd flick the ball just over the net so his buddy couldn't reach it. I loved the arch of his back when he'd stretched up for a serve.

He slammed one serve so fast I didn't even see it. Neither did his opponent; the ball whizzed right by him. Dad won the point.

"Way to go, Dad!" I shouted. Every pop that ball made when he hit it was a little burst in my heart that made me feel more alive.

"Fifteen-love," he said.

Love. That's exactly what I was feeling.

My body twitched with excitement. I didn't know how they didn't trip. I sure would have. Everything was so quick.

When they took a break over by the big tree, Dad wiped sweat from his face with a towel. I think I was sweating as much as he was. My hands stung from clapping. I jumped up despite the jolt of pain in my hip I knew would come. I didn't care. A new hope tingled in my heart.

On the drive back home, I asked Dad, "Would you teach me how to play?"

"Oh, I don't know. It's . . . it's too risky."

"Please, Daddy. I can do it. I know I can."

He kept his eyes straight on the road. "Not now, honey."

"I'm almost eleven. I want to have fun like that, too."

"Maybe someday, Lucie."

Later that evening I was in bed and thumbing through Dad's book about the U.S. Tennis Nationals at Forest Hills. There was a side-view photograph of Alice Marble arching her back to serve the ball. She looked so graceful. I'd never heard of her. Mom came in to say goodnight.

I showed her the book. "Have you ever heard of Alice Marble?"

"Oh, yes. A famous tennis player years ago. She won Wimbledon."

"What's Wimbledon?"

"The most famous tennis tournament in the world."

"Oh, wow." I scooched up in bed. "She must've been really good."

"Yes, she was. Photographs of her were in all the newspapers and magazines. Here are the blouses I've finished ironing. Since you're already in bed, I'll hang them up for you."

"Thanks."

Mom took her sweet time in my closet. She finally said, "Why are these all the way in the back of your closet?" She turned around, holding my leg brace.

I was supposed to wear them every night. "I don't like them." That was a fib—I hated them. "The metal bar stiffens my ankles. It's hard to sleep with them."

She sat down at the edge of my bed. "You need to wear them. Doctor's orders."

"But whenever I try to turn over, the screw on the brace snags the sheet. This hot pain shoots up my leg. I get all tangled up."

She rubbed my legs. "Maybe your father can smooth out the screws."

I couldn't look at her.

"Lucie, don't you wear them at all?"

I gave a half-shrug with one shoulder. That was pretty much the truth. "Some days I do, but they don't do any good."

"You don't know that sweetie. You need to give it time."

"How much time?"

"I don't know for sure. You're just starting your second year wearing them. Small changes become bigger changes. After a while, you'll notice a difference. It will get better."

"Promise?"

She nodded. "Here, let me help you put them on." She kissed my forehead, and before she closed the door she said. "Sweet dreams."

I flipped through a few more pages of Dad's book until I came to another photo of Alice Marble. The caption read, *Miss Alice Marble from California, the 1940 US Nationals Ladies Singles Champion.* That night, I dreamed that my body had grown so strong that, one day, I'd be able to play tennis just like Alice Marble.

∼

At my next appointment with Dr. Fetner, I asked if I could try playing tennis. He said not yet. I was about to crawl out of my skin with impatience. If I was going to be a competitive tennis player, I'd need to start training soon.

I stood up from the examining table. "So when, then?"

"Well, you can give it a try, but wait until midsummer," the doctor said. "Start slow and easy. Do your stretching exercises before and after you play. Continue your physical therapy. The goal is to minimize your hip from over-rotating." He paused. "One last thing, Lucie. Don't stop wearing the leg braces at night."

With Dr. Fetner's cautious go-ahead, Dad brought me to the club tennis courts two months later to run and swing at the tennis ball. The mid-July afternoon was bright with a gentle breeze. We started slowly by playing half-court, hitting the ball from the service line.

I took to the sport immediately. Something about tennis freed me. I didn't feel self-conscious about how I moved. I ran until I'd trip over my own two feet, which was often. No matter; I'd pick myself up and try again and again. When I focused more on the ball rather than on my hip or feet, I usually hit it over the net. What an exhilarating feeling to hit the ball clean and pure. We played for about twenty minutes, gradually working our way back to the baseline and starting a rally from there.

When I started to trip, Dad said I'd had enough. But I didn't want to stop! I had a fire in my belly that I'd never known before. As a compromise, he suggested I hit against the club's fenced-in backboard. "To develop a feel for stroking the ball," he said. I loved hearing the ball hit the racquet strings over and over.

That summer before entering sixth grade, I hit against the backboard every other day. I began by setting my feet properly, about ten inches apart, and pushing off with one foot then the other. Sidestepping drills proved frustrating as I couldn't figure out how to stop stumbling. My steps were either too narrow or too wide. I tried to hear Joanne gently telling me what I was doing wrong and encouraging me when I was successful.

Running short, wind sprints forward and back were easier for me. After the footwork routine, I'd hit forehands and backhands against the backboard, and then sprinkle in a few quick volleys. My legs were exhausted, but I enjoyed it too much to stop. Backhand balls sometimes flew over the fence, as my skinny arms didn't seem to have the strength to swing the backhand correctly. That's when my temper flared. Frustrated, I chucked my racquet against the wall and broke it.

Later that day I received my first punishment and lecture from my parents about respecting property and controlling my temper. They were kind enough to buy me a used racquet, but they warned me that the next time I broke a racquet, I would have to pay for it on my own. Fair enough.

I kept hitting against the backboard that summer, hoping to improve my footwork and swing. To my delight, hitting the ball seemed to soften the hurt of losing Joanne. One afternoon while I was practicing against the backboard, the club's tennis pro, Mr. Martin, approached me. He was a soft-spoken man, tall and lanky.

"Hi, Lucie," he said with a big smile. "Want to come on the tennis court and hit a few balls for fifteen minutes until my next lesson comes?"

"Are you kidding? Sure, Mr. Martin." I was so grateful he'd asked.

The ball came across the net more slowly than when hitting against the backboard, which gave my legs time to reach the ball and swing freely. Mr. Martin gave me two pointers: get the racquet back sooner and keep my eye on the ball. Those fifteen minutes raced by, and I knew that this kind man could help me become a much better player.

The following week, on my eleventh birthday, my parents surprised me with a gift: thirty-minute tennis lessons twice a week with Mr. Martin. I thought I'd die of happiness! During those weeks of lessons and practice, my legs ached, but I felt them getting stronger, so I decided to stop wearing the leg brace. Mom, ever protective, scolded me when she found out.

"No brace, no tennis," she declared.

From then on, I laced up the brace every night, and I played tennis that summer as often as my legs, Dr. Fetner, and Mom would allow.

Each day, I hoped to find a letter from Joanne in our mailbox, but none ever came. It was time for me to forget about her. Tennis became my new best friend.

I continued practicing every other day against the backboard and occasionally with Dad. Down-the-line forehands and backhands, cross-court forehands and backhands, net play, and the serve. I hated the serve. I could never toss the ball up to the same place and hit it squarely each time, and I could never get my right hip around like Mr. Martin wanted. Tossing the tennis ball hundreds of times into the air at the same place so that you hit the serve consistently bored me. No wonder I didn't practice the service motion very much. It became my worst stroke. No surprise.

As my legs became stronger, so did my strokes, allowing me to rally for longer periods with Dad or Mr. Martin. But often I'd shorten a rally because I feared tripping and possibly falling—Mom's worst nightmare. It was mine, too.

At the end of that summer, Tullamore Park sponsored community-wide track races. Since running straight didn't seem to bother me too much, Dad thought it a good idea for me to enter a race to see how I would hold up for distances. I ran the twenty-five-yard dash. One girl, Peggy, towered over me. As we headed toward the finish line, I was in the lead. Then I felt Peggy gaining on me. When I turned to see where she was, she ran right by me and won.

After the race Dad came over, hugged me, and said, "Let's get some ice cream at Carvel's."

Since the weather was topping at ninety degrees, he parked the car under the shade of an oak tree and opened a window to let in the cooling breeze. We licked our cones and chatted.

"I'm proud of your effort," he said. "Remember when you turned your head toward the end of the race?" I nodded. He smiled. "Never look back."

Chapter 5

With Dad's advice, I tried to look forward to seventh grade. But the 'It' teasing and jeering continued, despite my improved walking gait. I was skinny as a chopstick, and some classmates reminded me about that whenever I walked down the hall. Fortunately, I had three teachers who were kind, smart and energetic. They made me feel safe and happy in their classes. Though I did well in science, history and music, my heart wasn't always light. I continued to withdraw from classmates, uncertain of myself and how to make new friends.

Throughout the school year, I continued the hip exercises, along with weekly physical therapy sessions at the local hospital. Dr. Fetner also instructed me to "point the feet outward" to help straighten my pigeon-toed gait. In our backyard, I walked backwards to strengthen my thigh muscles. All I could think about was playing tennis once school let out. But one of my classmates had other plans for me on the last day of school.

The final bell rang, and all the students near my locker rushed out the side door to catch the bus home. I took my time gathering my stuff. Another girl was also gathering her things at a slow pace. She edged closer to my locker.

"So 'It'" she began, "what're you gonna do this summer?"

I ignored her and placed a few things inside my book bag.

"Hey, 'It', you deaf?" Her face was now six inches from mine.

"I hear you. I'm gonna play tennis."

Her laughter pierced my ears. "Good luck with that. You're skinny, you walk funny, and you're a weakling."

She turned to walk away. I gritted my teeth and slammed my bag into the back of her knees. She hit the lockers and crumpled like a rag doll.

I walked casually toward the hallway exit. "Who's the weakling, now?" I called over my shoulder.

~

Summer was tennis. I loved playing on clay courts—sliding to reach a forehand or disguising a drop shot. I continued practicing—especially the volley, backhand cross-court, and the serve. After each day of practice came two days of rest. Good thing, since my hip was awfully achy at times. The routine was designed to keep me healthy and happy and to keep Mom from yelling at me. Around mid-July, Mr. Martin suggested that Dad and I enter the low-key Parent-Child Tournament on Labor Day weekend.

What a thrill it was for me to have my father by my side. He punched deep volleys and sliced wicked drop shots, which drove our opponents crazy. He had a great touch with the ball because as a mathematician he understood the geometry of the game—all ratios and angles. Dad was so happy when he hit the ball, and that joy infused me as well. I loved the mental and athletic skill tennis required, which drove me to improve my footwork and my serve.

Maybe those leg braces were helping all along.

~

"Nice and easy," said Mr. Martin, the club pro. He was skinny like me, and he always wore a polo shirt with an upturned collar that looked even whiter next to his dark tan. He never wore a hat, even on the sunniest of days. "Swing through the ball. That's it. A few more forehands, then I'll hit some backhands to you. Concentrate on turning your shoulders . . . good. That's it. How does it feel?"

I grinned. "It's great hitting with you again, Mr. Martin."

"Call me 'Coach.'"

Coach? My gosh, he believes I can compete. All those years in physical therapy, practicing against the backboard, watching Dad play, and learning from Coach Martin have added up to bring my dream to fruition. Maybe I'll be a winner like Alice Marble!

"Sure, Coach." I beamed.

"I'm going to move you around the court, now. We'll take it slow and build from there. Let's begin."

We rallied back and forth from half court for a good ten minutes, then hit full court for another ten minutes, which accelerated my rhythm and confidence. My strokes were smooth despite my difficulty getting to the ball early enough.

"Let's spend time up at net with your volley. You have great eye-hand coordination. We should take advantage of that; in coaching terms, we call that having 'great hands.'"

Coach hit forehand and backhand shots, some wide and others straight. Volleying at the net was easy for me because I didn't have to move too far laterally.

"Shorten your backswing and hit out more with a little slice under the ball. That's it, do it again. Now you're getting it!"

As I bent my knees low to retrieve Coach's ball, I winced and mishit the ball, sending it straight into the net. I rubbed my left hip as I straightened up.

"Are you going to be okay?" he hollered.

"Sure, Coach. I'm fine."

Mom had arrived early and sat down on a nearby bench to watch the end of the lesson. As we wrapped up the session, I said, "Thanks, Coach. My mom's here."

"Okay," he replied. "Next lesson, we'll play a few games."

"Sounds great! I walked over to Mom and sat down next to her.

"I saw you limp when you straightened up. Are you in any pain? How's your hip? Talk to me," Mom fired away.

"I'm just tired. Let's go home."

I plopped down on the front seat of the station wagon, loosened my sneaker laces, and asked, "Would you stop staring at me? I'm fine."

"Okay, but you'll need to take more than two days off."

"Why?"

"So you don't overdo it. Give your body a good rest."

I slammed the car door shut, giving my sore hip a good twinge in the process.

"I need to return a book to the library that's due tomorrow," Mom said after dinner. "Want to come with me? Maybe you could check out some books for summer reading." I was not used to her gentle voice.

"Sure. I've got nothing better to do."

We drove to the public library where I moseyed through the stacks of books. I came across a title in the sports section about the female tennis player, Alice Marble. I was super excited to read about her, as I still had Dad's tennis book with photos of her on my nightstand. I checked out the new book and headed home with Mom.

I devoured the read. Alice Marble was from California. At the age of nineteen in 1933, she traveled across the country to play in a national tournament in East Hampton, New York. In one day, she played 108 games in 100-degree weather. She lost twelve pounds—my bones would have melted. She suffered severe heatstroke and had to stop playing for eight months. When she competed in an America vs. France team tournament in Paris the following spring, she collapsed on the court. She was rushed to a hospital, diagnosed with tuberculosis, and told she would never play tennis again.

How awful to be so ill at such a young age. To think that you could never again play the sport you loved. Her experience put my enforced rest days into perspective.

The next chapter in the book had much better news. Alice Marble fully recovered from TB. Although it took two long years, she eventually won in 1940—the Wimbledon singles, doubles, and mixed doubles championships. Given her respiratory condition, she developed a quick, attacking game so she wouldn't have to endure long, drawn-out rallies.

That strategy could work for me as well: to end points more quickly, giving my legs a momentary rest. I tried the new strategy. I sensed it could work, but it caused me to rush my strokes, lose points, and throw my racquet.

One time when I threw my racquet in the net, Coach Martin asked, "Does that make your tennis better?" He didn't wait for an answer. Instead, he placed squares in different locations on the court. I hit those squares until I could direct the ball to any point on the court a dozen times in a row. I got to number eleven and had to start all over again until I reached the magic number. By the end of the drill, my thigh muscles fired heat and I almost collapsed.

"Break time, Lucie. Sit for a bit and drink some water," he smiled.

"Phew, I'm pooped!" I said and toweled off the sweat from the nape of my neck and forehead.

~

Every lesson for the next two months included the squares drill, except the magic number became twenty. Coach also drilled into me the belief that correct footwork was the foundation for solid ground strokes. Both my backhand and forehand "groundies" were fluid, but lacked power—no surprise there, given my build. Toward the end of the summer, however, as my balance, agility, and consistency improved, Coach entered me into two regional tournaments; one in Connecticut, the other in upstate New York. The two-week interval between tournaments would allow me to rest my body, yet still manage a few light workouts.

We constructed a game plan around my ground strokes and return of serve. And for the most part, it worked. I made it to the finals in both tournaments, earning me a number two ranking. In the final game of the final match in New York, I ignored the twitches in my right hip and decided to quicken the pace of play. In succession, I hit sharp angles to bring my opponent up to net, hoping to end the points with passing shots down the line. In response, she punished her winning volleys right at my feet. On match point, I attacked the net, but her exquisite passing shot sealed her victory. It was my first taste of real competition. I wanted more.

A week before ninth grade started, Mom called up from downstairs to say I had mail. I hurried down the stairs, sure it must be a letter from Joanne. Even after all this time, my heart—currently in my throat—had never given up.

The letter wasn't from her. My parents, at the table looking through their own mail, watched my face as the return address registered. I ripped it open.

It was a letter from the Eastern Lawn Tennis Federation, inviting me to participate in an indoor, development program for a small, select group of junior tennis players in the New York City Tri-State area. The program started the first Saturday after Labor Day and finished after Memorial Day weekend.

With no Joanne to hug, I shoved the letter in my dad's face. "Can you believe it? They believe in me—hot dog! Sweaty persistence and discipline paid off, Dad!"

"That's right, kiddo!"

Mom was already pursing her lips to form the "B" in "But" when Dad said. "It's an incredible opportunity. Let her try, Isabelle."

"What if she gets hurt?" Mom said.

"That's always a possibility for any athlete," he responded. I was glowing with pride and possibility—my dad had just called me an athlete. "Give it a month, and let's see how Lucie feels."

She glanced over at me. "Very well, one month. Then we reevaluate."

Chapter 6

My eyes popped open at the sound of the clock's annoying *bzzz* at four-thirty in the morning. I bolted out of bed, washed and dressed in a fraction of the time it usually took me: my favorite cotton polo shirt, navy warm-up outfit, and white, Tretorn sneakers. With athletic bag and purse in tow, I walked down our dimly lit street, brightened only by the soft glow of neighbors' front porch lights, and arrived at the station platform in less than ten minutes. I boarded the train at 5:15 a.m. to New York City. It pulled into Penn Station an hour later at 6:15, in time for me to grab a bite of scrambled eggs, wheat toast, and orange juice at the local diner. It was September 1965.

Across the way stood the looming, canvas bubble of indoor courts. Practice began promptly at seven and finished exactly at nine. I was home by ten-thirty, the time most of my classmates were eating their Saturday morning breakfasts. This ritual played out over the next four years.

I strengthened my body and my game. I inched up the ladder of the junior circuit, achieved a national ranking, and dreamed of playing in the European tournaments. Giving up a lot of my free time on the weekends didn't bother me too much because I loved the game of tennis. My goal was to be a top competitor.

I quickly learned how highly competitive the girls in this indoor program were. Some weren't particularly nice to be around, forever trying to edge each other out for the coaches' attention, annoyed if they were overlooked. One of the players, Karen Mitchell, whispered to me, "How did you get selected to the program? You're so puny. You'll never last." I turned away and waited for my time to practice cross-court backhands.

My temper erupted when I missed a shot, and I chucked my racquet in the net. The coach yelled, "Lucie, pick up your racquet and sprint to the end of the line."

I reined in a smart-ass comment and did as he said. I wasn't mad at him, anyway. It was just that I'd waited so long to start tennis, and I was so eager to improve that my shortcomings frustrated the heck out of me.

That night, after I told Dad what happened at tennis, he said that losing one's temper was poor sportsmanship and a waste of energy. *A hard lesson for a feisty, impatient athlete to accept.*

At the close of the first month of the junior development program, Mom insisted that Dr. Fetner check me out, to see whether he thought my body was holding up. I had no doubt it was. He examined me, took some x-rays, and found nothing alarming. I was thrilled.

"Just remember to always strengthen, stretch, and rest," he said.

I replied, "Promise."

At the end of practice the following Saturday, when all the girls were in the locker room packing up their things, a book, *The Secret at Shadow Ranch,* fell out of one girl's gym bag. I recognized the book cover.

"Hey, Donna, you like Nancy Drew mysteries too?"

"The plot is always simple, but they relax me. Nancy and her two friends hike the Grand Canyon and ride horses. They get stuck in a flood. Have you ever ridden a horse?" she asked.

"Yeah, a few summers ago when we went to a family camp in New Hampshire. Just around the paddock a few times. Haven't ridden since, but I enjoyed it."

"My aunt and uncle board horses in West Virginia. I've been visiting them for the last three summers."

"That sounds like fun."

"It is." Donna checked her watch. "Gotta go; my mom is waiting for me downstairs. See you next Saturday."

∼

While on the train I was so involved in finishing the Alice Marble book that I almost missed my stop. The kind conductor recognized me after so many train rides to New York City, so he tapped me on the shoulder. "Missy, I think this is your stop." He helped gather my things and stretched out his arm to balance me as I stepped off the train. I turned, thanked him, and waved.

When I returned home, I asked Mom. "Can we go back to the library to see if they have any more photographs of Alice Marble? I think seeing photographs of her playing would help me visualize her strokes."

"Sure, once you've finished your lunch and rested your legs for another hour."

That was my mom—a broken record.

We set off for the library two hours later. When Mom asked the librarian at the front desk if the library had issues of *Life* magazine from the late 1930s to the early 1940s, I cocked my head, thinking, *Who cares?*

"We keep old issues for twenty-five years. Are you looking for anything in particular, ma'am?"

"Yes. In the early 1940s, I remember *Life* magazine had articles with photographs featuring famous athletes. My daughter is interested in Alice Marble, a famous tennis player. Maybe they have pictures of her."

"I'd be happy to check, but it will take some time, as the back issues are in our basement. Can you come back on Monday afternoon?"

Mom looked over at me. "Sound good to you, Lucie?"

"Sure does," I smiled at Mom, then thanked the librarian before we left the library.

I couldn't help noticing how interested Mom had become in my tennis. Up until now, she seemed so strict.

On Monday, after school, we returned to the library. The librarian had a stack of back issues sitting on the front counter. On the top was an August 28, 1939, *LIFE* issue with Alice Marble on the cover.

"Look at this!" I held the magazine up for my mom. "At the cool cap she's wearing! I'd like to check out the magazine."

"Sorry, only books can be checked out," the librarian said. "You'll have to read the magazine here in our reading room."

"That's fine. Thank you for finding this!" I was itching to read it.

While Mom went to the grocery store, I read how Alice Marble came back from the horrible disease, tuberculosis. She worked closely with a coach to increase her stamina and improve her overall game. Reading the article reminded me of the tennis lessons with Coach Martin and how instructive and supportive he was. Our lessons always came late in the day after he finished with his other students. Hitting tennis balls in the gathering twilight, when shadows angled across the court, forced me to concentrate on seeing the ball and nothing else. Maybe that's why he chose to teach me late in the afternoon.

∾

A few months into the junior development program, the coaches focused on doubles play and teamed Donna and me as partners. Our playing styles were different: Donna patiently hit forehands and backhands, while I preferred to end a point quickly with angled shots—something I learned from watching Dad play doubles. That strategy also meant that I didn't have to run wide and worry that I would trip. Lately though, my legs felt heavy. I couldn't seem to rotate my hip and swing freely. So, doubles suited me; I didn't have to run around so much. Donna noticed I was acting impatient and cranky.

"Are you okay?" she asked.

"Not feeling too good today, sorry. I'm having trouble moving sideways to the ball."

"That's okay. When I'm not feeling too good on the court, I try to bend my knees more. Maybe that would help."

"Thanks, I'll try that." But nothing seemed to work. I tried to ignore it, and for the first time I kept looking up at the clock waiting for the session to be over. Finally, practice was finished. We all said our good-byes as Memorial Day weekend ended our first year in the indoor program.

Pain crept into my knees as I boarded the train back home. I was happy and relieved to simply sit and stare out the window. One cold, high-rise building after another rolled before my eyes, with little surrounding grass or shrubbery to soften the gray cement and steel landscape. It made me realize how lucky I was to live in a town where every home had a garden and a grassy front yard.

I was incredibly fortunate to have been selected into the junior development program. Would it all come to an end, if this new pain persisted?

I kept the pain to myself. When I felt alone in my thoughts, I'd sometimes think of Joanne and how supportive she'd been. Donna reminded me of Joanne. Though Donna and I were both shy, we laughed a lot, and like Joanne, I never heard Donna say anything unkind about anyone—except Karen.

Chapter 7

I turned fourteen at the start of year two. Every Saturday morning, from September through May, the coaches continued to work us hard. They combined the two-hour sessions with technique instruction, rigorous drills, and strategy sessions. Intricate crossover footwork drills were particularly challenging for me because sometimes I'd still trip over my own feet. When this happened, one of the coaches would take me aside to break down the progression into smaller movements. Though the coaches were demanding and never let up, they were encouraging and gave us concrete feedback on how to improve. I loved every minute of these Saturday mornings, even though I needed to be careful and rest my legs as Dr. Fetner and Mom kept reminding me. When pain deepened, I would go for a light bike ride. It seemed to calm my nerves and gently lengthen the leg muscles.

Trouble started in year three, the very first day in the locker room after the two-hour session ended. One of the coaches had introduced a new player, Angela Overby. She was Black, tall, had high cheek bones, and she possessed a beautiful serve. The other girls in the program completely ignored Angela. When she walked too close to their lockers, Karen tripped Angela, sending her racquet and purse flying. Angela kept her balance and looked up at Donna and me. Donna ran over to pick up Angela's things and I stood there, stunned. Slowly, I made my way to Angela but had no idea what to say. My eyes were wet, and all I could mutter was, "I'm sorry, Angela."

"It's not your fault. They just don't like me, that's all."

"The girls don't even know you. How would they know they don't like you?"

Angela shrugged her shoulders and tried to smile. We gathered our gear, closed our lockers, and headed for the stairwell leading to the street. Angela hummed a beautiful tune, sounded like some kind of hymn. We said our goodbyes before I could ask her what she was humming.

Angela's incident with the other girls reminded me of a particular day back in fifth grade. A classmate had slammed me against the hallway locker so that she could pass. I hit the steel hard, collapsing to the ground. No one was around to help, so I leaned against the locker, pushed up with both hands, and steadied myself before walking to class. She did it because no one was in the hallway. It happened many times in my childhood, but Joanne and other classmates always helped me if they were nearby. I knew my walking looked very different from other kids; I guess that's why they called me 'It.' That name really hurt then, even more than my achy hip and legs did now.

On the train ride back home that day, I remembered reading in Dad's tennis book how Alice Marble had fought for a Black tennis player's right to enter all-white tennis tournaments. When I got home, I looked in the sports encyclopedia and found they had more about the story. The Black player's name was Althea Gibson. She won many tennis tournaments in the Black American Tennis Association league, but was not invited to play in the 1950 all-white US National Championships until Alice Marble wrote a long letter in the July 1950 issue of the *American Lawn Tennis magazine,* entitled "A Vital Issue."

She argued that Miss Gibson should be allowed to play in the championships. The letter influenced the United States Tennis Lawn Association's decision to allow Gibson to compete in the national tennis championships at Forest Hills, New York, later that summer. The encyclopedia's article quoted directly from that letter:

> If tennis is a game for ladies and gentlemen, it's also time we acted a little more like gentlepeople and less like sanctimonious hypocrites. If Althea Gibson represents a challenge to the present crop of women players, it's only fair that they should meet that challenge on the courts.

How brave to stand up for someone that most people wouldn't bother to help.

Alice Marble's letter supporting Althea Gibson was written in 1950. It was now 1967. Why does it take so long for people to accept one another despite their differences? It made no sense why the tennis officials would not let her play. They should have judged players by the quality of their play and sportsmanship, and nothing else. Seven years later, Althea Gibson went on to win the US Nationals and Wimbledon.

I was determined to earn that kind of respect as well.

At the next Saturday morning tennis session, Donna and I were discussing how best to support Angela, but she didn't show up. Donna and I waited until practice was over to approach one of the coaches.

"How come Angela didn't show up today?" I asked.

"Is she okay?" Donna said.

"We really enjoy playing with her. She's nice, and a really good player," I said.

"Well, girls, we're not too sure. We will let you know next week." Coach walked away.

In the locker room, the other girls were saying that Angela didn't belong with the group anyway, so they were glad she was gone.

"What do you mean?" I hissed. "Angela plays well and has a terrific serve. She belongs here as much as any of us do. In fact, she could probably beat every one of us."

"Then she should play with her own kind," Karen whispered.

Donna and I heard every word. I glanced at the clock. If I didn't leave now, I'd miss the train back home. "Gotta go, don't want to miss my train. Bye, Donna."

Barely making the train, I plopped down on a seat and closed my eyes until the train was out of the railway tunnel. As the train gained full speed, I looked out the window and noticed swallows perched on the telephone lines, and I envied their balance. How steady they all were, even as the train whizzed by. I couldn't play as steady as Donna and Angela, and that bothered me. But what upset me the most was how awful Angela must feel. She shouldn't feel excluded because she's Black. We were a group of talented and lucky athletes with an opportunity to excel at a sport we loved. Why should Angela be treated any differently by the other players?

When I returned home, I read more from Miss Marble's letter to the *American Lawn Tennis* magazine:

> If she is refused a chance to succeed or to fail, then there is an ineradicable mark against a game to which I have devoted most of my life, and I would be bitterly ashamed. We can accept the evasions, ignore the fact that no one will be honest enough to shoulder the responsibility for

Althea Gibson's probable exclusion from the nationals. We can just "not think about it." Or we can face the issue squarely and honestly. . . . She is not being judged by the yardstick of ability but by the fact that her pigmentation is somewhat different. . . . To me, she is a fellow tennis player and, as such, deserving of the same chance I had to prove myself. I've never met Miss Gibson but, to me, she is a fellow human being to whom equal privileges ought to be extended.

How inspiring and gusty that Alice Marble supported someone she didn't even know.

⌇

The following Saturday, Angela had already arrived and was waiting on the court. Donna and I walked over to greet her.

"Hey, Angela, glad you're back," I said.

"Thanks," she replied with a big smile. "Want to warm up together before we start our drills?"

Donna looked at me. "Sure," we said together.

Angela and I played against Donna because she was like a backboard. Every shot came back. Donna moved effortlessly, squaring her shoulders before serving, delicately bouncing on her tiptoes when returning a serve, and casually touching a volley with great spin and angle. Everything about her was balanced. Sometimes I paid more attention to Donna than my own game. She was *that* good.

The other girls eventually arrived—all nice and polite, as if nothing had happened a few weeks earlier. For this session, the coaches separated the groups and paired us with girls we hadn't played doubles with before. All the teams played nonstop for one-and-a-half hours with a ten-minute bathroom break. For the last half hour, we focused on our groundstrokes. I loved every minute of this practice because it taught me endurance and match-play skills. In the long run, you can drill hitting hundreds of balls, but if you don't apply the skill by playing real games, you're not going to win matches—let alone tournaments.

Toward the end of the session, Karen slid wide going for a drop shot and hit her shoulder on the edge of the bench. Her partner, Angela, ran over immediately and extended her arm to comfort Karen. She grimaced in pain, snubbed Angela, and sulked alone on the bench. The rest of us waited while Coach Roberts ran over to check on Karen.

"Keep playing girls. Focus, focus. Karen will be fine." He spent a long time talking with her, even after our session finished.

In the locker room, Donna pulled me aside. "I don't know what's going on with Karen. Do you think we should ask her, or ignore her?"

"I don't know. Maybe the bench knocked some sense into her." I smirked.

Angela walked over to us. "Hey, just wanted to say goodbye. I hope to see you next week." She smiled and headed through the main lobby and into the gray hustle and bustle of the New York City streets.

The only thing I didn't like about taking the train was that I was always rushing. It never gave me a chance to hang out and get to know Donna and Angela better. We lived thirty miles from each other—only a river and a bridge separated us. Yet, I felt something drew us together, something more than just endlessly hitting tennis balls.

Rain slashed at the windows, causing the train to frequently slow to a crawl. It allowed me to finish my math homework.

I also had time to think about the encyclopedia article about Alice Marble that I had read a few days before. Alice figured out how to use the American Twist to shorten points in a way that would put her at an advantage. It's a type of serve that's hard to return because, when the spinning ball lands in the opponent's service box, it rises and tails away after the bounce. It starts out in one direction and ends up traveling in the opposite direction. This serve has a slower speed, which allows the server extra time to get to the net. For Alice, it was the perfect remedy. She served and volleyed to win points quickly.

I wasn't sure I could serve that way. My painful right hip had trouble rotating enough to get that twisting motion.

The article also noted that Alice's doctor suggested she wear a brimmed cap with a cabbage leaf inside. Laborers in the desert put cabbage leaves under their hats to prevent sunstroke, he said. She tried it and discovered her head always remained cool. From that point on, Alice Marble played with that signature cap, the very one on the cover of *Life* magazine I read at the library.

When I stepped off the station platform, the rain stopped and the air smelled sweet with honeysuckle, a sure sign that spring had arrived. I was anxious to have more tennis lessons at the club with Coach Martin. I walked home quickly and explained to my parents that I wanted to work on my movement and serve, and hoped to have a few tennis lessons during the summer. Dad agreed, on the condition that I babysit more to help pay for my lessons.

Mom added, "Another condition is that you practice every other day. You must rest in between."

"Yes, Mom. You're like a broken record." I walked away shaking my head.

Chapter 8

Our fourth and final year of the Junior Development Program began with a disappointment. The head coach signaled to our group to form a circle near the first court baseline. We hurried over, eager to hear what he had to say.

"Angela's mother called and asked that I explain why Angela would not be here today. The Harlem Central Hospital is honoring Angela's father who was a decorated fighter pilot in the Korean War and spent his final days at Harlem Central."

My legs shook.

"Are you okay?" Donna whispered.

"I don't know. What can we do for Angela?"

She gave me a pat on the shoulder. "We'll think of something."

"That's all, group," Coach said. "Now, line up single file at the baseline."

I was already standing right on the baseline until Karen pushed me away. "Move, I'm first up."

I stumbled but pushed back. "No way, I was here first."

She pushed again. "But I'm bigger than you."

"So what!" I pushed her hard.

"Lucie, Karen back of the line," Coach shouted.

"You know, you're a real piece of work. Just play and shut up," I said. Karen's eyes shot me an angry, unmistakable glare.

Coach continued his instruction. "For each player, I will hit a short ball to bring you in to the net and then follow it up with a volley. The balls will come quickly, so be in your ready positions and on your toes. Ready? Begin." He fired balls at us for ten minutes, pointing out what we were doing wrong or complimenting us when we hit with control. This drill was particularly challenging to me because sometimes my left foot would turn-in causing me to trip ever so slightly and keep me off balance when I'd hit the volley.

We rested for five minutes, thankfully.

"Okay group, places," Coach announced. "Our last drill will be just the reverse. You will start at the net. I'll hit you one volley, then a high lob. You will race back to the baseline and hit either a forehand or backhand down the line. This drill is tough, but I know you all can do it."

Fifteen minutes later, Coach stopped the drill. I bent over, exhausted. My drenched head band dripped on the court. *So, this is what it takes to be a ranked player.*

"Okay, that's it for today," Coach said. "You all played well. Have a great weekend!"

Donna and I walked off the court together and gathered our things in the locker room.

"What was that between you and Karen?" Donna said.

I jammed my racquet in my bag. "She pushed me to get first in line. I pushed her back, hard. I just don't like her."

"So that's why Coach told you both to get to the back of the line." Donna shook her head.

"Yep."

We said our usual good-byes and walked down the steps to the noisy Manhattan streets, where we went our separate ways. The train ride home was noisy, too. The compartment door was partially open so all you heard was the squealing of the steel wheels. My nerves were on edge thinking about Angela's loss and Karen's malice.

～

In the final two months of the program, our coaches worked us harder than ever before with full-court drills and match-play scenarios. It was a fitting end to four long years of becoming a competitive tennis player; years full of sweat, pain, laughter and joy. I was grateful beyond measure to the coaches who taught us the habits of discipline, problem solving, and self-reliance. I was also grateful for the friendship developed with Angela and Donna. To celebrate that friendship, I invited both of them to play tennis at our club after our high school graduations.

The third weekend of June, I drove to the train station to pick up Donna and Angela and eagerly waited for them on the station platform, fidgeting with my watch the whole time and hoping they would have a good time playing doubles. I had arranged for another girl to round out our foursome. The train was unusually late, making me even more jumpy. Once they stepped off the train and smiled, I felt certain all would be fine.

The tennis club was located at the edge of the town's wooded park and parallel to the Long Island Rail Road tracks. The tennis club felt like home to me. When the sun shone and I was playing on red clay, all was well with the world. I hoped that Donna and Angela would feel the same way.

But first, I led my friends down a brightly lit corridor to the kitchen where I would introduce them to Harry. He was the commander of the kitchen and looked after us youngsters from time to time. He was a crotchety, big man who made the best fresh orange juice drink in town. For years, every time I finished playing tennis, I sat at the shiny kitchen counter and the two of us talked and talked. I felt safe with Harry and always watched enthusiastically as he concocted his special brew of fresh-squeezed oranges: ice chips, water, and tons of sugar he poured straight from an aluminum canister. He took a martini shaker and blended all the ingredients with such flair that when he poured the drink into tall glasses, it foamed and tasted incredibly delicious. I wanted my friends to enjoy the same sensation once we finished playing doubles.

When we entered his kitchen, Harry looked surprised in seeing Angela because no one ever brought a Black person to the club. Harry, a Black man himself, greeted us with his characteristic big grin and bellowing voice. "Well, Lucie, who do we have here?"

I beamed. "Hi, Harry. These are my friends, Donna and Angela. We're going to play doubles with Mary."

"Real good to meet both of you. Be sure Lucie stays out of trouble today."

"Can't guarantee that, Harry," I quipped. "We'll be back later for some orange juice. Come on girls. Let's hit the courts."

"Bye, Harry. Very nice to meet you," Angela and Donna said in unison.

As we walked out of the kitchen, Angela glanced over her shoulder toward Harry and smiled. He nodded in return.

Stone pathways led us to the last court where Mary was waiting. She looked dumbfounded as did other players on the adjoining courts when Angela walked onto the court. The other players stuttered to a stop, staring. I introduced Mary to Donna and Angela with little fanfare. I teamed Mary with Donna to avoid any awkwardness in the event Mary didn't want to play with a Black girl. She kept staring at Angela. We warmed up for ten minutes, hitting a variety of shots and taking practice serves. All seemed fine.

But Mary's mother didn't think so. Apparently, she was none too happy with what she saw. She yelled, "Mary get off the court."

Mary walked off, shrugging her shoulders at us, and said nothing.

Now what?

Lucky for us, Coach Martin, my beloved club pro, walked over. "Been watching you girls for a few minutes after my lesson finished. May I join you?"

"Sure, Coach, that would be great." I introduced him to Donna and Angela.

With his ready smile, he extended his arm to shake their hands. "Good to meet you both." He looked over at me. "Let's get started."

The four of us played one set, exchanging long rallies and punching back deep volleys with an occasional drop shot here and there. Despite being nervous playing with Coach Martin and worried we'd make stupid mistakes, we had tons of fun. We got lucky when Coach gave us a mini lesson on the overhead, an essential shot for doubles.

"Prepare to hit the overhead by tracing the arc of the ball with your free hand up and point at the ball until you hit it with your racquet. Like this."

"It's like using a protractor in geometry class," I said. Donna and Angela rolled their eyes at my observation. "Thanks for playing with us, Coach!"

Afterward, we headed straight for Harry's kitchen. It was too dark, not like Harry to turn off the lights.

"Harry." I called out, "where are you?"

He appeared from the back room. "Sorry to keep you waiting, I was in the storage area getting more ingredients."

We sat on the stools, elbows on the counter, and watched Harry concoct three foamy orange drinks.

"Here you go, girls. Drink up."

No one spoke, which made me a bit nervous, until Donna said. "This is delicious, and it's got a fizz."

"Glad you like it. So, where you girls from?" Harry asked as he wiped the counter clean.

"I live in central Jersey, town called Chatham," Donna said.

"And I live in Harlem," Angela said.

"Whereabouts?" Harry asked.

"South Harlem," she answered.

"I have relatives there. Live across the street from Mount Neboh Baptist Church."

"I know where that is. My mother and I worship at Memorial Baptist, a few blocks up."

"Heard there was some commotion on the courts with Mary and her mother," Harry said as he looked at Angela, then at me.

"She was incredibly rude." I didn't know what to say next.

He filled up our glasses. "Things like that happen all the time to us Black folk." He shook his head.

I squirmed in my seat. "Same thing happened to Angela on the tennis court where we trained at a junior development program in New York City."

He shook his head.

We got up from the stools to leave and said goodbye. Harry signaled Angela to come to the far end of the counter. Donna and I waited in the hallway. We heard them talking and laughing.

Angela then joined us in the hallway. "You know what? Harry told me not to worry about Mary not wanting to play tennis with me because I was Black. He said, 'Angela, you can't give up in life, and never doubt that dark clouds do break.' Wise man, I'd say."

"Couldn't agree more," I replied.

Chapter 9

It was a breezy July day when I stepped off the bus at 125th Street in Harlem. I looked around, a little nervous after what my mother had said, which was essentially "No" to Harlem, until my dad interceded and gave me specific instructions for which train and bus to take. Mom had said there were riots in Harlem after Martin Luther King, Jr. was assassinated this past Spring. She'd been nervous for me going up to Harlem. But then I saw Angela standing near the light pole just a few feet from the bus stop. She introduced me to her mother, a tall woman with honey-colored eyes and beautiful, high cheek bones, just like Angela's. She wore an A-line, collared, violet dress.

"I've heard so much about you, Lucie," she said sweetly.

"It's really nice to meet you," I responded.

She smiled. "We thought you might enjoy walking down a few side streets to see the beautiful brownstone buildings. Then we'll have lunch in our apartment. After that, we'll go to the tennis courts where Angela plays and gives tennis lessons to local kids. If there's time, we'll show you the church where we worship. Faith is important to us."

We left the loud music emanating from a nearby radio and turned down a tree-lined street, far enough away from the honking cars of 125th street to enjoy the pretty day.

"See these brownstones?" Angela asked. "When I was a kid, I'd hang out on these stoops and play with the other kids in the building."

"They're so different from anything I've ever seen," I said with astonishment. "The stoop is so wide and high."

"This is our building. Come, let's go inside, Lucie," Mrs. Overby said.

Inside their apartment, high ceilings and brightly lit rooms greeted me. The tall, narrow windows gave the living room airiness, a cheerfulness to the apartment that was undeniable despite its small, square footage.

"I'm not used to high ceilings; they're beautiful." I ran my hand across the paneled walls. "The woodwork is gorgeous. My father would love this; his hobby is woodworking."

"Thank you, Lucie. We'll eat shortly, girls."

$\sim$

The stroll to the public tennis courts was unnerving. People stared at me. Awkward, different from the stares and whispers when kids ridiculed the way I walked. Down at the corner of the street were four young men, standing around and smoking cigarettes. They whistled at us.

"Come, girls, let's cross the street. Just a few more blocks to the Harlem Tennis Center," Angela's mother said.

"What a difference from your street Angela," I said.

"That's my life. I go back and forth between quiet and loud, beautiful and ugly."

I said nothing. I knew very little about the life Angela lived. It was better to keep my mouth shut.

"Here we are," Mrs. Overby said. "Angela usually practices on Courts One or Two with the boys. She gives lessons on Court Six, under the watchful eye of the head pro."

I looked at Angela. "Do you prefer clay or hard courts?"

"Not sure, but hard courts wear out my feet quicker than clay."

"Yeah, I know what you mean," I said.

The three of us sat down on the splintered wood bench, flanked by tall hedges, and watched the adults play doubles. It was a nice respite and a chance to get to know Angela's mother a little better.

"Do you play tennis, Mrs. Overby?"

"No, honey. My husband did and loved the game. It's Angela's connection to her father."

"But Dad died when I was four; I never got a chance to play with him."

My voice choked up. "I . . . I'm so sorry, Ange. You were so young when he passed."

She nodded.

I turned to Mrs. Overby. "Angela told me that you're a nurse at Harlem Central Hospital. What kind of nurse?"

"I'm in the pediatric ward. Been there almost fifteen years, and I love it. It's hard work, but worth every minute."

"I bet the kids love you."

"Well, I hope so. You know, we should get going. Don't want you to miss your bus and train. We'll take a short-cut by walking through that alley." She pointed toward the end court. "It will save some time."

In the narrow alleyway, I stretched my arms wide and touched the buildings on both sides and felt the curves of the bricks. We didn't have homes like these in my hometown. The contrast between our lives was sharp. Yet I believed that despite the differences in our backgrounds, our budding friendship seemed to come naturally through playing a sport we loved and enduring ridicule we did not deserve.

～

Throughout the summer, I played in as many tournaments as my aching hip would allow. Donna and I were a regular doubles team, winning many of the summer tournaments on the East Coast. We earned a number two ranking, good enough for us to be invited to the 1968 Girls Nationals in Austin, Texas that began the last week in August. Although Angela was a terrific doubles player, she could not find a partner willing to play with her.

The truth was, Donna and I were already entered into a minor tournament in Virginia before the Nationals. Given how much my knees and hip were aching and inhibiting my movement, it no longer made sense for me to play both. Before withdrawing from the tournament, I called Donna to see if she'd consider playing doubles with Angela.

My suggestion was met with silence.

"Come on, Donna. You know she's a great player. You two will probably win the tourney."

"You're right. Okay, I'm in. Let me know what Angela thinks."

Angela warned me that some tournament directors wouldn't feel comfortable with a Black girl playing doubles partner with a white girl. "But we're all God's children," Angela said. "I have every right to play in any tournament I qualify for. That's what my mother told me, and I agree with her."

Angela agreed to enter the tournament with Donna, and eight days later, the two partners called me. "We won the doubles championships!" they yelled over the phone.

"Way to go!" I answered. "That's great. I knew you two could do it. Congrats." I was thrilled for them, though I felt a pinch of envy knowing that Donna and I could've won the doubles. During our conversation, Angela mentioned that she wouldn't be entering the Girls Nationals in Austin, citing financial reasons. I was disappointed for her; she certainly qualified to enter the Nationals. I didn't know why the governing board wouldn't award traveling scholarships for those who couldn't afford the expense. Didn't seem fair at all.

I could appreciate Angela's financial situation. Several years ago, Mom took on a new job with longer hours and better pay when it became clear that I was serious about tennis. My intentions meant increased expenses for tennis lessons, equipment, and additional therapy sessions to keep my body healthy for competitive play. She often worked on Saturdays as well, and insisted that I do as much babysitting as possible.

That evening after dinner, I explained to Mom and Dad why Angela would not be going to the Nationals.

"I'm sorry to hear that. She's worked hard for the right to enter," Dad said.

"It's not fair at all," Mom said. "I need to remind you, Lucie, to continue helping out with your tennis expenses," she continued. "If you don't get more babysitting jobs, you're not going to the Nationals either. Period."

That was a motivator for sure.

"One more thing," she added. "Increase your rest periods; otherwise, you may never make it to the Nationals."

"Ouch, that hurt Mom."

For the remaining weeks of August, I practiced hard for the upcoming Nationals, but soon became discouraged as my hip and knees continued to ache. I found myself asking, *What would Alice Marble do? Work her butt off, that's what!* That's exactly what I did: more drills, more practice games, more physical therapy, and more rest in between. That's what serious athletes do; we work at it.

It all paid off. I made it all the way to the singles semi-finals but lost in three long drawn-out sets—to Karen, of all people! Defeat is a frequent companion in sports, but I told myself what Coach Martin had once said: "Defeat will not defeat you." It didn't. The next day, Donna and I won the Girls National Doubles championship. She was a great doubles partner, always consistent, balanced, and calm. We understood each other's moves and moods, and we laughed a great deal.

After the Nationals, Donna invited me to spend a week at her aunt and uncle's home in West Virginia. She'd spent several summers horseback-riding there, but stopped when she started to play tennis seriously at the age of fourteen.

"Maybe you'd like to ride horses," Donna suggested.

"I don't know," I said as I considered the possibility. "I'd probably fall off."

"Why do you say that? I'll be riding next to you."

"Cause my thigh muscles are kinda weak."

"They can't be that weak; you're a tennis player."

"True. But when you have a hip problem, the inner thigh strength you need for quick lateral shifts is a hard thing to work on, because lying on your side on the floor to do the exercises hurts . . . a lot.

"Well, horseback riding really built up my inner thigh strength because you've got to squeeze your thighs a little just to keep your balance. Maybe give it a try," Donna persisted.

"Okay." I'd do anything to get stronger.

That decision would change my life forever.

Chapter 10

Donna's family loved to ride horses and boarded two of them at the local equestrian center in White Sulphur Springs, West Virginia. Nestled in the foothills of the Allegheny Mountains, the center had four barns and miles of riding trails.

Donna and I walked the graveled road for half a mile to the equestrian center where her Uncle John waved from the small A-framed barn. He had already saddled the horses, and behind him, Donna's Aunt Lilly greeted us with a ready smile.

"Welcome to our little bit of heaven," she said.

"We're glad you're here, Lucie," added Uncle John.

"It's great to be here. Thanks for inviting me," I said with a big smile.

Aunt Lilly handed me a soft brush to stroke my horse, Pie.

Pie was a bright, chestnut colt with braids of ginger hair and a diamond-shaped white mark across his forehead. I loved brushing his coat; it calmed my nerves. I hadn't been on a horse since riding Dakota at camp many years ago. I whispered something in Pie's big ear, like they do in the movies, and gave him a soft pat on the neck. I placed my foot in the stirrup, but I couldn't swing my leg over him. My hip wouldn't rotate easily. Seeing my difficulty, Uncle John smiled, cupped his two hands together, and gave me a lift.

"Up you go, Lucie. Enjoy the ride. It's a beautiful day."

I beamed a big "thank you." Pie snorted impatiently and eyed Donna curiously as we waited for her to mount. She did so with the same balance she displayed hitting a tennis ball. I nudged Pie forward, a little behind Donna, so that he could follow her lead.

"You'll love Pie; he's gentle," Donna reassured me.

I needed to hear those words.

"Before we head out to the trails, I'd like to show you how to post to trot." She gave a demonstration and explanation. Post forward and up simultaneously, then down and back up again. "As you rise, your pelvis should go forward and up, keeping your back straight. Then as you go down, sit softly into the saddle for a second then rise again. The control comes from your thighs," she said. I followed her instructions and repeated the actions until Pie and I found our rhythm.

"We'll ride slowly at first to get a feel of our horses and the terrain," Donna said. "To pick up a little speed, lightly kick the sides of Pie. And squeeze those thighs! He'll obey you."

"Hah," I chuckled.

"To steer him, lay the reins on one side or the other to signal which direction you want Pie to go. Any questions?"

"Nope. Got it." I squirmed a bit against the saddle to get my hips comfy and focused on my posture.

It was a glorious day—warm and sunny with a slight breeze tickling our faces. The trails took us parallel to the golf course, with its gently rolling fairways and deep sand bunkers. Donna and I crossed a dirt path and came upon a canopy of woodland leaves where other riders and their horses stood drinking in the shade of the large trees. The two of us slowly trotted past them, waved, and continued onto the meadow that stretched before us. I had never seen anything like this—an open space of rolling green grasses, their taller blades leaning against the cool breeze. The sun was radiant, light finding every corner of the meadow.

Donna's aunt was right; this was a little bit of heaven. It was just what I needed after a long, summer tennis season.

We rode for about an hour before making our way back to the barn. I stumbled a bit after I dismounted Pie.

I rubbed my thighs, deeply, up and down. "Phew, they're sore."

"Thought they might be," Donna said.

～

We got up early the following morning. Boy, was I stiff and sore—but eager to ride again. Sore muscles meant I was working them . . . and getting stronger. Surely it would help my hip and my tennis movement.

When we arrived at the barn, Uncle John had the horses ready for us.

"Thanks for tacking up our horses again; you're the best!" Donna said.

"You bet, Donna. Have a good ride, you two," he said as he waved us off. The countryside lay before us wrapped in a quiet mist rising slowly from the ground. We could hear nothing except the horses snorting and our own voices. The silence scared me a little, but Donna reassured me not to worry—the way Joanne used to years ago. We rode for about half an hour when Donna stopped at the end of the trail before turning onto a different path.

Donna pointed to her right. "We'll take that trail."

"This posting sure works the thighs," I said.

"Uncle John and Aunt Lilly taught me to post. It's helped my posture and balance even for tennis." She looked down. "See, they're pretty firm."

"Yeah, you always had great balance on the court."

"Thanks, Lucie," she smiled.

As we trotted alongside one another, the sunlight flickered through the orange-colored leaves with the dense mountain forests surrounding us. I felt relaxed, a peacefulness settling in. It must have been the beauty of the woodlands that captured me. Donna noted an eagle spreading its wings above us as if to say good morning. Various bushes lined the dirt path, and one yellow flowering bush caught my eye. I bent forward to get a closer look. Out of nowhere, a deer bolted in front of us. Pie reared, sending me skyward. All I could see were the tips of the tall pine trees before I slammed onto the ground. Smack on my back. Breath forced from my lungs. Pain seared through my spine. My body wouldn't stop thrashing. The pain then stopped, and I felt nothing.

"Oh my God, oh my God, Lucie!" Donna jumped off her horse, dropped to her knees, and placed her gloved hands on my legs, steadying me and eventually calming my screams. "Are you alright?"

"I-I can't move my legs."

She looked around in desperation. "I'm going to get help!" Donna yanked her horse around and left at a gallop.

For now, it was me, my pain, and Pie. Looking up, I saw this huge body with deep chocolate brown eyes. I was terrified that Pie would step on me, but I was powerless to move. Instead, he inched closer to me, bowed his head, and remained absolutely still. "Oh, Pie, what am I to do? What about college? What if I never walk again? No more tennis, no more joy—no more anything."

Sirens pierced the silence in the distance. Pie turned his arched neck toward the sound and waited by my side until I was lifted onto the stretcher and into the ambulance.

Chapter 11

"Why can't I feel my legs or wiggle my toes? What's happened?" I blurted to the doctor and nurse hovering over my hospital bed.

"I'm Dr. Albertson. You've hurt your back. I don't know exactly when the feeling in your legs and feet will come back. We'll have to wait and see."

"How long will that be?" I muttered.

"We're not sure. It's important that you rest now. We'll be back later to check on you." He closed the door behind him.

I cried myself to sleep and wanted my parents by my side. When I awoke, I didn't know what day it was. Sunflowers decorated the hospital room, and books perched on the windowsill. Donna sat near my bed.

"Hey, Lucie." Her voice was as light and delicate as wind chimes. She came to sit on the edge of the bed. Tears welled in her eyes. She leaned in, smoothed out my bangs and whispered. "I'm so sorry. How are you feeling?"

"Okay, I guess." The pain pills made me drowsy, irritable, and feeling sorry for myself. My eyes felt puffy.

Donna handed me a box wrapped in bright purple and yellow paper. "Here. I've brought you something. How about if I open it for you?"

"Sure."

She held up a tan, soft-leather, calf-skin journal and placed it in my hands. "The buckle-strap also holds a pen or pencil. Cool, huh?"

"It's beautiful." I ran my hand across the cover. "It's so smooth. I love it. Thank you."

"You're welcome. Can I pour you some water?"

"No thanks."

We chatted for a while until the doctor and nurse returned.

Donna touched my forehead. "See you tomorrow, then."

Dr. Albertson checked his clipboard then looked up at me. "I see you're eighteen, same age as my daughter. How are you feeling?"

"Drowsy and confused. What's going on?" I mumbled.

"You have what's called a fracture-dislocation, which means a break in the bone and damage to the soft tissue in the area. The L4-L5, S-1 vertebrae have moved a bit out of their positions."

"Is that the low back?"

"Yes, Lucie. The bones in your lower back."

"Now what?"

"We have you on strong medication because you were in severe pain when you arrived in the emergency room. I'm going to reduce the medication a little to gauge your pain tolerance. I also need to move your hip and legs a little to see how your body responds." Before the doctor left my room, he patted me on the shoulder and said, "It will take some time to heal."

"How much time? I'm a tennis player. I've got to get back to training."

"We won't know for several days. Try and be patient."

Easy for him to say. "Where are my parents?"

The nurse inched toward my bed. "They'll be here by noon tomorrow."

∽

I could hear the door open and someone tiptoeing, but I was too drugged to know what was going on until his voice filled the room.

"Dad." My eyes were so puffy, I squinted to see him.

"Yes, dear. Mother and I came straight from the airport." He kissed my forehead.

"I brought Lambie." Mom snuggled the small, frayed, pink stuffed animal in the palm of my hand. I caressed my soft friend.

"Thanks, Mom."

Dr. Albertson entered the room and introduced himself to Mom and Dad. They discussed my back for several minutes before he introduced another person who was patiently waiting. "This is Laura Richards, the physical therapist who will be working with Lucie."

"Hello. Nice to meet you all." Her warm smile was calming.

"The doctor needs to examine you now, sweetie. We'll be back a little later." They both kissed me. Mom squeezed my hand before she left.

"How's your pain?" Dr. Albertson asked.

"I'm starting to feel a sharp, quick pain in my lower back. Goes away though. But I can wiggle my toes!"

"Let's take a look."

He poked around with a small hammer-like instrument with a rubber top at one end.

"Why are you using that?" I asked.

"The reflex hammer? To test your deep tendon and muscle reflexes, to make sure your nervous system is working properly. There should be some movement of the ankle; the muscle should contract. Let me know if anything hurts."

He tapped the left ankle area first. No response. Then he tried the right ankle. A slight response.

"It didn't hurt, but there wasn't much movement. How come?"

"Slight movement is a good sign, Lucie. Not to worry. Give

it time. Laura and I would like to check your range of motion by gently bending one knee toward your chest and bringing it down slowly. Then we'll repeat the sequence with the other knee. Let's begin."

The two of them moved my leg around just as he had described.

"Any pain, after what we just did?" Laura asked.

"Nope," I lied. I wanted to get going with physical therapy.

"Good," she said.

Dr. Albertson concurred. "It's a good sign that you can wiggle your toes. Feeling in your legs and feet will gradually return." After jotting down a few notes in the chart, Dr. Albertson stated that he and Laura would come by in the morning. "We've given instructions to the night nurse for your care. Sleep well," he said as he patted my shoulder.

~

Dad stayed for a few days, but needed to return home to Long Island and to his job. Before leaving, he said. "Listen to what the physical therapist and doctor tell you to do. You'll be fine, Lucie. You're a fighter."

I hung on to his every word.

~

For ten days the physical therapist and doctor had monitored my pain levels, performed additional range of motion exercises, and charted my progress.

Today, however, would be different. Laura and I would go for a walk. I grabbed her arm and slowly rose from the bed. I attempted a step, a bit shaky. I hesitated, wondering whether I could stand up straight, yet grateful and relieved when I took a step forward, then another, and then another.

My mother was cheering me on. "That's good Lucie," she said joyfully.

Laura was beside me with each step I took. "Let's try walking out to the hallway. Do you think you're up to that?"

"Sure." I'd been robbed of my physical freedom and would try anything to get it back. We ventured out into the windowless hallway with its white walls and closed doors.

"Will you be okay, Lucie?" Mom asked. "Don't go too far."

"Let me try." I walked several steps halfway down the hall, then stumbled. Laura caught me mid-stride. "Maybe I should go back to my room."

As the three of us approached my room, Dr. Albertson appeared around the corner.

He opened the door. "I have an update."

Laura helped me back to bed before he spoke.

"The new set of X-rays reveals that the fracture is bilateral. You'll need to stay in the hospital another week or so to heal enough to travel back home."

"When do you think I can . . . play tennis again?" I asked. It came out as a stutter.

"Let's not worry about that just now. You have a long road ahead. Laura will be back later this afternoon. Try to rest." He and Laura walked out together and closed the door.

I could barely look at Mom. "'Try to rest.' That's all I ever hear. What good will that do? Please leave, Mom. I want to be alone."

"All right, dear. I'll be back later, sweetie," she said.

I heard the door click closed.

"A slight chance," the doc had said. Good God. I had come far since the early days of swiveling hips and faltering gait. *Please, God, give me another chance. Tennis has given my wonky body hope, purpose, and joy. Please don't take that away.*

"Time for your therapy," Laura said. She entered my room and adjusted the blinds to let in the bright and giving sun. She explained that my physical therapy this week would focus on gentle stretching and strengthening of my abdominal and lower back muscles that support the bony spine and discs. "These rubbery cushions act as shock absorbers and tough ligaments that hold the vertebrae of the spine together." I needed something to absorb this new reality, that's for sure. I felt like I'd been kicked back to kindergarten.

"Let's start with the Pelvic Tilt. I'll explain what needs to happen. Lie down straight on your back with your knees bent. . . That's good. Tighten your abdominal muscles and gently press your lower back flat against the mat. Hold for three seconds to stabilize, then gently lift the back to the starting position. One . . . two . . . three. Easy, easy. Be gentle and slow."

"I'm an athlete. I don't like slow."

"If you want to be an athlete again, you'll have to learn to be patient. Remember, when you start the Pelvic Tilt, inhale to relax, tighten your abs, then exhale as you tilt your pelvis down. Hold three seconds, then come up slowly. Try it now. Do five repetitions, or 'reps' as we call them."

"I did it." Phew.

"Good. Now do five more reps." I dug in and completed the reps.

"Next," she continued, "I'll stretch your back, as I have done before. Then we'll walk."

"Okay, got it."

Five minutes later we were ready to walk the hallways.

"Try getting out of bed by yourself. I'm right here if you need help."

I swayed a little when I straightened up out of bed and took her arm to balance me.

"Time to walk the long hallway." She was a task master but was always nice. "Let me tell you about those different abdominal muscles."

"Okay." *Why I needed to know was beyond me.*

"Stop for a minute. The multifidus is a muscle that helps to hold your spine upright and assists in rotating your spine. The traverse abdominis is the deepest layer of your abdominal muscles, which stabilizes your lower back and pelvis." She spread her hands across my waist to demonstrate.

"Why are you telling me this? Why should I care? I can barely pronounce mutifid . . . whatever!" I giggled.

"Good question," she said, smiling patiently. "Those muscles work together to create stability and strength. They will help your back and, ultimately, your tennis game."

That caught my attention.

"Why have you stopped walking? Keep moving," she instructed.

I looked up. "Hey, Mom. Laura was explaining different muscles to me. Says they'll help with tennis. Good news, huh?"

"Yes, dear," she said in an unconvincing voice.

"We'll schedule another PT session for tomorrow morning and the afternoon. In the meantime, keep walking twice a day and watch your posture. She nodded to Mom. "She's coming along. Good day, Mrs. Sampson."

By the end of the week, I had all of the feeling back in both of my legs. My pain level was still high; Dr. Albertson had cut back on the meds so I could tell when I went too far in physical therapy. Based on my progress, he finally decided to discharge me from the hospital. He told Mom and me that he spoke with my hometown orthopedist, Dr. Fetner, about the injury and treatment options.

"Here's a back brace to stabilize your spine." He handed it to me. "You'll need to wear it during the day, but not at night."

Great. Another brace.

"Good luck. I wish you all the best." He smiled and gave last-minute instructions to Mom, then he closed the door behind him.

Within an hour, we left the hospital grounds. I felt the warmth of holding Mom's hand and hoped that soon everything would be all right.

Chapter 12

I recuperated at home after being in West Virginia nearly a month, and I felt terribly isolated as my high school friends and Angela were now in college. Stretch, our dachshund, was my willing partner when I performed exercises in the backyard. He watched me walk backwards, then up and down the portable steps as part of my rehab. When I'd complete the routine, Stretch would knit his brow and tilt his head, stealing my heart as he always did.

Dr. Fetner insisted that I wear the back brace and continue the daily walks. The alternating muscle contractions would help my back. After breakfast each morning, except when it rained, Mom and I would walk down one street, turn around and walk back home. The following day another street was added, then another and another until, little by little, my back began to straighten. The pain subsided, though I still took pain medication and looked forward to the day when I could return to the courts. That was my goal.

For several weeks, I underwent physical therapy sessions three times a week at the local orthopedic clinic, about fifteen minutes from our home. Since it wasn't safe for me to drive yet, we planned the sessions around Mom's work schedule. I wished that the sessions would end soon, but I knew I had a long road ahead of me with a new group of back and hip exercises set to begin: the Cat-Cow pose and the Clam Shell.

The Clam Shell exhausted me the most—an exercise for strengthening the deep, external rotator muscles of the hip. To perform this exercise, I would lie on my side with knees bent at a ninety-degree angle with my leg and ankle stacked on top of each other.

"Lift one knee in a hinge-like motion, resembling a clam-shell," Nicolas, the physical therapist, instructed. "Keep your ankles together. Don't let your body roll backwards. Hold for two seconds. Repeat eight times. . . . Excellent. You've got the hang of it. Do another set of eight reps."

"Can I rest for a minute?"

"Not yet. Turn over and do the same routine again. Two sets of eight reps."

Nicolas supported my back and encouraged me as I fought through the tiresome ordeal. No matter how difficult the therapy exercises were, the worst part came at the end of every session.

I took a shaking breath, stepped into the four-by-five-foot aluminum tub, the Bath from Hell. Ice water shot into my feet, shocking every nerve. My slim frame trembled as I fought against submerging my body. My stomach tightened with queasiness.

Nicolas played my favorites, the Four Tops, The Beatles, the Beach Boys—anything to distract me until the eight freezing minutes were up. Despairing of how much longer I would have to endure all this throbbing, numbing pain, I popped another pill.

I kept my emotions inside and closed myself off from family, friends, and even myself. I really didn't know why I kept things buried. I tried writing in the leather notebook Donna had given me, hoping to feel better. Eventually, I gave up writing.

When Mom returned from the public library one rainy day, she stacked several books on my desk.

"You trying to dictate what I read?" I asked.

"If you don't like the books, I'll take them back." She left my bedroom shaking her head.

I picked up each book, and two struck me: *Strength to Love* by Martin Luther King and *Le Petit Prince* by Antoine de Saint-Exupery. I knew something about King's assassination and was curious to know more about him. The other book was in French, whose author I couldn't even pronounce. But the back cover had an intriguing quote: *"Voici mon secret. Il est très simple: on ne voit bien qu'avec le cœur. L'essential est invisible pour les yeux."* I knew some high-school French and translated. "Here is my secret. It is very simple: It is only with the heart that one can see rightly; what is essential is invisible to the eye."

But how was it possible to see rightly when your heart was broken?

As leaves began to fall that autumn, I wondered what winter's chill had in store. Time is different when you can't move easily. Days seem to inch along; they seem all the same with one flowing into the next. On a gray, chilly afternoon, feeling pitifully sorry for myself, I turned to the writings of Martin Luther King in his collection of sermons, *Strength to Love*, the book Mom brought home from the library and renewed for me at my request. I happened upon his 1967 Christmas Eve sermon. He wrote: "You can't give up in life. If you lose hope, somehow you lose that vitality that keeps life moving, you lose that courage to be, that quality that helps you go on in spite of all."

I'd heard that line, "you can't give up in life." But where, when had I heard it? Was it what Harry said to Angela a few years ago when she and Donna visited the club? Alice Marble certainly never gave up, even though the odds were stacked against her.

No matter how hard I worked on the exercises, dark edges of loneliness set in again as the months lingered. Everything had been difficult: getting out of bed, standing up straight, going downstairs, walking without a hitch. It had been three months since the accident, and a restless spirit can't be idle very long.

Dad had a sixth sense when things seemed out of balance with me, and so it was no surprise when, one November weekend morning, he said, "Bring your coffee and come downstairs. I want to show you the latest piece of furniture I've been working on. A night table that needs some smoothing around the edges. I could use your help."

"Okay," I said as I took his arm.

Dad's basement workshop was a treasure trove of saws, vices, nuts and bolts, chisels, different grades of sandpaper, and several planes. Coils of wood shavings covered a small area of the floor. Tiny particles of dust hung in the sunlight, shining through the window that he always kept partially open for ventilation.

I loved watching him shape a piece of wood and put all the pieces together. I took a deep breath. "It smells so sweet."

"That's cherry, my favorite wood," he explained.

We spent almost two hours down in the basement, measuring the wood for a nightstand, smoothing out the table legs with sandpaper, and then vacuuming the remaining cherry shavings.

"Woodworking takes good eye-hand coordination, creativity, and patience," Dad said as we walked upstairs for lunch.

"Like tennis," I said.

"That's right," he said with a nod.

~

Mom and I continued our daily walks, even when snowfall hushed the world; it was too peaceful not to be outside. Reading comforted me and offered a glimpse into different worlds— places I couldn't pronounce, people who shared their joys, tribulations, and cultures with distinct customs. I decided to write again in Donna's soft-leather notebook to outline my progress and create match scenarios.

Angela sent me a postcard from college and asked how my back was. She also wrote that since the women tennis players were so easy to beat, she played mostly with the guys. She ended with, "Miss you and GET WELL SOON!" It brightened my spirits to hear her voice in my mind . . . but only for a moment. Nothing was happening "soon."

Each day, weather permitting I walked by myself farther around the neighborhood, feeling my back loosening up and praying for the day when I no longer had to wear the back brace. Until I was able to return to the red clay and feel the ball touch the strings of my racquet, I remained moody and irritable.

I returned home from a walk around the neighborhood a few days before Thanksgiving, when Mom stated, "It's time for you to start thinking about others, not just yourself. "

I planted myself at the edge of the sofa where she was sewing in the family den.

"The Scripture says, 'Encourage one another and build each other up.'"

"Give it a rest, Mom. I'm not ready to do anything."

"Too bad. Why not volunteer at the public library a few hours a week and read to children? They're always looking for volunteers."

"Not yet!" I protested.

Mom continued mending clothes, sitting by the mahogany end table that edged close to the bay window. She didn't seem as relaxed as she usually was when sewing.

"Darn, that hurt." Mom exclaimed. Blood trickled down her index finger to the palm of her hand. "Get me a towel from the kitchen, please."

I handed her a towel and a cold washcloth.

"Thank you, dear." She wiped away the blood and wrapped the cold washcloth around her finger.

"You okay, Mom?"

"It's just a prick."

"I mean, you seem edgy."

"Well . . . today a letter came from Aunt Lucie. She wrote to say that she's not feeling too well." Aunt Lucie was my mother's aunt whom she adored, and my namesake. She was French and lived in Normandy, France.

My voice tightened. "What's wrong with her?"

"Something about pain in her stomach. I'll call her soon to learn more."

"Good idea, Mom."

She looked away for a moment, then turned to me. "Now about volunteering?"

"I'll think about it," I replied.

For the next several months, I read to second and third graders at the library on Saturday afternoons. For the most part, they'd sit quietly on the carpeted floor in a circle, resting their elbows on their knees, listening to different stories. Sometimes the kids cheered loudly for the good guy, or sighed when a puppy broke its foot, or laughed at me when I'd act out a part. One day I read a few lines from the poem "Birches," by Robert Frost.

When I see birches bend to left and right
Across the lines of straighter darker trees,
I like to think some boy's been swinging them.
But swinging doesn't bend down to stay
As ice-storms do.

One of the boys jumped up and started swinging and swaying, almost losing his balance.

"Is this how the trees do it?" he asked.

"Pretty much, Jimmy. Don't bend too far over, just a little bit. Watch, like this." I demonstrated and they all giggled. I continued reading and stopped at the line, "The boy always kept his poise."

I looked at the group and said, "Let's all stand up and try it, like what the poem says."

"What's poise?" little Rebecca asked.

"Watch as I bend sideways slowly with both my feet solid on the ground. See, I don't lose my balance. That's poise . . . steady and balanced." Ironic—these were the two traits that challenged me.

Rebecca and the other children followed suit, bending slowly down and up several times, being careful not to fall over. They were adorable and terrific. The impulse to bear children of my own beat within me.

Chapter 13

I enjoyed sharing my interest in reading with the children and settled into a weekly routine with them throughout the winter months. I also continued working on all the back, hip, and leg exercises my doctor and physical therapist prescribed. Life took on a more hopeful outlook as spring approached.

Mom entered my bedroom late one morning. "Want to go for a walk?"

"Sure. Let's walk to Tullamore. It's longer than my usual walks, but it's nice and sunny."

"Bring your sweater, though," she cautioned. "The temperatures are still cool."

"Must you *always* tell me what to do?"

"That's what mothers do."

~

We walked in silence, noticing the delicate new petals of purple crocus and the upright arch of budding yellow forsythia in our neighbor's gardens.

Mom broke the silence. "Received another letter from Aunt Lucie. She's not feeling any better and the doctors haven't agreed on a diagnosis yet."

"Oh, Mom."

"I'd like to visit her in Normandy. Also, the French Open in Paris begins in two weeks. Would you like to go?"

"Of course!"

"You'll need to pay for your airline ticket."

"Yikes. Well, I still have some babysitting money left over in my savings account. I haven't touched it. Should cover an airline ticket, no?" I asked.

"Just about, dear."

"Will Dad be joining us?"

"No, he'll be working. We'll spend two days in Paris at the French Open, then travel north to Normandy for a few days. Thankfully, that region is safer than Paris since the riots."

Puzzled, I turned to face Mom and asked. "How could the Martin Luther King assassination riots have anything to do with France?"

"I'm referring to the student protests in May of '68, at the University of Sorbonne in Paris. They protested about overcrowded dormitories, outdated academic facilities, and other grievances."

"What happened?" I asked.

"It started out peacefully, but then students started throwing cobblestones at police. Disgruntled truck drivers and sanitation workers joined the student protesters. For weeks, there was no gasoline, no public transportation, and no garbage pick-up."

"Did the rioting affect the French Open that year?" I asked.

"Oh, yes. Streets were barricaded. Since very few taxi drivers drove their cabs, the players were often late to the tournament grounds, which created scheduling problems. Garbage piled up in the streets and tear-gas choked the air. Hundreds of Parisians wanted to forget about the riots and attend the tennis matches. They walked miles to the tournament, filling up the stadium for the entire two weeks. France was in the grip of civil unrest, yet the French Open went on despite the turmoil."

"That's quite a history lesson, Mom. And yes, I'd love to watch professional tennis players in person and meet my namesake."

∽

Our small Paris hotel was located on a narrow, cobblestoned street three blocks from the Sorbonne. Mom was reading the metro map in our sunny, street-view room, figuring out which train would take us to the French Open.

"The metro to the French Open is only a few blocks from here," she said.

"Great. Let's go."

While we hurried to the Metro, I noticed a young woman wearing a floppy, wide-brimmed, purple hat as we passed her. So fashionable! I turned to get a better look, but Mom tugged on my sleeve and pointed to the Metro entrance that would take us to the Metro stop, across the way from Roland Garros, home of the French Open.

∽

We took our time enjoying how the sunbeams peeked through the canopies of chestnut trees. Soon, more people of all ages crowded the Boulevard. We made our way to the tournament entrance, which was framed by red geraniums and flags from different nations. I burst into tears at the huge *"Bienvenu"* sign. "Welcome," in blue, white, and red.

"What's wrong?" Mom asked.

"I miss tennis so much. Will I ever get to play competitively again?"

"I don't know. Maybe you'll be inspired by watching the players." She pointed toward some benches. "Let's go see that plaque over there by the wrought-iron benches."

I stared in awe at the six-foot plaque. Etched in brass were the names of all the previous winners since 1920.

"Mom, look. Althea Gibson won this tournament in 1956. Remember Alice Marble? She's the one who fought for Althea's right to play in any tournament for which she qualified. It's great to see Althea's name up there."

"Yes, it certainly is." She slipped her arm around me. "Let's get to our seats. We don't want to miss the match."

We followed the usher up several steps to the open portal. In the distance the famous Eiffel Tower soared, watching over pedestrians and players alike.

Once the matches started, players would tap the bottom of their sneakers with their racquets to dislodge any red clay build-up. They all had a seriousness about them, and I wondered whether they were having any fun at all.

First up, Ken Rosewall, one of the Australian greats, played against a lesser-known player. Rosewall was quick on his feet and rarely lost his balance. He punched volleys to the corners just like Dad. Rosewall's backhand simply glided through the air with accuracy and variety. Their long rallies went back and forth with cross-court backhands, down-the-line forehands, and then Rosewall hit a sneaky drop-shot to end the point. He had such feel for the ball, as if brushing it softly.

"What a shot, Mom!" I exclaimed. "This is great! Guess that's why my coaches had me hit hundreds of balls, day after day, so I would develop the ability to play by feel. Now I get it."

Mom smiled.

∽

"Bonjour Monsieur, deux pour petit déjeuner, s'il vous plait," Mom said.

"Mais bien sûr, Madame," the Maître d' said. With a turn of his arm, he showed us the way to a small table by the window.

Mom continued to speak French and ordered breakfast. She asked how far the Jardin du Luxembourg was and asked what else we might do before taking the metro to the second day of the tournament. He seemed delighted to speak with her and explained that the garden was not too far to walk. His eyes filled with delight when she spoke French.

Vegetable omelets and buttery croissants melted in my mouth. After a second café au lait, we left the restaurant to walk the short distance on the Boulevard Saint-Michel to the Jardin du Luxembourg.

The stillness of the early morning was a haunting throwback to the morning of my horseback-riding accident. But the Luxembourg garden was so beautiful, with its cedar and oak trees lining the perimeter and colorful flower beds, that I soon forgot about the accident. At the garden's central pond, two children raced their miniature, yellow sailboats, prodding them with sticks to see who would get to the other end of the pond the fastest. Their parents cheered them on. What fun they were having! Soon seagulls swooped down on the pond, reminding me of the summers spent with Joanne at Long Beach Island. We watched the graceful birds perch themselves on the boardwalk rails, waiting for crumbs left by beach goers who would settle on a nearby bench.

Mom and I walked to the other end of the park and took the metro to Roland Garros, which took about thirty minutes. As we approached the front entrance, my heart skipped a beat. Would my aching back ever hold up under the constant repetition of striking the ball over and over again?

We arrived early. Coach Martin always said to watch great players warm up. They hit as if the ball was in slow motion. Getting the feel for hitting a tennis ball was, according to him, the key to dictating play. He would often say, "Lucie, carry the ball across the net." That's exactly what these players were doing. One of the players was Evonne Goolagong from Australia. She stroked the ball with incredible ease and moved around the court like a gazelle.

"Mom, watch Goolagong's backhand. Doesn't it remind you of Rosewall's slice backhand?"

"It does. It's so fluid; she simply slides through the shot on these clay courts."

Goolagong's serve was beautiful. At the baseline, she looked relaxed; she bounced the ball once or twice before serving, seemingly unaware of the game's score. Then she'd slide her back foot toward her front foot as she prepared to toss the ball into the air. It would hang there for a split second longer than other players before she struck the ball. Her service motion reminded me of Angela's grace when she served—her best shot. Great variety was part of Goolagong's repertoire: full of angles, spins, depth, and the smoothest backhand approach shot I ever saw.

How exciting it would have been to see a match between Evonne Goolagong, a complete all-court player, against a serve-volley player like Alice Marble. My game was some-where in between—not quite the variety of a Goolagong, nor the quick serve of a Marble.

Goolagong won the first set, 6–3. There was a two-minute break so that spectators could stretch their legs. Directly across the stadium, I noticed a young woman with a purple hat stand up and make her way to the exit.

"Mom, there's that same girl we saw near the Sorbonne yesterday." I pointed in the direction of the girl.

"Hmm, maybe she plays tennis too, or is a student at the Sorbonne."

I focused on Goolagong's footwork as the second set unfolded. She quickly took that set, 6–1, winning the match by playing to her opponent's weakness—the volley. Goolagong, the steadier of the two, hit long rallies, making her opponent stretch on her backhands, then hit a short shot bringing her opponent to the net. Goolagong would then pass her with a lovely low backhand or a deep high lob. This frustrated her opponent, but Goolagong continued that tactic until the end, when she quickly took the last two games by chipping forward and attacking high volleys.

I tucked away everything I saw in the store of tennis wisdom I kept filed in my brain.

～

The next morning, we ate at the same restaurant as yesterday.

"Bonjour, Madame et Mademoiselle. Le petit déjeuner, n'est-ce pas?" He warmly greeted Mom and led us to the same table by the window. We had several rail connections to make before we arrived at Cany-Barville in the Normandy province where Aunt Lucie lived. We didn't linger at the restaurant as before, and ate quickly.

Having never met Aunt Lucie, my great aunt, I was anxious to know what she was like. She'd sent me a heartwarming get-well card after the riding accident and over the years had always remembered my birthday. Each year at Christmastime, a package from France would arrive on our doorstep, always the same delicious dark chocolates laced with a peppermint liqueur. Most years I remembered her birthday, and when I was younger, I would send her a homemade Easter card. Mom said that Aunt Lucie had a knack for storytelling so I was eager to hear what she might have in store for us. I wondered what mother loved so much about Aunt Lucie. I would soon find out.

Chapter 14

We arrived late afternoon in Cany-Barville. There was no trace of wind or heat; just a light amber sky with soft shadows spreading over the wheatfields in the distance. As we stepped off the train onto the station platform, an elegantly dressed woman stood at one end with a priest by her side. They walked slowly toward us, waving. Could this be my namesake? She wore a stunning A-line, light-blue, tweed suit with navy ribbon trim at the collar. A silver brooch pinned the suit's left lapel. Nervously, I watched as Mom hugged Aunt Lucie and kissed her on both cheeks. She had a gentle face with soft hazel eyes that brightened as Mom introduced her.

"Aunt Lucie, I would like you to meet my daughter, Lucie."

Aunt Lucie stroked her graying, wavy hair away from her face, looked straight into my eyes, and kissed both my cheeks. Her lips were as soft as a rose petal. She smiled, then introduced the priest as Father Lucien and said, "*Allons-y*. Let's go."

Aunt Lucie's family home, a half-mile from the center of town, lay at the end of a curved and narrow street. Flowering beech trees surrounded her two-story, stone masonry house with peach-colored, terracotta roof tiles and casement windows. As the four of us entered, Aunt Lucie unpinned her top jacket.

One large window and three smaller windows gave a natural, welcoming light to the living room. Despite the dark, exposed wood beams, an airy lightness permeated the room. The floors were made of gorgeous, beige stones with several small rugs scattered about. The room also served as the dining area. A series of still life paintings of yellow pansies and red poppies decorated an adjacent wall. A home full of life.

Once settled inside, we sat around the oval kitchen table and enjoyed some port wine, Normandy cheeses, and delicious Madeleine cakes, which really hit the spot after our long journey from Paris.

I gazed out the window. Her beautiful garden was full of pansies—purple, yellow, and orange ones. In the far corner of the garden near a tool shed was a cluster of yellow roses seeming to stand at attention waiting to be admired from afar.

Aunt Lucie must have noticed my fascination because she said, "Let us go and sit in the garden."

Father Lucien carried a tray of three glasses, a pitcher of water, some cheese and cakes and led us to a forest-green, wrought-iron table and chairs. We sat and listened to the calls of a lark in the distance. He smiled and returned to the house. Aunt Lucie had learned to speak English, although haltingly and with limited vocabulary, but we had little trouble understanding her.

"Ma petite," she addressed me, "how is your back?" She had the kindest face I'd ever seen.

"Not too bad. I think I'm making good progress with physical therapy. It's hard, and it can be boring sometimes, but I'm used to it. I started PT when I was a kid for my hip problem."

"Yes, I remember your mother telling me. It's good that you are making progress. Try not give in to any dark feelings you may have."

"It's hard not to, Aunt Lucie, but I think Mom would agree, I'm really trying."

"Yes, dear, you are," Mom affirmed.

Aunt Lucie continued, "Keep at it. Takes time to heal, *ma petite*. Now, tell me about this friend of yours, Angela, the girl you mentioned in your last letter."

"Angela's a really good tennis player and a good friend. We get along well, even though we're pretty different. She's quiet and calm when she plays a match; I'm temperamental. She's Black; I'm white. We both like history. Her father lost his life after suffering injuries when his plane was shot down in the Korean War; he was an Air Force pilot."

"I'm sorry to hear that. What keeps you two together?"

"Our love for tennis, I guess. Plus, we were both bullied a lot."

"Keep her close, *ma petite*." She patted my knee. "Do you have plans for college?"

"If all goes well, I'll start in September. I've been accepted to Florida State University."

"Felicitations," she smiled with the lilt of her voice.

Mom turned to Aunt Lucie and poured her a glass of water. "How are you feeling?"

She took the glass. "Thank you, Isabelle. I'm feeling all right, dear. We can talk about that later. But for now, I have something I want to share with you both."

Her hazel eyes were soft as she began to tell a story about Gabriel Durand who, at the young age of twenty-three, served in the French army during World War I as a stretcher bearer.

I leaned forward and said nothing as Aunt Lucie began. "Stretcher bearers were a team of four to six soldiers responsible for picking up wounded soldiers from the battlefields and carrying them on stretchers to medical aid posts. Under terrible circumstances, with machine-gun firing straight toward them, they would dodge and stumble until they could reach a wounded man and carry him to safety."

Aunt Lucie sliced a thin piece of camembert cheese for each of us, took a sip of water and went on to explain that each stretcher bearer was given a pannier—a canvas sack with a red cross painted on the side, containing a water bottle, gauze bandages with tail ends, packs of compressed bandages, and morphine tablets.

Mom asked, "Did the stretcher bearers have any kind of medical training?"

"Yes. Doctors and nurses trained them in how to bandage open wounds, apply splints to broken bones, and administer morphine when necessary."

Aunt Lucie excused herself and walked inside to the living room. I watched her. She slid open a drawer from the desk next to the window, retrieved something, and placed it in her skirt pocket. When she returned, she unfolded a partially torn, stained envelope from her pocket. She stilled her hand and said, "This letter was written by a stretcher bearer to Gabriel's parents. They gave it to me soon after they received it." She began reading.

> Monsieur et Madame Durand,
> We got to know your son well. He had this small grill that you gave him before he left for the Front. Once a week we gathered in his dugout and he cooked us sausage, beans, and cocoa. We laughed at silly jokes and told stories. His eyes brightened when he spoke about you and his fiancée, Lucie.

Aunt Lucie took a sip of port before she resumed reading.

> During heavy rains we'd be knee-high in mud. Gabriel always led the way. He was steady, strong, and selfless. Always making sure the wounded soldier we carried would not fall off our stretcher.

One day, after two hours in the cold and rain looking for injured soldiers, we finally made it back to the aid post in an abandoned stone farmhouse. When the doctor and nurse saw us coming with a patient, they ran to help, but not before a sniper bullet from the nearby forest pierced Gabriel's neck. It killed him instantly. We will never forget him.

Yours Truly,
Jean-Pierre Foubert
July 22, 1918
Battle of Soissons

Aunt Lucie wiped her tears and whispered, *"C'est tout,* that's all." She bowed her head in silence. She was my namesake and all I could do was sit there quietly while Mom knelt in the grass and placed her hands on Aunt Lucie's lap. It was impossible to imagine what Aunt Lucie's fiancé had gone through. She awakened in me a deep sadness and respect for what Gabriel and stretcher bearers had done to help their comrades, their friends, at any cost.

After breakfast the next day, the three of us took a walk, arm-in-arm, along a narrow path. It led to fields of goldenrod and then down a gently sloping street to the town square and a church. The sun was bright, the air crisp. Candles were lit in front of a statue of Joan of Arc to the left of the church's entrance. Little flames danced in the sunlight, pale and clear against the dazzling whiteness of the walls. Between two windows, the names of local soldiers who died in the "War to End All Wars" were etched in golden letters shimmering on a marble tablet. Aunt Lucie pointed to Gabriel Pierre Durand's name then sat down on the marble bench. I brushed my fingers across the marble, feeling the curve of the letters, and lit a candle.

I turned toward Aunt Lucie and looked into her kind eyes—eyes that took you in, comforted you, and promised that everything would be all right. I sat beside her in silence. Time passed slowly in that moment. I thought of Angela and her father.

Mom lit one last candle before she sat beside Aunt Lucie.

Aunt Lucie shared another story about her brother. Paul was part of a group of schoolteachers who fought the Nazis by joining the Resistance during World War II.

I whispered to Mom, "Why is Aunt Lucie so eager to tell us such personal stories? Is there a reason?"

"There must be," Mom responded softly.

Aunt Lucie kept telling her story. "The Resistance members were schoolteachers, doctors, housewives, priests, bankers—fighting for their country's freedom. After the war, we were told by a friend, who was also in the Resistance, that Paul and his group traveled by train between Paris and Arles in the south of France to obtain secret information about what the Nazis were planning."

"What was their mission?" Mom asked.

Aunt Lucie spoke slowly. "They were couriers who passed messages via train between the two cities. A courier would place a thin newspaper inside one of the lavatory signs. Another courier from the other group would go to the restroom, unscrew the sign, retrieve a note placed inside the newspaper, then replace it with his own message, and reattach the sign. The messages revealed locations of Nazi soldiers and weapons, and instructions on how to cut down communication lines."

"Ingenious—and dangerous," Mom said.

"Yes. The friend also said that when Paul's group entered the Porte d' Orléans station in Paris, the Gestapo captured them. They sent them to the Fresnes Prison located a few miles south of Paris. Paul died in that prison in 1944."

I mustered up some courage to ask, "Aunt Lucie, do you hate the Germans?"

"I hated them for a while. They took my fiancé and my brother. It was difficult to forgive. But I grew tired of being angry. I became bitter; it affected the way I treated people. What the Nazis did was horrific. Sometimes I still get angry, but I am not bitter anymore.

"But how do you bear the loss, the sorrow?" I asked.

"Long sorrow is fruitless. It yields nothing. If we are full of hate, there will be no room for love, there will be no future. In our darkest moments, we must focus to see the light."

"But how, Aunt Lucie?"

She motioned toward the main entrance. "Let's go inside the church. The sun is hot now." We settled into one of the back pews and welcomed the cooler air.

Quietly, she continued. "To get out of my darkness," she said, "I relied on my friends. I suggested to a small group of lady friends that we help young people whose memory of their war-torn country was still fresh. So, for the last twenty-five years, we have traveled down to Paris, to the Université de Sorbonne, the week before Christmas. We speak with students about the effects of war on the young. No point in being bitter and creating hatred. We serve them homemade chicken and split pea soups, apple pies and chocolate cookies. There are German, Dutch, and Italian students in the audience. They ask lots of questions and exchange ideas with their French classmates. It is uplifting."

We sat quietly in the pew admiring the stained-glass windows as the afternoon sunlight played with shifting tones of orange and red. I felt humbled by all Aunt Lucie had told us and heartened by her dedication to the younger generation. Perhaps that was the reason she shared her stories of friendship, service, and courage—to alert me to their importance. I loved her gentle and wise spirit.

Chapter 15

When Mom and I returned from France, a letter from Tallahassee, Florida, was waiting for me on my nightstand. I couldn't wait to hear what Angela had to say about her second year at Florida A & M University.

Hi, Lucie,

How are you? How's your back? I hope you're getting stronger every day. I really like my classes, especially Anatomy and History. But I don't like all the cliques here; either you're a jock, an artist, a musician, or a nerd, and the boys on the tennis team think they're God's gift to the world. Funny thing is, I can beat many of them. The men's team gets priority over the women's team in signing up for the tennis courts. Doesn't seem fair. Drives me nuts.

By the way, I saw Karen Mitchell last weekend at a big tournament in Orlando. She plays for Rollins College, not far from Orlando. She came up to me and had the nerve to say, "I hear Lucie had a bad riding accident. Least she won't be playing tennis anymore."

She rushed off as I yelled, "Don't bet on it!" Something's wrong with that girl, Lucie.

Angela also wrote how much she was looking forward to returning home this summer and for the two of us to start playing tennis again. I winced.

I hadn't picked up a racquet since the horseback riding accident almost a year ago, and had no idea how my back would respond to the demands of tennis. My back was stiff, and my hip clicked every once in a while. I knew I still had a long road ahead with hours of treatment and rest before I could even step onto a court. Tennis drills and the grind of practice would have to wait. But giving up wasn't an option. I thought of Alice Marble and all the setbacks she endured, yet she worked tirelessly on getting healthy so she could play tennis again. Then she won Wimbledon. What an inspiration!

I wrote back, saying how much I wanted to play tennis with her, but had my doubts as Dr. Fetner said it would be months before hitting the ball was possible. My physical therapy had to take priority.

And so it did. I handled the painful exercises and tolerated the dreaded Ice Bath from Hell. I kept reminding myself that these exercises would return me to the court—to slide on the red clay and to swing freely in midair. That joy was motivation enough.

I returned to the court in mid-August, three weeks before I would leave for college. The day dawned crisp and clear, bringing with it a new hope—that my body would hold up.

Coach Martin was waiting for me on the end court. "Ready, young lady?" he called and grinned his signature smile.

"Ready as I'll ever be!"

"Let's begin, then."

I moved gingerly at first, measuring the rhythm of our rally, one lovely beat after another. I soon trusted myself to change the beat and run quickly and swing freely. My back and thigh muscles felt smooth and hot. Oh, how sweet it was to be back where I belonged!

Coach and I hit for half an hour, moving each other forward and back, slicing backhands in one direction and stroking forehands in the other direction. When we took a break, I swiped the back of my hand across my face to wipe away the sweat. I loved the salty taste to my lips.

"Shall I try serving?" I asked.

"Let's wait on that for tomorrow," he advised. "Instead, let's hit some volleys at net then call it a day."

"All right, but I'm feeling stronger every minute."

"That's what I like to hear, Lucie. When you're in the locker room, be sure to stretch your back, shoulders, and legs."

"Will do. Thanks, Coach, see you tomorrow."

Before I left for college, Dad took a few days off from work to play singles with me and play some friendly mixed doubles with another father-daughter duo. Calm washed over me whenever we hit together, and these final days playing with him readied me for college.

As we walked off the court, he stopped, and said. "The riding accident has been hard for you. Your mother and I have watched you strive to find your way through it all. Life, unfortunately, deals us these setbacks. It creates cracks along the way, and sometimes holes in our hearts. Recovery will take time, Lucie. Longer than you want it to. You are strong, you are stubborn, and you are impatient. Keep your head high and you'll find your way back."

"I will, Dad."

Chapter 16

Like many serious tennis players, I chose Florida State University because I knew I could play tennis all-year-round. In Tallahassee, I wouldn't have to contend with Long Island's cold, snowy winters. A bonus was that Angela was at Florida A & M, a college predominately for Black students, just over a mile away.

While my back fatigued the first few weeks I began playing at FSU, I gradually resumed a semblance of quick movements and smart shot making. The tennis court's surface was hard, cement-like, tough on the knees and back; nothing like the softer, forgiving surface of red clay. I would need to carefully monitor my daily workouts, given the hard courts. But nothing would keep me from playing the sport I loved.

I enjoyed my classes, especially Comparative Literature and Art History. My early interest in reading paid off as I found myself deluged with heavy reading assignments in British, Spanish, and Russian literature. In my art history class, the professor introduced us to photography as a way to better analyze paintings. We were given loaner cameras so we could experiment first-hand with light, composition, and focal point. I took to photography immediately and soon realized the patience it required, a skill I badly needed to cultivate. Another skill I needed to master was the balancing of all these interests.

~

"Have you heard about the tournament in Gainesville? It's in November. Both our men and women's teams are entered," Angela said one Sunday late in September, as we sat over coffees and bagels at Oscar's coffee shop, a convenient midpoint location for both of us.

"I heard," I replied. "Our men's team is going, but the women's team still must get permission from the director of athletics to enter. I'd love to go. Our team's a bit disorganized. We're coached by an unpaid graduate student who has little coaching experience, but who thankfully has a passion for tennis."

"Same at A & M. But our grad student is an excellent player. I'm hopeful."

"Me too. Guess we expected coaching by professionals like we had at the junior development program. By the way, does your team have uniforms?" I said.

"No."

"Neither does ours, so we decided to sew white and garnet trim, the university's colors, on our tennis dresses. Makes us feel a bit more like a team. Of course, the men's team have uniforms, plus they play on six brand-new, hard courts. Our women's team plays on four cement courts located at the other end of the athletic complex."

"We're stuck sharing ten courts with the men's team. It isn't fair," Angela said.

"Can't agree more. The male players can qualify for scholarships, but there's no money for female players. It's as if were second-class citizens."

"We are, and it's just not right. Listen, Lucie, I need to get to the library. Lots of studying still to do," Angela said.

"Me too." We left together. "See you next Sunday, Ange."

~

Eventually, the FSU director of athletics gave permission for us to play in the Gainesville Invitational. Our coach drove the team in a six-seater VW van, and in less than two hours we arrived at the University of Florida campus. Four other teams were invited, including Rollins College where Karen Mitchell, my old adversary from the junior development program, played on their team. Throughout the weekend, each team member played a total of four singles matches and four doubles matches. My doubles partner who hailed from Miami was a perky, talented girl with a lovely serve and quick hands at the net. We enjoyed playing together and had won all of our three matches so far. My back ached as the brutal consecutive singles and doubles matches took their toll. We had one last doubles match to play. We were scheduled to compete against Karen and her partner.

From the corner of my eye, I saw Karen stride onto the court, nose up in the air, and twirling her ponytail.

She drives me nuts . . . still, after all these years.

She walked straight toward me. "Hah! I heard you were back. Still trying to be someone you'll never be."

"That's right, Karen. Just watch."

Our doubles match proved to be a battle of endurance, running down shots, smashing high overheads and angling sharp volleys. We won the first set 6–4 and were ahead in the second set 5–3, with Karen serving to me at match point. I focused on her ball toss and anticipated the serve out wide; I took the ball early and stroked it hard down the line. Karen scrambled to retrieve it, but the ball wheezed right by her. She didn't have a chance. We won the point, the set, and the match. I soaked in the applause from our teammates who were watching from the courtside bleachers.

As is customary, the four of us shook hands at the net, but Karen only whispered in my ear, "This isn't over, Lucie."

"What isn't, Karen?" I laughed.

She snickered and walked away.

~

Two weeks after the Gainesville tournament, I went to a Saturday night frat party. At nine o'clock, I walked into the noisy, smoky living room and saw a tall man with wavy, strawberry-blonde hair standing by a beer keg. When he turned sideways to grab a beer, I tilted my head to get a better view of his buns. I chuckled at how tight they were, but hesitated to cross the room. This was new territory for me, but it was time I explored a different social scene. I was captivated by his style and stood helpless with indecision. Finally, I caught his eye. He smiled back and motioned with his hand to come over. I zigzagged around people to the far end where he was waiting.

"I'm Henry Logan. Can I get you something to drink?"

"Hi, I'm Lucie Sampson. What do you suggest?"

"How about a screwdriver—vodka and orange juice."

"Sounds delicious."

"I saw you on the tennis court the other day; you've got a wicked backhand," Henry said.

"Thanks. I'm on the women's team."

"Cool. I play for the men's team."

My heart skipped a beat. "Maybe we can play together some time?"

"You ready to get beaten?"

"Ah, it's a match, then," I said with a smile. "Yeah, I'll take you on!"

"Hah!" He handed me my drink.

We talked and laughed for a while, and after a few more drinks, decided on a walk around the fraternity's property. I felt comfortable in the easy balmy evening, but soon realized it was eleven forty-five, just fifteen minutes before dorm curfew.

"I've got to get back to the dorm by midnight. If not, it's an infraction. Sorry, Henry, I need to leave."

He grabbed me, kissed me hard, and let me go.

～

The next morning Angela and I met at Oscar's. I sat down at our usual spot, the last booth next to a window with checkered curtains.

"Hey, Lucie, how are you?" my friend asked. "You look tired. Party last night?"

"With lots of drinking. Feel like crap."

"Well, you look it. Let's order some coffee. Can your stomach take breakfast, or you still hung over?"

"I need some breakfast, for sure."

"I've never seen you hung over," Angela grinned, "or know you to drink before."

"I met a guy, Henry Logan, on the men's tennis team."

"What's this Henry guy like?"

"Handsome, great smile . . . great buns too!"

Angela shook her head. "That's it?"

"For now. He's a pretty good conversationalist." I poured cream into my coffee and averted Angela's fixed stare.

"Right. Time to change the subject," Angela said. "I've decided to give Black kids free tennis lessons on Sunday afternoons. Want to help?"

I looked up from my coffee mug and leaned back in the chair. "Uh, yeah, I guess. Where?"

"There are two courts at Barrett Park, off Madison Street, about a mile from here. Closer to you. There's a dog park across the way."

I took another sip of my coffee before asking, "*Every* Sunday?"

"Yeah. I checked with the tennis coaches. They said the university doesn't use the courts anymore for competition, and if I coordinate the outreach and update them every Monday morning, they said it's a go. Plus, they'll provide the balls, good used ones."

"Sure, I'll help you."

"Great! It'll be fun."

"What about advertising?" I asked.

"You're the English major. Write something catchy to get kids' and parents' attention."

"I'll work on it. We can put up some posters to generate interest. By the way, how you'd come up with this idea?"

"Well, Florida A & M students staged several sit-ins in front of City Hall, which blocked the entrance. Police would come and disperse the students with tear gas. The protests happened over and over again with no immediate effect. I wanted to do something where I could see results."

"Good for you, Ange."

"Now, we also need to figure out how to get extra tennis racquets. Kids won't have them. Can you check with the FSU coaches? In case we can't find enough racquets, I think we should limit the clinic to four to six kids for now."

"Agreed."

Ten days later, Angela and I gave our first one-hour tennis clinic, to one girl and three boys. It was a warm October afternoon with cloud cover, ideal for tennis. The two tennis courts had a ten-foot, chain-link fence bordering the perimeter with only a few cracks near the net posts.

The ten- and eleven-year-old children arrived with two other adults. After introductions, Angela and I had the students "run the lines"—a fun way to build anticipation and get students' blood flowing by having them run the lines of the tennis courts. Their laughter filled the air. We then progressed to the forehand, demonstrating the movement of the stroke with and without a racquet. The kids practiced their swings for several minutes as Angela and I walked around to adjust their technique.

To keep it fun and improve hand-eye coordination, the players dribbled the ball with their racquets. Some stumbled at first, but they all worked toward a consistent dribble to see who could get the most dribbles without making a mistake. Next, for several minutes we tossed each of them a ball to hit. One boy couldn't make contact with the ball at all and finally gave up, slouching his shoulders and hanging his head.

"Angela, could you take Jessica into your group for a few minutes?" I said.

"Sure."

"Hey, Jackson, let's play catch without the tennis racquet."

He said nothing.

I walked up to him smiling, "What's wrong? How can I help?"

"I can't hit the ball the way you showed us. You put the racquet in my right hand. I'm left-handed."

"Oh gosh, I'm sorry. My mistake. Thanks for telling me. Let's practice gripping the racquet in your left hand and swinging on your left side."

Jackson progressed beautifully and was soon contacting the ball and even hitting it to the back fence. I loved teaching these kids, especially seeing them smile when they knew they hit a solid shot.

For the next two months, the four students showed up at two o'clock every Sunday afternoon, eager to run around the court and hit tennis balls. One windy December afternoon, Jackson hit a ball over the fence and struck a policeman on the top of his head. Jackson froze.

The policeman turned toward the court. "Hey, kid, did you just hit me? You come over right now." He pointed his finger at Jackson. "And you too, young lady." He looked straight at me and sneered. "Why are you here? You don't belong with these people." He stood with arms crossed, jaw locked.

"It's okay, Jackson," I said and signaled him to join me. I took Jackson's hand and walked off the court toward the officer. One of the other parents joined us and placed his hand on Jackson's heaving shoulders. Angela stayed with the other three kids.

"My friend, Angela, and I have permission to use these courts to give free tennis lessons to local children," I explained to the officer. "We've been doing it for two months now—"

"That's no excuse. Can't you control these people?"

Angela ran over to us, leaving the other parent to stay with the kids.

"But, officer, how can we control that? These kids are just learning. You can only learn if you swing at the ball and make mistakes," Angela said.

"And I'm supposed to trust the word of a nig—uhh, someone like you," he looked down at Angela.

"Excuse me, but what did you just say to her?" I said.

He stepped closer to me, about a foot from my face. "If you want to go to jail in her place, I'm happy to oblige. Why are you helping these people anyway?"

"Get out of my face," I snapped. "I'll do whatever I want. There's no crime against doing this."

"Oh, yes, there is. Turn around."

"What the—?" The officer clapped handcuffs around my wrists. "I did nothing wrong."

"You disrespected a police officer. Now get in the car. We'll settle things at the precinct. Move aside," he said to Angela. "You want to end up like your friend and come to the precinct?"

"Yes, I would," she stood her ground.

"Angela, no. Think of the kids. Finish the lessons. I'll call you later."

"Keep your mouth shut or I'll throw your friend into the car too." He slammed the door.

Angela turned to Jackson and asked, "Did you apologize?"

"No, ma'am."

The officer raised his voice another octave. "See? You people have no manners!"

"Jackson . . ." Angela motioned to him.

"I'm sorry, officer. Didn't mean to hit you. I just lost control of the ball," he said quietly.

"Yeah, but you did, and I don't appreciate it, boy." The policeman got in the car and drove away with me looking out the back window at a fading view of Angela and Jackson standing on the sidewalk.

∼

"Hey Ange, it's me."

"Where are you?"

"Still at the precinct. I was charged with disrespecting a police officer. But after sitting two hours in a dark, cold holding cell, the sergeant finally took me into another room. He grilled me with lots of questions, including whether I had ever been involved in the student civil rights protests. I said no. He eventually dropped the charges and let me go. As I walked out of the precinct, he said, 'Next time you're picked up, we'll book you.' I apologized to him and left."

"What now?" Angela said.

"It's too dark to walk back to my dorm. I'll take a cab. How'd it go with the kids?"

"Okay. They were frightened. Did mini-running drills and then a contest of who could pick up tennis balls the fastest. I tried to make it fun."

"Bet it was. What's next for them?" I asked my friend.

"I told them we'd continue after Christmas."

"Good idea. They want me off the phone now. Gotta go, Ange. See you next Sunday at Oscar's, okay?"

"See you then. Bye."

⁓

Angela looked up from the table when I arrived at Oscar's the following Sunday morning. "Good Lord, you look awful."

"Another party with Henry."

"Tell me, what do you see in him?"

"Well, besides tennis, we both like history and we get into some heated debates. It's interesting listening to him. And he's so good looking."

"Ah, I see," Angela said. "But listen, I've got some bad news: The university cancelled the tennis clinics and gave no reason. When I reported to the coaches the next morning to give them a report, they already knew about the incident. Very embarrassing. I wanted them to hear it from me first. I really wanted to continue working with those kids."

"So did I. They were improving and having fun. I really enjoyed the kids."

"Guess the incident gave the university too much negative publicity," Angela's eyes narrowed.

"I'm so sorry for making things worse."

"It's not your fault, Lucie. I don't know what else we can do right now. Sit-ins don't make much sense to me. I graduate in five months. My mom keeps reminding me that I've got a full-time job teaching tennis waiting for me back in Harlem."

"That's great, Ange."

"I just need to do well in my classes, graduate on time, and play number one for A & M. I don't want to jeopardize anything. I need that job."

"I'm really sorry it has to be this way. You'll make a difference teaching back home, for sure."

"Yes, suppose so."

Chapter 17

Angela graduated on time with a degree in Anatomy and Physical Education, finished number one for Florida A & M, and returned to Harlem to teach tennis. She wrote about how excited she was to be working under the supervision of a well-known tennis instructor, who had longstanding ties within the Black community. I missed our regular brunch meet-ups at Oscar's and the kids from the tennis clinic.

In my final year at FSU, I became increasingly bothered by the disparities between the men's and women's tennis teams at FSU. Our team received free tennis balls and new team uniforms, but it was 1973, and women still had no scholarships or a paid, full-time coach. As team captain, I felt an obligation to make an appointment with the director of athletics to discuss the low priority the university gave to women's sports. I approached the appointment with a measure of pride and fear.

"Please sit down. What can I do for you, Miss Sampson?" the broad-shouldered athletic director said from behind his desk.

"Thank you for meeting with me. As captain of the women's tennis team, I'd like to discuss an increase to our budget."

"I see."

"We barely have enough money to cover travel expenses, and we only have enough money to play in two AIAW sanctioned tournaments."

He shifted his weight and rubbed his mustache. "Go on."

"We're a good team, but we could be stronger if we had a paid, full-time coach and access to the athletic trainers. Just like the men's team."

"Tell me, Miss Sampson, how much revenue do you bring into the athletic department?

"None, sir." My stomach tightened.

"Exactly. The men's team does."

"But people hardly know we exist."

"My point exactly. I doubt the women's tennis team would draw any crowds. Be thankful we gave you new uniforms at the beginning of your season. They're pretty don't you think?" He chuckled.

"Pretty uniforms don't win matches," slipped out of my big mouth. "I mean, thank you. We work hard at our sport and represent FSU well when we play against other colleges."

"That is to be expected."

"But how do you expect us . . ."

"Expect what?" He began tapping his pencil on the desk.

"To improve. To be recognized. To be appreciated."

"You must be patient, Miss Sampson." He stood up from behind his desk. "Just because you are the captain does not mean you can demand things. I'm sorry, but you will not have a paid coach nor any more funds for travel, nor access to our athletic trainers. Good day." He stood.

I remained seated. "But why do men get it and women don't? It's not fair."

Be patient for what exactly? I wondered.

"People are interested in watching male sports, not female sports. That's the way it is. Thank you for coming, Miss Sampson." He didn't move from his standing position.

I pushed up from the leather chair, thanked him for his time, and left his office. Furious.

A few days earlier, I had read an article by Billie Jean King, a great tennis champion. She talked about women's sports and believed that if we don't get enough exposure, people won't know who we are. Influenced by her words, I wrote an editorial in our college newspaper. It was published the next day.

Recently, I met with the athletic director, who told me that "Fans are interested in watching male sports, not female sports. That's the way it is." But that should not be the way it is. A lack of opportunity and funds force women's sports to be squeezed out. This is certainly true for the women's tennis team. We don't have a paid, full-time coach, nor access to athletic trainers, nor a budget for out-of-state tournaments. Female athletes are just as dedicated to their sport as our male athletes.

We want to be recognized and appreciated. How much longer do we have to wait for our fair share of the athletic budget, for something real, lasting and secure?

Signed,
Lucie Sampson
Captain
FSU Women's Tennis Team

～

The following week after practice, when my teammates had left the court, our coach took me aside.

"Lucie, let's talk over there in the shade."

"What's up?" I asked.

"The director of athletics asked to see me in his office."

"Why?" *This can't be good.*

"He's disappointed and offended by your behavior. The editorial placed him, the athletic department, and the university in a bad light. He called it 'behavior unbecoming of a student athlete,' which violates the student athlete code of behavior.'"

"Coach, I was just telling the truth. I quoted him correctly and, well . . . you know how much money our team gets. It's a joke."

"That's not the point, Lucie. You disrespected a university official and in a very public way. The director of athletics carries a lot of weight around here."

"I meant no disrespect. None at all." *Oh, what have I done now?*

"Because of your impertinent attitude in his office and the 'brazen' editorial you wrote—those are his words—you have been benched from competition for the rest of the season."

Every part of me paused while my thoughts caught up, my words unwilling to take flight.

"Lucie, did you hear what I said?" There was an odd gentleness to his voice.

"Yes," I finally uttered.

"You will remain on the team and practice with the team, but that's it. Learn from this, Lucie." He wiped his brow and walked off the court.

I was dripping with humiliation. Playing tennis for the women's team had been an honor. Tennis is an individual sport, so being on a team meant that you were part of something bigger than yourself. I was confused because I'd been trying to help the team. Dad warned me about my impatience. I strike out, never fully realizing the full impact on others.

And so I sat on the bench and cheered on my teammates as they played against other colleges. I hid my shame. Other than rooting for and practicing with the team, I kept to myself. There was no physical therapy for the kind of pain I was feeling; I had to figure out a way to heal.

Chapter 18

At the age of twenty-two, I was a college graduate who wanted to be a professional tennis player. That had been my goal. But now I knew how the sport would challenge me, emotionally and physically, and what it meant to give it my all. Some people thought I was on a fool's errand, given my orthopedic history; others were not surprised, given my passion for the sport. Moving back to Long Island meant I'd have the opportunity to receive first-class rehab at a new sports medicine clinic just fifteen miles away from my parents' home; I'd get to see Angela; and I could continue working-out with Coach Martin.

I had lots of catching-up to do with townspeople, and one of my favorites was Harry. I'd missed chatting with him these past few years and decided to pay him a visit to his kitchen at the tennis club.

He was making sandwiches and welcomed me with a broad smile. "Well, I'll be darned, look who's here." He wiped his hands several times with his apron.

I beamed. "Hi, Harry! How are you?"

"Well, how are *you*, Missy? It's been too long. Word has it you broke your back. Rough time, I'd imagine?"

I nodded. "It happened while horseback riding in West Virginia. I got thrown by a horse and landed on my back. Been tough, but I'm doing pretty well."

"Glad you're getting better."

"How about a glass of your famous orange drink?" I asked, and sat down at the shiny counter on a new, red-padded, aluminum stool. I felt comfortable sitting across from Harry. Same ol' gruff voice but kind face. His hair had streaks of gray around the temples now, and deep lines wrinkled his forehead when he laughed.

He handed me a large tumbler. "Here ya go, Missy."

"Thanks, Harry. I always loved your special drink."

We chatted for a while about his daughter's successful first year at the state college, about the new rules for bringing a guest to the club, and about me.

"I hope to start playing tournaments again. My parents are making me find a job to pay for part of the travel expenses and entrance fees."

"Well, you should pay. No such thing as a free lunch."

"Yeah, I know. But I don't know if I can take on a job, prepare for tournament play, *and* continue with rehab; it's all so overwhelming."

He leaned forward and topped-off my drink, then said gently. "You need to pay your way. Lots of people are in the same boat."

"What do you mean?" I asked.

"Sometimes we have to juggle three or four responsibilities. You know—school, work, family obligations."

"I see."

"Why not check in with Coach Martin. You two go way back."

"I think I'll do that. Thanks Harry," I smiled.

"Don't worry, Missy, things take time. Just work at it. And remember, there's no free lunch." He waved me off with a big grin. "Now go, I need to finish these sandwiches."

❧

A few days later I visited Coach Martin. When he wasn't giving tennis lessons, I always knew where to find him. I entered quietly from the back entrance to the shack where, on one wall, he organized tennis racquets by brand; on another wall, he stacked cans of tennis balls three feet high. Coach had a stringing machine, a small refrigerator, and a comfy couch that I'd relaxed on many times after a hard day smashing overheads and slicing drop shots in the sun. The junior players called the shack "Marty's Place," though we never said it to his face.

I found him sitting on the couch overlooking the red clay courts. I allowed the sight of him to warm my heart for a few long moments before I spoke. "Hi, Coach."

Without even turning, he said, "Hi, Lucie! I'd know that voice anywhere." He turned, got up, and extended his hand. "Great to see you. How's your back? Everyone at the club and around town heard about your terrible accident. Come, sit."

He took my arm and led me to the middle of the couch. Other than some graying around the temples, Coach looked to be the same tan, slim maestro of tennis I so adored. We talked for about half an hour.

The sun cast shadows across the courts. Coach Martin said, "Remember how those shadows gave you such trouble? You'd lose the ball in the darker section of the court. You seem to be in those shadows now." On the court, Coach fired off technical details rapidly; but in here, he spoke in slow, measured sentences.

"Guess I'm not sure how to get out of the shadows."

"You're feeling sorry for yourself, is that it?" His eyes met mine.

"I want to be a professional tennis player, but my parents want me to get a full-time job to offset travel expenses. How do I balance the two?"

"Your ambition to play the professional tour doesn't surprise me, but I have to say, I agree with your parents. I could offer you a job. I do need an assistant for the group lessons which start in two weeks."

I sat forward, eager to hear more. "Doing what?"

"First, there's housekeeping responsibilities."

After having the role of women in sports so recently explained to me, I got the picture. "I suppose you mean vacuuming and washing dishes?"

He chuckled and shook his head. "No, not that. You'll need to make sure all students have a racquet and proper tennis sneakers, keep the water jugs full, and pick up stray tennis balls. You'd also demonstrate proper stroke technique and hit tennis balls back to the players during drills. It would mean down-time for you, too, so your back and hip can rest. Interested?"

Things were looking up.

"I'll pay you minimum wage, plus lunch, and a brand-new tennis racquet. How's that sound? I'll need you from July first through Labor Day weekend. Monday will be your day off. Tuesday through Friday from ten to four, and weekends from noon to five. Think you can do it?"

"That's great. Thank you, Coach. And thanks for the new tennis racquet."

"One more thing. Before we begin, let's take a look at your game. You up for it?

"Sure am!"

We hit back and forth on his teaching court. I was nervous because I wanted to play well. My ground strokes were solid, even when he ran me wide. My serve, however, was another matter. He reworked the twisting motion that aggravated the lower part of my spine where it had been broken. The more changes we made, the weaker my serve became.

I needed to figure out whether it was the mechanics of the service motion or the limitations of my body that was the cause of my weak serve. Coach decided it was better to simplify the service motion and concentrate more on my groundstrokes and volley. During several private lessons I took from him throughout the summer, he'd place squares on the court and have me practice groundstrokes until I hit the squares. Then we'd do the same thing for the volley at net. It was all about precise technique. Coach told me, "It takes hours of practice and care of your body to compete at the highest level."

My spirit was willing, but I was beginning to wonder if my body could hold up to the strain.

Chapter 19

I looked forward to Angela's visit on the last Monday of July. Although we shared a love for history and tennis, there was something else. At an early age, we were deeply hurt because we were different— the taunting Angela withstood because of her skin color and the bullying I endured because of my faltering gait. Being different made for painful moments no matter where we were, on the tennis court or in the schoolyard. The insults stung—like when a bee attacks your arm without warning or remedy. They linger.

We played singles for almost two hours before we stopped to have lunch under a shaded tree. We ate tuna sandwiches with sliced tomatoes, their juices dripping down our wrists, and enjoyed juicy green grapes for dessert. About forty-five minutes later, my Father arrived at the club and asked if he could play Canadian doubles with us, two against one.

Angela smiled at me.

I motioned him to the court. "Let's do this."

We rotated partners every three games and had a blast hooting and hollering when one of us hit a winning shot. I lost big-time when Dad and Angela played against me. With his wicked drop shot and Angela's big serve, I didn't stand a chance. It didn't matter. It was great seeing Angela joke around with Dad and win most of the points. Soon, the late afternoon sun shadowed the court, making it difficult to see—or at least, that was my excuse for losing so badly.

"Thanks, Mr. Sampson. I had so much fun beating Lucie."

I laughed. "I bet you did. Nice friend you are!"

Thirty minutes after Angela showered and changed her clothes, I drove her to the train station. She wanted to be home before dark set in. Angela continued giving tennis lessons at the Harlem Tennis Center from nine to four, Tuesdays through Sundays. "I love working with the kids and the adults. Keeps me alert to differences," she would say.

When I returned from the train station, I retreated to my bedroom and settled back into the stillness of my world. Though I could feel the pain in my lower back from playing too many hours that day, I realized how much fun I had playing tennis and playing well.

How fortunate I was to have the job with Coach Martin. He had a knack for communicating with people, and he had a generous spirit. During my lunch breaks, I'd sit on a bench—the one closest to his teaching court—and watch him instruct the juniors. He enjoyed every minute helping them become better players and gaining self-confidence along the way. I learned a great deal by observing him—about patience, grit, and purpose.

When I was younger, Mom often would say, "Brighten someone else's corner." The expression irritated me as I saw it as a form of lecturing. I wondered if maybe there was something to that saying after all. Some purpose. Perhaps that's why she had me sell those Christmas napkins to benefit the March of Dimes and volunteer at the library reading to the kids. It was all about the other person, not about me.

Tennis, on the other hand, is a selfish sport and mostly about the individual. A woman has coaches to guide her along the way, but she doesn't have to worry about anyone but herself. For the most part, she is on her own when playing a match. It makes her independent and self-reliant, yet also more distant from friends and family.

Dad's tales about his rowing days in college told a different story. "Crew is different from tennis," he'd explain. "Each rower is dependent on his teammate for the success of the boat, and each teammate must adjust to the needs and skills of the other rowers. If not, the boat flounders." Imagine that. The team was what mattered, not the individual. I learned that the hard way at college.

I had been too wrapped up in my own pain to appreciate those sweet days when the world was not all about me. Maybe it was time to brighten someone else's corner. But how? I still wanted another chance at competitive tennis. How could I play professional tennis and help others at the same time?

I left the security of my bedroom and headed down to the kitchen where Mom prepared dinner and Dad read today's mail. I slumped down in the chair.

Mom turned from the stove and peppered me with questions. "What's the problem? Are you upset? Don't you like teaching with Coach Martin?"

"I enjoy teaching tennis . . . a lot. It's fun and hard. So is playing tournaments. I'd like to enter some after I finish work at the end of the summer."

"Oh, no! Is that possible? You think you can?" I heard the doubt in her voice.

"Yes."

"Seriously?" she persisted.

"Well, I won't know unless I give it one more try," I snapped.

"Your body might not hold up."

"Thanks for reminding me, Mom." I looked over at Dad, but he remained quiet. "Look, you both have given me everything I've ever wanted. You have taught me to work hard and never give up, even when I was hurt and scared."

"I see." Mom glanced at Dad who looked up from the mail.

"It's not just a lot of fun. It's creative too, like chess, setting up your shots and maneuvering your opponent around to win the game.

"True enough," Dad finally chimed in.

"Coach Martin said tennis players must learn to improvise, especially with a disability. Some shots you can't get to or even attempt . . . like a decent serve. Mine's a joke, but I do the best with what I've got. I need to give tournament play another try."

"Isabelle, we've raised our daughter well," Dad told Mom. "She understands to never give up."

"True, but it also makes her stubborn," Mom replied.

"And you too, perhaps," Dad said.

Mom frowned at him. "Charles," she said in a lower key.

He rubbed his forehead and looked over at Mom. "It's her decision, dear."

"Very well." She chopped up the carrots at a furious rate.

Chapter 20

After Labor Day of '74, I decided to train with Coach Roberts, Head Pro at the Westfield Tennis Academy on the north shore of Long Island. It was about forty-five minutes from home. Coach Martin was a master technician, whereas Coach Roberts focused on the subtleties of match play. Their personalities were different too. Coach Martin, a man of few words who explained things with precision, was kind and encouraging, but very demanding. Coach Roberts, on the other hand, was flamboyant and blunt, yet understood the psychology of match play and how it affects shot selection and performance. I needed that to compete in the demanding tour of professional tennis, and I was excited to begin.

One day, after a tough cross-court forehand and backhand drop shot drill, Coach Roberts and I rested for a few minutes. He said, "Look, you've survived the horseback-riding accident and years of physical therapy, so I expect you to survive our drills. Buck up. Let's try the drill again. Remember to carry the ball when hitting it." He headed back to the baseline ready to fire away at those cross-court shots.

"Carrying the ball" meant to keep it on the strings a little longer so you felt the ball hit the strings, directing its path instead of just swatting at the ball and hoping it would land deep in your opponent's court. That saying, "carry the ball," really helped me.

Coach Roberts decided it was time for me to play against men. They played with more power, which would improve my reaction time and concentration. Just as important as playing well was sportsmanship. Both coaches, especially Coach Martin, emphasized fair play, respect, and humility as did my father. Sportsmanship to Dad was more important than winning.

Back and knee pain paid me a visit in early November about the same time that Coach Roberts decided to enter me in a key tournament, the Maryland Open. Ranked players, both men and women, came from nine states—from Connecticut to Texas. Players knew that, if we made it to the semi-finals, tournament invitations from the prestigious Federation of International Tennis would soon follow. I desperately wanted to play well, but was uncertain if I could cope with the pain. So I took a few pain killers—just enough to take the edge off.

I had been playing well throughout the Maryland Open and now faced Janet Thurston in the quarter-final match. Pain entered into each shot I hit. We rallied back and forth for ninety minutes. She won the first set and was ahead in the second set, 5–4. Janet's next shot was a "sitter" that hung softly in the air. I attacked with a quick, backhand drive, cross-court, that passed Janet, winning the point. Janet's next shot glided across the net and dropped right on the sideline.

"Nice shot. Too good, Janet," I shouted across the net.

It was now match point in Janet's favor. She returned my serve with a solid backhand, down the line. I was off balance and lunged for the ball; I struck a half volley that floated back to her. She responded with a huge swing and drove the ball crosscourt so fast that I couldn't react quickly enough to get my racquet on the ball. Her shot landed right on the baseline, winning the point and the match.

Even though I tried to end points quickly like Alice Marble, I waited too long in doing so. Janet won fair and square. Feeling dizzy, I inched toward the net to congratulate her, but my left knee buckled. I smacked onto the red clay. After what seemed like an eternity, Janet and the tournament director picked me up and walked me over to the bench behind the referee's chair.

"Here, take some water," Janet said.

I shook my head and felt like throwing up. *So this is how it's going to end?*

The tournament director then offered me a cool towel. "Take a few sips of water now, slowly at first. You're probably just dehydrated."

Janet handed me the cup of water, and sat with me for the longest time, but her ride finally came. We shook hands. "Thanks for everything," I said. "Good luck tomorrow."

And then she was gone. Janet had played well and simply wore me out. I laid down passing shots in the match. I couldn't move to the ball without limping or faltering. I ignored physical pain while playing, but once it interfered with movement, I was forced to change my game. I started taking shortcuts, rushing points, losing balance, and stumbling. I knew it might be over— that tennis was lost to me. I had suffered enough.

Someone touched my shoulder from behind. "Hey, Lucie. I watched your match from the grandstand. You played well. How are you feeling?"

I turned, surprised to find Henry, my off-again, on-again boyfriend from college.

"Hi. I didn't know you entered this tournament."

"I didn't. Two good friends did. They're trying to make it on the tour." Henry poured some more water from the large jug next to the bench. "Here. Drink up." He sat next to me and placed his hand on my thigh. "What have you been doing since we graduated?"

"Giving tennis lessons on Long Island and continuing my physical therapy. This is my first pro tournament. You?"

"After I graduated, I moved to Virginia. I work for a commercial real estate development company. Pretty exciting stuff. We're looking to expand our business in Southern California. Pay is great."

"You said you always wanted to make a lot of money. Good for you."

Henry glanced down at his watch. "Sorry. I've got to leave soon. Train back to Richmond leaves in thirty minutes." We swapped phone numbers and then he rose. "Take care." He kissed me on the cheek and was gone.

~

My knee seemed okay, and since my train back to Long Island wasn't scheduled to leave for a few hours, I decided to head for the Anacostia River, just a block from the tennis courts. I followed the signs leading to the riverbank, eventually finding a bench that looked out over the horizon. What a view. Two great blue herons skimmed the water, almost as if they were announcing what would follow. Two rowers moved in unison as their boat glided through the calm waters. I thought of Dad and his days rowing in college where he learned that two is better than one. I was alone again with only my thoughts for company. Sadness and anger grabbed my stomach. This was not at all what I had planned. I had fought hard, and what good had it done?

All those years of tennis drills, physical therapy, unspoken sacrifices that committed athletes know all too well, and little to show for it. I wanted to win and loved the sport too much to walk away. There had to be another path forward. What would

Dad say? And my coaches? I needed to figure things out myself. But how? I dripped with sweat and confusion.

Swallows flew low over the river's edge, their wings tapping the water, then quickly taking flight toward the setting sun.

Chapter 21

Given my poor movement at the Maryland Open, I decided to see Dr. Fetner for some advice. After his thorough physical examination and a new set of X-rays, he announced. "You need surgery, Lucie. A lumbar discectomy. I've seen very good results with my patients who are in a lot of pain, though they have not been athletes."

"What's involved?"

"I would remove the damaged lumbar discs, which would relieve pressure on the nerves in that region, thereby reducing your pain. Let me show you."

He got up from behind his mahogany desk and moved a skeleton from the corner closer to me. After adjusting his black, horned-rimmed glasses, he pointed to one disc that was bulging, another that was herniated, and a third that had a bone spur.

"Because you have three damaged discs, the surgery could cause some nerve damage."

"Will the procedure stabilize my back?" I asked. "What's the recovery period like? Will it work?" My left leg started to twitch as I spoke.

"The lumbar discectomy will probably stabilize your back and reduce your pain. The recovery is usually three to four months, plus physical therapy. Some surgeons, however, do recommend decompression and fusion for greater stability. That procedure comes with added risk. There's little research on its effectiveness for athletes." He shrugged. "Wish I had better news for you. We can schedule the surgery later in the month if you like." He returned the skeleton to its dark corner. "Think it over and call my office when you've decided. If there are no more questions, I need to see my next patient."

"Is there no alternative to surgery?"

"Rest, try medical massage, and stop playing so much tennis."

He left the room, leaving the door and my decision wide open.

The uncertainty of choices gnawed at me. The decision needed to be mine alone, and it terrified me. Should I take the pills and play with no pain, play with pain and hope for the best, or have the surgery? What if I make the wrong choice? Check with my parents? I'll call Angela. She always had a knack for calming my nerves.

I called Angela and explained the details about a discectomy surgery, and how Dr. Fetner said he had very good results with his patients, but there were risks. "There's really no guarantee that my movement would improve significantly or that I would be pain-free."

"Why the heck would you have the surgery, then?" Her emphatic voice surprised me.

"Because the doc said the surgery could stabilize my back. I don't want to regret not having the surgery if it gives me the best chance to play the pro circuit. I made it to the quarterfinals at the Maryland Open and played well. The pills stopped the pain, but also made me slow to the ball. Guess that's why I lost."

"Ya think? That should tell you something. If you're slowing down on the court because of the pills, maybe surgery might help the pain, but . . . I don't know. . . sounds risky to me."

"I have a second opinion coming up soon. I'll let you know. Thanks for listening, Ange."

Chapter 22

I scheduled a session with Coach Roberts to analyze my movement. Halfway through the lesson, rain sprinkled the court. Fearing the rain would damage the racquet strings, we gathered our equipment and rushed inside the clubhouse before the rain worsened.

"Coach, can we go to your office? There's something I need help with."

He led me to his office, off the main lobby. "What's on your mind?"

"My doctor has recommended back surgery. There's this procedure called discectomy where they remove a damaged lumbar disc to relieve pressure on the nerves." I shared with him all the details Dr. Fetner explained to me.

"So you're in a lot of pain?" he asked.

"Every time I hit the ball."

"I see. It's not a tough decision. Just have the surgery and reduce the pressure. You think too much, Lucie. As an athlete, you know that if you're in less pain, you move more freely and win more matches. At the pro level, it's all about movement."

"Yes, I realize that."

"I have high expectations for us, you know. I'm taking you to the pros and need you to be in great shape." His voice was clipped and edgy.

The insistence in his tone bothered me. "I like working with you, Coach. I've really improved, but I don't know if the surgery is right for me. Lots to think about."

"Well, don't take too long. Do it now and get on with it." He led me to the door.

Startled, I just nodded and left without a word. In the lobby, a doubles foursome complained about the rate increase for both private and group tennis lessons. They said Coach Roberts also reduced the number of teaching pros. Something about financial difficulties at the Westfield Tennis Academy.

Rain pelted the windshield as I drove home and reflected on Coach's reaction. Something didn't sit well. I would measure his advice against Coach Martin's later in the week.

～

"I've heard about this kind of surgery," Coach Martin said. "Some turn out fine; for others, not so much. What athletes need is fluid movement, as you know all too well. Will your movement improve because of the surgery? Over the years, we worked around your movement limitations by perfecting your technique. It's given you the foundation to build a strong, versatile game."

He furrowed his brow and rose from the couch to get some water.

"Why have the surgery?" he continued. "If the procedure is unsuccessful, you lose out on playing professionally and, possibly, teaching the sport you love. Not very good odds. Here, drink some water. You're dehydrated. Still in those shadows I suspect." He smiled and sat again.

I agreed. "Those shadows! You chiseled away at my technique until I got it right. What a piece of work I must have been. You have the patience of a saint."

He laughed.

I leaned against the wall in his shack overlooking the tennis courts, listened to my mentor, and watched two girls playing. One girl reminded me of myself when I first started to play . . . running clumsily around the court, swinging freely. I hadn't given any thought to having to relearn techniques that had been tailored to this body of mine.

Both coaches agreed on one thing: Movement was key. The lumbar discectomy was high risk with no guarantees. If the operation was unsuccessful and worsened my movement, forget the pro tour. But surgery could also limit my ability to move well enough to coach. Teaching tennis had brought joy and purpose to my life the summer I assisted Coach Martin. If that were taken away, tennis would be lost to me forever. This was not an easy decision; I wanted those shadows to just disappear.

I underwent more testing and an examination the following week for another opinion. The second orthopedist believed the surgery was too risky.

Several days later, I explained to my parents the details of Dr. Fetner's recommendation, and also that the second physician did not agree with him. Despite the conflicting professional opinions, I decided to play the prestigious Southwest Clay Court Open and see whether my body would hold up.

"We've been through this before," Mom said. "You keep saying 'one more tournament,' 'one more tournament.'"

I couldn't tell whether she was irritated or anxious for me. "Yeah, I know," I replied. "But I played well at the Maryland Open until my movement gave out. I didn't rest enough. If I rest a bit more between tournaments, maybe it'll make a difference."

"I'm not keen on you playing any more tournaments." Mom didn't move from the kitchen counter.

"Why?"

"Because you might end up hurting yourself. I couldn't bear that again."

"I'm sorry, Mom. But it is my body. The tournament is at the end of February in San Antonio, two-and-a-half months from now. I plan to rest more to see if that makes any difference in my game."

Mom looked over at Dad. "Charles, I don't want Lucie to jeopardize her health."

"Well, I agree, playing another tournament after her loss at the Maryland Open could be risky. But I guess she won't know unless she tries."

I sat down at the end of the table and took a deep breath. "I don't want to upset you both. You worry enough about me. I'm just angry about the Maryland Open results. I wish surgery would solve my problem, but there's no guarantee it'll make me stronger. I'm stubborn; I know that. I need to be sure I can make it on the pro tour. It's what I want."

"Do you have a plan?" Dad asked.

"Yes. Rest my body for three weeks . . . just some stretching, footwork drills, and walking. Then for the next three weeks, practice an hour and a half a day. Then two weeks before the tournament, practice two hours a day and have a lesson twice a week with Coach Roberts. I'll pay for the lessons, and I'll use what's left in my savings to travel to the tournament. What do you think?"

"Seems like you've given this a lot of thought." Dad glanced over at Mom, looking for confirmation, perhaps. "You'll need to line up practice sessions with some of the men at the club. And yes, you will pay for all your expenses," Dad said.

"Definitely," Mom agreed.

"I will."

This decision was a risk, even I thought so. I'd be scraping my savings account down to zero, and for what? More pain, to go down in a blaze of glory, or failing big time? Who knew. But I'd come this far, and tennis and I weren't done with each other yet.

~

"Come in," I said.

Dad opened the door to my bedroom and sat at the edge of the bed. "Been thinking. Remember when you were around eleven years old? You came in second place in the twenty-five-yard race at Tullamore Park because you looked back to see who was gaining on you."

"Yeah, and she passed right by me."

"After the race we went for Carvel ice cream, and on our way back home, I told you . . ."

"Never look back."

He smiled. "I'm thinking you need to look ahead now."

"I know, Daddy." I hadn't called him that in years.

Chapter 23

A few days later, I drove to Westfield Tennis Academy to tell Coach Roberts my decision. He finished up his lesson with a promising young boy, a lefty. I waited on the bench adjacent to the court until he signaled me to meet him at the net.

"Hey, Coach. I wanted to tell you that I've decided not to have the surgery."

He shook his head, then stared right at me. He raised his voice. "Well, I wasn't expecting that! After all I've done for you! I'm very disappointed in you."

I flinched. "I'm sorry you feel that way, Coach. I've got to do what's best for me."

"No, what's best for you is to have the surgery and have me as your full-time coach. I have great plans for us."

"That may be what's best for you, but not for me." My voice cracked. "I thought you'd understand."

His jaw hardened. "Understand? You're making a bad decision."

I couldn't fathom his response. "Maybe I should leave now." I turned to walk off the court, but hesitated. "Thanks for everything you've done for me. I mean that, Coach."

He said nothing. I left his court for the last time with a cold shiver, and walked to the parking lot.

I swung open the car door, threw my racquet in the back seat, and cried until I was dry. Several minutes later, I switched on the radio and cranked up the Rolling Stones as I drove away. I hoped someday everything would be all right.

Chapter 24

I played well in the early rounds of the 1975 Southwest Clay Court Open in San Antonio. It was common on the tour to see many of the same players enter the same tournaments. As fate would have it, Karen Mitchell was my quarter-final opponent. I won the first set and was down 2–5 in the second set. I fought my way back, but not enough to take that set. Karen won it, 7–5. The third set would determine the winner.

This final set will be mine; it's got to be.

"Out," Karen yelled.

That ball couldn't be out. It hit the baseline with chalk flying. I walked closer to the net so she could hear me. "The chalk flew up. The ball was on the line."

"No, I called the ball out."

"You called it before the ball hit the ground. It was in, and you know it. Can't call a ball until it hits the ground. You know the rule. My point. 40–30."

I wish we'd had an umpire for the quarterfinals.

"You're wrong. The ball hit the ground, then I called the ball out. There was no chalk dust."

I shook my head and walked back to the service line. "Oh, forget it, Karen. 30–40."

"That's the right score." She smiled and readied to return serve.

The game seesawed for several minutes before I lost the game along with my cool. Karen was winning the third set, 2–1. As we changed sides, I started to mumble to myself, *I can't lose to her, no matter how much my back hurts. Crap, I've got to beat her; I can't stand her. Okay, breathe. Her backhand is weak. Attack it. 'Carry the ball.'*

I won the next game.

"2-all!" I announced.

I looked across the net before serving a slice to Karen's backhand. She netted it.

"I wasn't ready. Play the point over," she griped.

"Forget it. I looked at you before I served. You were in ready position."

"No, I wasn't!"

I hollered loud enough so other players heard every word. "You're a cheater, Karen. Do you want me to call over the director so she can ref our match?"

"Serve the next point."

Ha, gotcha. "Ready, Karen?"

"Yes." She netted the return, again.

"30-Love," I called out.

"I know what the score is."

"I'm just following the rules." I smiled nicely.

I stood at the baseline and looked up at her to make sure she was ready. I served the ball which landed in the net. My second serve also found the net—double fault.

A few points later, I served a slice to Karen's backhand. She returned cross-court to my forehand. I answered with lots of underspin. The ball landed mid-court. Karen countered with a backhand down the line.

"Out." I yelled, not sure if the ball was actually out.

"No way." She ran up to the net shaking her finger right at me. *Ha, she's pissed—great!*

"That's how I saw it. The ball was out. 40–15."

Karen took forever to get into ready position, trying my frayed patience.

"Ask for the Tournament Director, if you like," I said with some sass.

She stomped her right leg in anger. "Forget it."

"Ready?"

She nodded.

I couldn't believe it. I aced her with a wide serve to her forehand. Game over.

I was in the lead with the score at 3–2, but I needed something to distract me from the pain traveling through my back and hip. As we changed sides, I sat briefly at the side chair and retrieved some Chiclets chewing gum from my bag. I shook out two pieces and chewed furiously on my way back to the baseline, ready to receive Karen's serves. I decided to keep hitting deep balls, pushing Karen way back behind the baseline, which gave me greater control. I also tried hitting the ball early, taking away her time to adjust her feet and get set; that way, her timing would be off, making her uncomfortable and forcing weaker shots. It worked. I was ahead 4–2, but Karen won the next game, making the score 4–3 in my favor.

Crap, she's catching up.

The sun and humidity had been tough throughout the tournament, with the temperatures hovering around eighty degrees— unseasonably hot for mid-February. Since the sun was behind me now, I used it to my advantage. I hit a short shot, causing her to run to the net. So I threw up a lob right into the sun, which blinded Karen, causing her to miss the ball and lose the point. I tried the same shot again, sending another lob into the sun. She pointed to the ball and smashed it straight into the net. Game over, 5–3.

Karen was now serving and missing most of her first serves. Since her second serve was weak, I moved in a few steps and returned the ball with a defensive lob. It forced her to look straight up at the sun again to hit the overhead. She netted her shot.

Great, I've got her now.

She walked slowly back to the baseline. Before she served, she wiped her brow with her wrist band, straightened her ponytail, and tied her left shoelaces.

Typical Karen stalling.

I crouched behind the service line, ready to receive. Karen missed her first serve. I inched forward to receive the second serve and smacked a crosscourt return, but she scrambled for the ball and whipped a forehand down the line. Desperate, I ran toward the ball and hit another lob into the sun, praying Karen would net it. She smashed it right at me and won the point. The next two points, however, I won.

This is it; just one more point and I win the match.

"Match point," Karen stated. She hit a huge first serve, but the ball landed in the net. She then puff-balled a weak second serve. I returned it with an extreme underspin, forehand, crosscourt that dipped barely over the net, unreachable for her. I won the point—and the match! Without coming to the net for the customary handshake, Karen quickly picked up her gear, sneered at me, and ran off the court.

I had beaten my nemesis and regained my confidence. I won!

The next day, the San Antonio heat lifted for my semi-final match against Lydia Benson with an umpire to call the match.

The first set score was 5–3, in my favor. Yet, pain visited deep into my back and left hip, and with each subsequent swing of the racquet, the pain dug a little deeper. I couldn't move to the ball without limping.

Just two more points and I'll take the set.

On the next point, I hit a wicked short ball which brought

Lydia up to the net. Her return volley skidded just inside the baseline, yet I found a shot she wasn't expecting—a low, cross-court, passing backhand winner.

Great! One more point, and the set's mine.

I slowly walked back to the baseline, bounced the ball twice, and looked across to Lydia to make sure she was ready to receive the serve. Then I gently tossed the ball up in the air, arched my back, reached toward the sky and served as hard as possible. It was an ace. I had won the first set, 6–3. But pain cut across my lower back.

I dropped to one knee. Frozen. I eventually used the butt of my tennis racquet to steady myself and rose slowly.

Then I did something I had never done before in my short playing career. I walked to my opponent's side of the court. "I'm so sorry, Lydia, but I can't finish the match." My voice quivered as I tried to continue. "I can barely rotate my hip to stroke the ball. Good luck to you in the finals."

She consoled me, putting her right arm around my shoulder, and wished me well. I gathered my things and walked off the court. I sat down at a nearby bench and slammed my bag down on the cement. I wanted to scream. My shoulders trembled. Tears stung my cheeks.

How could I walk away from the sport I loved and all that I ever wanted and worked so hard for?

I sat for the longest time, trying to calm down, and then I walked over to watch a men's semi-final match. One of the players kept missing his forehand volley because his wrist slapped at the ball like a buggy-whip snap instead of hitting the volley with a firm wrist. Like Coach Martin used to say, "Punch your volley; don't flick your wrist." It was frustrating to just watch: I wished I could talk to the player.

Chapter 25

My decision to forfeit the semi-final match at the Southwest Clay Court Open was humiliating. I had worked hard to finish matches, certainly not to give them away. Unable to complete that match signaled to me that the pro tour would never be possible. My sweet, battered body had provided the answer.

When I returned home, I was eager to pay Coach Martin a visit. Winter had lost its icy grip on Long Island and the wind had lost its bite. I waited outside Marty's Place, alongside the humble dandelion that peeked its head through the dry grass. The mid-day sun warmed my spirits.

Coach finished his lesson and walked toward me, dressed in navy warm-up pants and a matching sweatshirt. "Welcome, Lucie! Glad to see you're standing guard."

He always made me laugh. "Hey, Coach! Are you through for the day?"

"Yes, I am. Let's go inside. What's on your mind? Have you made any decision about surgery?"

I followed him inside and sat down on his couch. "I've decided not to have the operation. Coach Roberts disagreed; he was actually angry with my decision."

"Thought he might feel that way. I don't know for certain, but I believe you made the right decision."

"Thanks, Coach, that means a lot."

"So, do you plan to continue playing competitively?"

I told him briefly about why I'd had to forfeit to Lydia in the semi-finals after the first set.

He pulled up a chair in front of me. "That must not have been easy for you," he said gently. "Always remember what tennis has given you. More than simply matches won and lost. Tennis taught you to problem-solve, to persevere, to follow through."

"I realize I can't play the pro circuit. But I don't want to walk away from the sport I love. You've been such an inspiration to me for so many years, and I want to be that for other up-and-coming players. I want to coach."

"Hmm, they say timing is everything," he said.

"Coach?"

"A new tennis club in Southern California is looking for assistant teaching pros. My close friend and doubles partner in college, Jack Simmons, is the director of the tennis center in Palm Springs. He said the teaching pros make a nice salary out there. He also owns several apartments he rents to his staff." Coach stood up to fill his water glass. "Might you be interested?"

"Do you think I'm ready?"

"Absolutely! I watched you teach the juniors when you were my assistant. You can be impatient, but you explain things in a simple way that students understand. That's a gift. And you demonstrate perfectly what you explain. You'll be challenged by strong players because of your limitations, but you'll figure it out along the way. You always have."

I realized what I'd always hoped was actually true; I was not defective or defeated.

"What about your friend, Angela? I remember several years ago when she visited the club. We played a few games of doubles. Her strokes are beautiful, and she's now coaching tennis in Harlem. I think that's what you told me a while ago."

"Yes, that's right." I sprang from the couch and shook his

hand. "Thanks, Coach! This is unbelievable. I'm in! I'll check with Angela."

"I'll call Jack and put in a good word for you; Angela, too. He mentioned to me that he'd cover transportation expenses for the best candidates he needs to interview. So, you probably won't have that to worry about."

"That's fab!"

∽

Angela and I spoke at length about making such a big move and being so far away from our families. We talked about expenses, like rent, utilities, food, car, and insurance.

"I don't know, Lucie. I don't think so. Not too many Black people out there. I'm used to mean stares and comments from white people, but living in a sea of them . . . I just don't know. Need to talk with my mom about this. It's a big move." Her voice trailed off.

"But it's not like you're moving out there by yourself. You'd have me," I said enthusiastically, trying to convince her. "And our airline expenses for the interview would be paid for by the director."

"Oh, that's good to hear."

"Plus, we can rent separate apartments the director owns."

"That sounds pretty good, too."

"And the weather is fantastic! We can teach year-round."

"That's true."

"I'm going for it! Tell you what, Ange, when you're ready, give me a call and let me know what you've decided."

"It all sounds great, Lucie, but I've got a good thing going in Harlem. Possibilities for Black women are limited. Let me think whether to apply. I'll let you know."

∽

Ten days later, Angela and I arrived at the front entrance to the Palm Springs Tennis Center, which opened to an expansive garden of desert plants we had never seen before. We shaded our eyes from the sun, as not even a wisp of a cloud softened the bright rays.

The exotic landscape made this new opportunity all the more exciting. To secure the coaching positions, we needed to pass a rigorous playing test and then demonstrate our teaching capabilities by giving lessons. I was confident and calm—until I saw her.

"Oh no! It's the cheater."

Angela's head was buried in a magazine. "Who?"

"You know who."

She plopped the magazine on her lap and looked up. "Good Lord. No, it can't be."

"It's Karen, all right. What the hell is she doing here?"

Karen sauntered toward us, tennis bag in hand. "You two coming to learn how to play?"

"We're interviewing for the coaching positions, as if it's any of your business. And what, may I ask, are you doing here?" I said.

"Same." Karen looked down at Angela. "You don't belong here, just as you didn't at the junior development program."

Angela stood, her magazine falling to the ground. "You're a racist."

"Call me what you like. I don't care."

"You haven't changed at all, Karen," I said, shaking my head.

"My UCLA coach said I was a shoo-in for this job."

"UCLA?" I rolled my eyes. "We know you were at Rollins."

Karen squared her shoulders. "I transferred my senior year. So, I know the tennis scene around here. You don't."

Karen was about to continue when a man dressed in tennis whites emerged from an office. His fit physique and wavy salt-and-pepper hair gave him a distinguished look.

"I'm Jack Simmons, the director at the center. I see you girls have all met. Welcome. I'm glad you're here. This is the plan for today. Separately, you will hit with Michael for thirty minutes. Then you will each give Luke a thirty-minute lesson. After that, a thirty-minute lesson with me. And finally, I'll interview each of you. Both Michael and Luke are assistant tennis pros at the Center. I will be observing throughout. Are there any questions?"

"Yes, how many positions are open?" Karen asked.

"Two," Jack said.

I shot Angela a look that I hoped said, *We've got to do our best.*

"That's correct, two. We'll begin the process in an hour. Please meet on Court One. See you then."

Karen strutted off. "See you later, girls."

"Ange, I didn't know there would be another candidate today, and of all people."

"Surprised me, too. We'll be fine. Just need to forget about Karen."

"You're right. Let's go back to the hotel. I'd like to call my father."

"I think I'll stick around here and eat lunch at their café. Okay with you?"

"Sure. See you in a bit." I sauntered off.

～

"Hello?" my mother said as she answered the phone.

"Hey, Mom."

"Hi, dear. Everything okay?" she asked.

"Sure. Is Dad home?"

"Yes, he just got back from playing doubles." She passed along the phone to him.

"Nice to hear your voice," Dad said. "How was your trip? What's on your mind?"

"There's another candidate for the job; it's Karen Mitchell. You remember her?"

"Yes. Isn't she the one who had a reputation for cheating?"

"Yeah, that's the problem. I think I should tell the director, Jack, about her. What do you think?"

"Why would you want to do that?"

"Because she's a cheat and Jack should know this."

"Maybe he already does."

"I can't take that chance."

"Wait a minute, Lucie. Do you want to tell him because it might help you get the job, or because you know it's wrong to cheat?"

"Well, both."

"Do you want to get the job by belittling someone or get the job on your own merits?"

"I don't like her; Angela and I spoke with her earlier, and she hasn't changed. She's just plain nasty."

"Why tear her down? Let Jack figure it out; it's not your place."

"Listen, Dad, I've got to go. We're supposed to start at noon. Love to you and Mom."

"Bye, honey."

∽

The three of us withstood an intense afternoon of playing sets with Michael and giving beginner tennis lessons to Luke and advanced lessons to Jack. Plus, an interview with Jack. We gathered under the canopy where Louisa Alvarez, the receptionist, placed water glasses, orange slices, and granola bars on the octagonal table.

"Hi, girls. Jack will be with you in just a few minutes. In the meantime, enjoy the goodies and the shade."

"Thanks, Louisa," Angela and I said in unison.

"Oh, Louisa, this is so thoughtful of you. How kind," Karen said.

"You're very welcome."

Angela and I just rolled our eyes. Typical of Karen to feign kindness. Jack returned several minutes later and stood by the table.

"Well, girls, this is a difficult decision. You all played and taught extremely well. Very impressive. When I hire people, I also look for qualities beyond tennis skills, what we call the 'intangibles.' For me it's trust, work ethic, and honesty. I am on a committee at The Federation of International Tennis which has proposed that all rounds for junior tournaments now have a referee, not just for the semi-finals and the finals. Cheating among the juniors is becoming a problem which needs to be fixed.

Karen squinted at me through her hardened eyes. "Nothing worse than a cheater." She said between her teeth.

"Quite right," Jack said.

I clenched my jaw to avoid bursting out with the truth.

"I will call each of you by six o'clock this evening with my decision." He shook our hands and smiled. "Thank you all for your interest in our program. You're each very talented."

The next morning, Angela and I stepped into Jack's office beaming. We were too excited to speak. We had been offered the two teaching positions.

"Welcome aboard," Jack said.

"Thank you for choosing me—and Lucie, too!" Angie was bursting.

"Yes, thank you for the opportunity. We won't let you down." I said.

"I expect you won't," he smiled reassuringly.

A loud bang on the door unhinged the happy atmosphere. Karen stood rigid in the door frame. "Jack, excuse me. I need to say something. Do you really think a Black tennis instructor is going to be accepted in Palm Springs? Why would anyone want to take lessons from her? Why would you hire someone like her in the first place? Besides, she's not a better player than me."

Angela and I looked at each other with eyes wide. Dad was right; the truth always comes out.

"Sorry you feel that way, Karen. Based on her teaching and playing skills, plus those intangibles I mentioned earlier, Angela's the right choice."

"Well, I think you'll regret your decision. One bruised teaching pro and the other a Black one. No one will take lessons from either of them." Her eyes simmered with hate. She turned and left.

Angela exhaled, her lips trembling.

"You alright, Ange?" I asked.

"Will be."

Jack got up from behind his desk and closed the door. "No question about my decision, girls. You have my full support."

"Thank you, Jack." Angela said.

I nodded to him.

He sat across from us. "Now, let's get down to business. I'd like for you to begin in early April. That's a little over two weeks. Okay with you two?"

"It's short notice, but I think I can manage it." Angela said.

"Just need to pack a trunk; that's all." I said.

"It's all settled then. See you both in a couple of weeks." He shook our hands and saw us to the door.

"Let's go celebrate and have a drink at that local tavern we passed earlier," I said.

"You're on. Some California sparkling champagne?"

Chapter 26

We arrived at the Palm Springs Tennis Center in April 1976, anxious, proud, and eager. It had been a long haul up to this point and I was grateful for my good fortune.

Jack met Angela and me at the large patio. "Please have a seat and enjoy some fresh lemonade." He smiled and pulled out two wicker chairs from the table. The shade from the green awning and the crisp, cold drink relaxed us.

"Spring is beautiful here," he continued. "Mild temperatures, plenty of sunshine, with all kinds of colorful flowers native to the desert." He took two sips of lemonade before he explained what was in store for me and Angela. "We have different kinds of clientele. Some are only in the desert for six months of the year, called 'snowbirds.'"

"Why snowbirds?" I asked.

Jack chuckled. "People who live in colder, northern states come to the Coachella Valley where its warmer. Usually from October to May."

"Never heard the term before," Angela said.

"Me neither."

Jack continued. "Local families who live here all year round and are keen on learning the sport come to the center. We also have guests from Los Angeles and Santa Barbara who like to come on weekends. There's been talk about holding some college tournaments, and in June, the tennis center is sponsoring a tournament for Coachella Valley high school players."

"Sounds like things are busy around here," Angela said.

"It can be, and that's good for business." He smiled broadly at Angela and brushed back his hair as he adjusted his ball cap. "Now, let's review your responsibilities. First, housekeeping duties: welcome the patrons, sweep the clay courts twice a day, and keep count of the tennis balls that find their way into the desert garden. You will also teach three group lessons in the morning and two in the afternoon. Also, on weekends, I might ask you to play doubles with folks from L.A. who need doubles partners."

"What about private lessons?" I asked.

"Be patient. It'll be ten-twelve months before you start giving private lessons. I need for you to be fully accustomed to all that goes on here. Any questions?"

"Everything sounds good," Angela said.

"It's just great to be here, Jack," I said.

"Excellent. I'm delighted you're both here. You'll add a great deal to the tennis center.

$\sim$

About three weeks into our new positions, when Angela and I were combing errant balls near the wildflower beds, a woman yelled at Angela. "Hey, what are you doing?" she asked. "Those aren't your balls. Get out of the garden! You're stepping on the flowers!"

Angela stiffened, turned, and smiled. "Good morning, ma'am. I'm one of the teaching pros. Tennis balls always fly over the fence into the garden. Every day we go looking for them. Might this be one of your balls?"

"No, never mind," the woman said. She walked away muttering to herself.

Angela continued looking for errant balls. She took a long time, and I never could figure out why, until today. She turned to me. "The gardens calm my unease. I notice the simple beauty of the arid landscape. They are God's miracle, and they lift my spirits. But sometimes, I get these nasty looks from people or mumbled snide remarks. I can't actually hear what they're saying. I don't have the energy to respond. When I'm here in the garden, no one talks back to me. Until today."

I nodded. "It's really peaceful here. Have you spoken to Jack about this?"

"Nope. You know me. I keep things to myself. It's a trait we both share, for better or worse. We keep things inside, maybe too much."

"True enough."

"It's the same old thing," she said. "Nothing new. I get tired of people still looking at my skin color before anything else. I want to scream sometimes. Other times I turn the other cheek. My mother tells me to walk away with dignity—not to lose my temper and start an argument. She says, 'Have you ever seen Arthur Ashe lose his temper or throw his racquet, young lady?' That always stops me in my tracks."

"She makes a good point, Ange."

"Yeah, I know. But you should talk. Remember your temper flare-ups?"

"Yep, sure do. I remember when Dad and I attended the U.S. Open at the Westside Tennis Club in Forest Hills in 1970 and watched Arthur Ashe play in the quarterfinals. Dad admired his beautiful strokes and went on and on about how Ashe never lost his temper. Eventually it sunk in."

"I got a letter from my Mom the other day," Angela said. "She told me about her recent promotion at the hospital to Head RN in the pediatric ward; I'm thrilled for her! But then she asked how my temperament was and to remember to look for the good in people. It reveals the indwelling Holy Spirit within us. Mom's faith is important to her, and it is to me too."

"Wow. 'The indwelling Holy Spirit.' I never heard that before," I said. "Congrats to your Mom on her promotion. Maybe you should talk to Jack about that rude woman. Want me to go with you?"

Angela ignored my suggestion. "Want to hit some balls," she said.

"Yeah, okay. Need to get my racquet. Meet you at Court Six."

The staff prepared for the high school tournament, slated for the second weekend in June. Angela and I were responsible for contacting the local high school tennis coaches to extend invitations to a round-robin format tournament. Jack believed that kind of format was great for building community spirit because it was the fairest. It gives each player the same opportunity to play, and it prevents one poor game from eliminating a team from the competition.

Six high school teams accepted the invitation. The grandstand bleachers, which held 250 spectators, were freshly painted in forest green. The maintenance crew and gardeners took great care to ensure that all areas throughout the tennis center were clean, safe, and welcoming to the public. Michael and Luke, the two other assistant pros, oversaw tennis balls, court equipment, water stations, sliced oranges and sodas.

The tournament started promptly at nine on Saturday morning, June 19th. I approached the bleachers to watch and passed two parents on my way.

"What's that colored girl doing over there?" She pointed at Angela.

I turned around and asked, "Excuse me, may I help you, ma'am? Which girl are you referring to? There are dark-skinned players in the tournament."

"They're Hispanic. I mean that one, over there. Are you blind?" She smirked and pointed her index finger toward Angela.

"I can see clearly. Angela is a terrific instructor. Maybe you'd like to take a lesson from her?"

"Who do you think you are? I want your name."

People were circling in, paying more attention to the woman and me than to the boys and girls playing their hearts out. The whole point of the tourney was to bring people together in a beautiful setting to enjoy each other's company while watching the students play tennis. I cringed at the scene we were making.

Softly, I said, "My name is Lucie Sampson. I'm one of the teaching pros here, like Angela. The director's name is Jack Simmons. You can find him over there near Court Number One, under the green awning." I pointed in that direction and smiled.

She stomped away.

I waited for the round-robin exchange to finish on Court One before I headed to where Jack was sitting.

"What was that noise over there on Court Five a while back?" he asked.

I sat down and faced Jack directly. "That woman was nasty when I explained to her that we have several darker-skinned players on the courts. She asked for my name and yours to report me. I was just trying to be factual and smiled throughout our conversation."

His arched eyebrow told me he wasn't too happy. "Were you smiling out of sarcasm or out of respect?"

I squirmed in my seat. "A little bit of both."

"That won't do. We have all kinds of people living here in the desert, with different attitudes and different points of view. You may not agree with some people, but they have the right to express their opinions."

"But, Jack, she was obnoxious."

"Too bad. Turn the other cheek."

"Yes, sir. I will. I apologize."

How disappointing. I had expected Jack to stick up for Angela.

We then reviewed the team standings and the detailed plans for the ceremony. "I'll announce the winning team at the end of the day. I've already contacted the local newspaper. They've promised a reporter and photographer to cover the afternoon. Any questions, Lucie?"

"No, Jack."

The same woman returned later in the day. She hovered near Angela who was sitting courtside, making sure the players were calling their lines correctly. I was sitting one row behind the woman.

"That ball was in," she yelled.

I tapped the woman's shoulder, leaned in and asked her not to yell.

She shouted again. "That ball was in."

Other parents shushed her. Angela came over to the woman. "Ma'am, please do not shout. It's disrespectful to the players. I have been watching this match closely. I see no cheating."

By now, Jack wondered what the shouting was about and sat down next to the woman to introduce himself. "Jack Simmons, the director here."

"Hello, I'm Jennifer Livingston. My son's in the orange cap." A minute later she started to complain and turned to Jack. "That Black girl is not watching the lines clearly. My son is losing because of her."

Jack calmly stated. "Is that so? Let's watch the game together, shall we?"

For the next twenty minutes, the two boys exchanged long rallies punctuated by a few big serves and deft net shots. All the while, Angela was glued to the court, waiting for any wrong calls by the players.

"They seem to be enjoying themselves, wouldn't you agree?" Jack asked.

"But my son is supposed to be winning. That's more important right now. College scouts are looking at him."

"Winning is important, but so is enjoying the sport. The more you enjoy it, the better you play. The better you play, the more matches you win."

"Is that so?" she said.

"Yes. Your son plays very well, but he's a little weak with his backhand. If he continues to practice hard, he'll improve enough to play college ball. We're delighted your son is playing in the round-robin. But please, no more shouting. It's unfair to the players. And Mrs. Livingston, Angela is not the reason your son lost the match. He is."

She said nothing.

He tipped the brim of his cap to her and left.

At five o'clock sharp, all the players, coaches, and parents gathered at the west end of the garden. They sipped cold beverages, chit-chatted, and waited for the director to announce the winning team. Jack stepped forward from Court One to address the crowd.

"Thank you, all. We have two awards to give out this afternoon. One for the most points earned in the round-robin, and the other award to the team which best demonstrated sportsmanship. Congratulations to Palm Meadows High School for coming in first place. Would the players and their coach please come forward?" Applause and cheers ensued. "I am pleased to announce the Team Sportsmanship award *also* goes to Palm Meadows High School! Coach, please come and stand next to me so I may present you with this plaque."

The newspaper photographer then gathered together the

coach, the players, and the tennis center staff for a photo op before Jack made a few final remarks.

"We hope you enjoyed the tournament as much as we enjoyed watching the competition. It's the first tournament in the Coachella Valley focused on our youth." He turned to the players. "I'd like to share a few observations. First, remember that only you are responsible for the outcome of your match, no one else. Second, don't let up when you're ahead; momentum and scores can quickly change the other way. Third, keep practicing. It's the only way to improve. Keep up the good work." He turned to face the crowd. "Thank you all again for coming. See you next year."

A reporter tapped me on the shoulder. "I'm Fred Beckwith from the *Desert Chronicle*. What's this I hear about a parent yelling at a Black girl?"

Annoyed by his question, I responded. "What about it?"

Fred pressed. "What can you tell me about the incident?"

I wanted to talk about the young players, the tournament, the possibility of holding more tournaments in the future. He wanted the scoop on the latest sports gossip.

"Look, if you don't want to answer the questions, I'll just ask someone else," he snipped.

"Okay, maybe we got off on the wrong foot. My name is Lucie Sampson and I'm one of the pros here. My apologizes," I then explained what had occurred.

"Anything else to add?"

"Well, I told the woman that shouting is unfair to the players and that Angela had nothing to do with her son losing the match." I hoped that was the end of the interview.

"Isn't the woman being biased because Angela is Black?" he asked.

"You'll have to ask her." I got up from the bench and shook his hand. "Thank you for reporting on the tournament. We appreciate the coverage." I hurried over to the players and thanked them for participating in the tournament.

When everything had settled down, I walked back to the first-floor staff office. I sat down, a heaviness weighing me down. Like in the junior development program all those years ago, once again I witnessed how narrow-mindedness puts such a burden on innocent people.

Chapter 27

"Lucie, it's Jack. I know it's your day off, and it's still early in the morning, but I need to speak with you. Can you come to my office in one hour?"

"Okay. Everything all right?"

"See you soon."

I slumped in my chair and could barely sip my morning coffee. *Oh crap, what did I do?*

~

I arrived promptly at Jack's office and knocked. He opened the door and signaled me to sit in one of his soft-cushioned chairs. When he went behind his desk instead of taking the other chair beside me, I sensed a confrontation in the air.

"Remember Mrs. Livingston? The mother with whom you had an uncomfortable conversation at the high school round-robin? The one who accused Angela of not calling the lines correctly during her son's match?"

"Yes." My stomach was in a knot.

"Well, she called me early this morning with some distressing news about you that I never knew. You were arrested a few years ago in Florida. Care to explain?"

I swallowed deeply. "In college, I was arrested for disrespecting a police officer. The charges were dropped by the precinct sergeant that evening. Since the charges were dropped, I saw no reason to tell you or Coach Martin."

"No reason." I could hear the anger in Jack's voice. "Imagine how I felt when I learned this from Jennifer Livingston. Her husband is the district attorney for Palm Springs, and at his wife's request did some sleuthing about you and Angela. Tell me what happened."

"Angela and I were giving free beginning tennis lessons in Tallahassee to a small group of Black kids. One day, a boy hit the tennis ball over the fence, and it hit a passing police officer on the top of his head. He was not happy and said some unkind words about 'those people.' We apologized to the officer, but then he got really close to my face and said something nasty. I snapped and told him to get out of my face. He handcuffed me for disrespecting a police officer. I ended up in jail for a couple of hours. I'm sorry, Jack. This put you in an awkward position with Mrs. Livingston. The whole thing was blown out of proportion." I bit my lip and bowed my head.

"I see. Well, you should have told me. I was ready to fire you on the spot. I must be able to trust you implicitly. So, I'm placing you on probation for the next six months, which means if you act in an untoward manner, I will let you go. After the six months, if you act professionally, I will keep you on. Any questions?"

"'Untoward,' sir?"

"Unprofessional, inappropriate, disrespectful behavior."

Six months. Suddenly I couldn't stop poring over every word I'd said to that journalist yesterday, wondering if my rebellious tongue might already have lost me this job. I pictured Karen on deck, licking her lips.

～

I was looking forward to my day off from work, but shame and regret stripped my energy. Angela, Luke, Michael, and I were to meet at the center by eleven to drive to Joshua Tree National Park, about an hour north of Palm Springs. It was already ten-thirty, so I hung around until the others arrived, unsure of what to do next. Unsure of myself, period. I heard the park had great hiking trails and beautiful desert landscape. Losing myself there sounded like a wonderful idea right about now.

~

Michael drove. The park entrance seemed lifeless, with hardly any trees, little vegetation, and no flora in sight. Sparse and rather forbidding until Michael took a hard right turn and stopped the Jeep.

"Let's get out and walk around, my legs are a bit stiff," Michael suggested.

We got out of the jeep and noticed nothing except the still air. It was absolutely quiet. We walked along a dirt path and up the slope of a hill. A field of gorgeous, orange-colored poppies and other purple and yellow flowers spread before us. We were speechless.

Minutes later a forest ranger approached. "Welcome to the Joshua Tree National Park. We're glad you're here. Would you like a tour of the south section of the park?"

We looked at each other and shrugged our shoulders.

"Yeah, that'd be great," Angela said.

"Follow me. There's a special tree I want to show you, up this way." He pointed toward a low wall of gray stone spanning the narrow canyon and explained that decades of cascading water made the stone smooth and that strong winds shaped the desert landscape. We all touched the stone wall and ran our palms across it.

"Smooth and curvy, like a woman's butt," quipped Michael. "So, where are those trees you mentioned?"

"Up there, about a quarter-of-a-mile beyond that north-facing cliff. See where the crescent-shaped shady area is? These large rock formations are favorite resting spots for hikers. Watch your step. Lots of smaller rocks can trip you up."

We hiked for a while and Mike hollered, "What are those clusters of weird-looking trees over there?"

"Joshua trees. Not really a tree, even though it has tree-like growths. It's actually a yucca, a perennial shrub that grows only in arid soils like this Mojave Desert," our guide said.

"Where'd they come up with the name Joshua?" Luke asked.

"Legend has it that Mormon settlers in the 1850s named it because the shape of the tree reminded them of the upstretched arms of Joshua, from the Bible. He led the Israelites into the Promised Land. The branches have a wide, upturned shape. Uplifting the settlers, so they said."

The ranger then went into detail about how the tree adapts to the desert: "Joshua trees rely totally on the female Yucca moth for pollination. The Yucca moth has evolved special mouthparts, making it possible to pollinate the flower of the Joshua tree. The moth's larvae feed solely on the plant's seeds, and the Joshua tree can't reproduce without the moth's pollination. The moth is dependent on the plant's seeds for the growth of the larvae."

Two stripe-tailed lizards bolted from beneath the shrubs, as if they were playing hide-and-seek. They saved us from the guide's tiresome explanation. I started taking photographs of the cacti in the canyon before the ranger brought us back to his lecture. "These big rocks cast shade and trap moisture in the earth beneath them. Seedlings are more prevalent in rocky nooks and crannies. Let's go to the top of that rocky cliff and take a look."

"What happens to those little seedlings?" Angela asked. "How do they survive and grow?"

"Well, young cacti are protected by the larger woody plants, such as the creosote bush and desert willow." He pointed to a creosote bush behind the cactus. "They mature and actually survive this hot, dry sun."

We thanked the guide, and looked around for a spot to eat our packed lunch. The guys wanted to check out a large stand of Joshua trees further up the hill to have their lunch. Angela and I found a large boulder that shielded us from the afternoon sun. We plopped down on the cool dirt, leaned against the smooth part of the rock, and ate roast beef sandwiches and fresh peaches. We rested and watched cloud shadows inch across the valley.

"You've been quiet," Angela said. "Hardly heard two words from you."

"Must be the natural surroundings," I said with a shrug. "Makes one reflect."

"What's going on?" She licked her fingers one at a time, after finishing her peach.

"Jack called me in his office this morning. He knows about my arrest."

"Good God, you never told him? How did he find out?"

"Mrs. Livingston, the rude mother who accused you of not calling balls out during her son's match. Turns out her husband is the district attorney for Palm Springs. She had him investigate us."

"What a piece of work," Angela said. "Why didn't you tell Jack about the arrest? What were you thinking?"

"Since the charges were dropped, I knew I didn't have a police record. Didn't think I needed to tell him or Coach Martin. Big mistake."

"What did Jack say?"

I shared the details of our conversation . . . that he went on to say that my "probation is for unprofessional conduct."

"Ouch. Will you still give tennis lessons?"

"Yes, so long as I don't screw up. After the six months, he'll decide to keep me or let me go."

"I'm so sorry."

"Me, too."

A few minutes had passed when I asked Angela, "I've been wanting to ask you about Mrs. Livingston . . . what she said about you."

Angela hesitated. "Remember when the guide told us, 'The great illusion of the desert is that it appears barren, but that there's life and beauty visible if you just look beyond the surface?'"

"No not really. My mind was wandering."

"That's how I feel a lot of the time. People judging me on the color of my skin. They don't look beyond that. The ranger also said that each plant tells its own story, and in the desert each plant or tree has adapted unique characteristics that help it survive in the desert."

"Wish I had been listening more closely. Lot of truth to what he said."

"I have my own story. I'm sick of it when people give me a rough time for no reason at all. I'm not sure what to do about it. Mother keeps telling me that we are all God's children, and no one has the right to hold you back. Turning the other cheek is hard for me when I get angry. Know what I mean?"

"Sort of," I said as I reflected on what she'd said. "You have it so much worse than I do. Some people still mock the way I walk or make fun of me when I trip. I ignore them. At least no one calls me 'It' anymore. Maybe you need to figure out what unique characteristics and strengths you do have and focus on those."

"How do you do it with your physical problems? Don't you get angry?"

"You're kidding, right? I used to throw my racquet out of frustration and anger. Dad warned me about losing my cool. In one match years ago, the tournament director bawled me out for unsportsmanlike behavior. In front of everyone!"

Her eyes bulged.

"It worked," I said. "I never threw my racquet again. I loved the sport, but could never be my best no matter how hard I tried. I felt cheated. Frustration builds up. The big challenge is figuring out how to not let the frustration and anger get the best of you. I still can be temperamental, though. You've been cheated out of things just because of the color of your skin. Makes absolutely no sense."

I chased an annoying fly away with my hand. "Sometimes when people are different, they create a world separate from the world they live in to protect themselves. Makes it difficult to trust people. But not everyone is out to hurt you. There are people who truly want to help."

Angela sat quietly, tracing sand circles with her forefinger. "That may be true for both of us." She stood and brushed off the dust from her shorts.

Luke appeared in the distance. "Hey, girls, ready to go?" He jogged toward us, zigzagging his way over the smaller rocks. Michael was right behind him, huffing and puffing.

"What's wrong, Michael, can't keep up with the youngster?" Angela teased.

So many thoughts and emotions swirled in my head as we drove back to Palm Springs. Angela and I sat in the back with the windows down taking in the cool, desert night air, enjoying the quiet drive home, letting the wind do the talking for both of us.

Chapter 28

Probation humbled me. I withdrew. Though teaching tennis gave purpose and joy to my life, I continued to struggle with pain, but more than just physical pain. I began to doubt myself. Drinking shots of vodka when I came home from a day on the courts didn't help the unrest in my heart. I was better than that and knew it.

During the six-month probation, I continued to work hard at my teaching craft despite the tendency to retreat into myself. Angela encouraged me to get out more. I took her advice by photographing the hills and flora around the Coachella Valley. I also joined a biking and hiking club.

A few months into my probation, a letter addressed to me at the tennis center came from Henry. He'd been transferred to Los Angeles from Virginia and had read a recent article in the *L.A. Times* about the tennis center. He wanted to get together. I responded with a short note: "If you're ever headed for Palm Springs, give me a call. Here's my phone number."

He and I spoke on the phone several times a month and tried to coordinate our busy work schedules so that we could see one another. A week before the holidays, Henry visited for the day. He looked fabulous with a California tan and trim physique, just as I had remembered. I gave him a tour of the tennis center, including a walk around the courts, the gift shop, my office, and the gardens. We decided to have lunch at the center's open-air grill.

"Nice facility here," he said. "Seems like a plush job you have here."

I smiled. "I'll take that as a compliment, I think."

He then proceeded to talk endlessly about the real estate market in southern California and how he could make a killing in rental properties and with high-end clients eager to purchase mansions. It seemed like a repeat of the conversation we had back in Virginia several years ago.

"I'd like for you to come to LA when the temperatures are warmer. It's a bit cool right now. I'll show you around. It'll be fun. Up for it?"

"I guess so."

"I'll set things up when I get back home." He gave me a long kiss before he left.

His personality lacked warmth, but his body had plenty of it. That much I could feel.

∾

It was 1977, the second year of our employment at the Center. I was twenty-five years old and, thankfully, no longer on probation. The day after New Year's, Jack informed Angela that she had earned the right to give private lessons. He also created a list of clients for her. A few days later, Jack asked me to take two of his private lessons while he attended two weekend conferences in Tucson. My heart leapt at his overture. What an opportunity.

"Of course, Jack. When and with whom?"

"The next two Saturdays at noon with Dr. Sean Wilson. He's a pediatric surgeon at the local orthopedic complex."

"I'll be there. Thank you. Any advice?"

"No, Lucie." I did a little jig down the hallway.

∾

Dr. Wilson was a few minutes late, but that didn't matter when he finally walked onto the court. His hair was a little long, and a strand hung down onto his forehead. When he introduced himself, his lips curved into a bright smile.

"Jack tells me you can help me with my volley," he said after we introduced ourselves.

I held eye contact longer than I normally would.

He noticed and winked at me. "Shall we begin?"

"Yes, of course. Take a position by the net. I'll hit different angles of the ball and see how you react with your volley."

"Okay," he said.

We exchanged volleys for several minutes before I made any comments. "You've got excellent reflexes. That's important for the volley. Right before you hit the ball, you tend to look where you want to direct the ball. As a result, you end up hitting the ball on the edge of your racquet frame instead of at the center of the strings."

"Makes sense. How do you fix it?"

"By hitting a punch volley. Focus on punching your racquet forward and slightly down, with a little backswing. This action adds underspin to the ball."

I demonstrated the stroke several times. "Try a few shadow swings, then we'll hit some more."

We volleyed for about five to ten minutes, hitting both forehands and backhands. "Well done, Dr. Wilson. I'd like to improve your backhand volley a bit more. Turn your shoulder a little, then punch forward. The shoulder turn will give you some power."

"Got it."

During the last fifteen minutes of the lesson, we hit full-court ground strokes with an occasional volley exchange. I'd hit a short ball, forcing him to run to the net and hit a series of punch volleys.

"Well, that's it for today," I finally announced.

"Thank you. Learned a lot, Lucie."

I shook his hand. "See you next Saturday?"

"Yes." He withdrew his hand with a light brush to my arm.

~

At noon the following Saturday, Dr. Wilson arrived with a bit of a stubble and aviator sunglasses. "Hi, Lucie. Beautiful day."

"Perfect for tennis. Ready to work, Dr. Wilson?" My gaze lingered on his face.

"Call me Sean, please."

"Very well."

"You can run me hard today."

"Okay, you asked for it. We'll work on the serve and the drop volley."

Sean had a natural rhythm to his service motion. Many players forget that both arms should rise together to create one continuous motion. I needed to correct his ball toss, however, which was too low, causing many of his serves to land in the net.

"Toss the ball as high as you can reach with your racquet. Try it, Sean." He gave it a shot. "Good, and again." A bit better. "Nice. Think of the toss as placing the ball up there with your fingertips."

For the rest of the lesson, we addressed the drop volley, a low-lying shot that just clears the net and drops down quickly on your opponent's court.

"Bend your knees low to hit the ball with an underhanded stroke and out in front of you."

"So the ball has some back spin to it," Sean said.

"Exactly. That motion causes the ball to drop just over the net. It's really a soft touch to the ball." The lesson went by quickly, to my disappointment. I smiled as I walked over to his side of the court. "That's it, Sean. Hour is up."

"Already? Really good stuff. And you did work me hard!

Thank you."

"You're welcome."

"Do you have time to get a beverage at the grill?" Sean asked.

"Sorry, I can't. Got another lesson in fifteen minutes. Another time, perhaps?"

"Another time. Great lesson. Thanks again."

I took a deep breath as he left the court. If Jack was giving me a test, Sean's enthusiasm and his improvement gave me hope.

The next day, I met with Jack for coffee at the center's café and asked how the conference had gone.

"Excellent, especially the food." He patted his stomach. "Sean told me you're a fine instructor who knows her stuff. You're certainly ready to give private lessons. On occasion, I'll ask you to conduct group lessons as well. Don't disappoint me, Lucie."

"I won't." I felt relieved, grateful, and ecstatic for the privilege of giving private lessons. I would not disappoint him or anyone else again.

∽

On my day off, I would often play with Michael, Luke, or Angela to keep my game sharp. Depending on my pain level, we'd play for one or two hours. When Angela and I practiced together, invariably she'd ask me to evaluate her game.

Today she said, "Hey, I could use help with my volley. Let me know what you think."

After observing a dozen of her volleys, I told her, "You're not getting low enough. Bend your knees, not your back. And abbreviate your backswing. That way you'll control the ball better. Try it."

We repeated the net-play drill for twenty minutes—a dozen backhand volleys, then forehand volleys, a quick dozen alternating forehands and backhands, before ending the drill with a base-line rally.

"Much better, Ange," I said. "Volleys are more precise. You have great touch."

"Thanks. Maybe another time we can work on my serve and volley set-up patterns. The serve is my best stroke and I'm feeling better about my net play."

"Sure thing, Ange. Happy to."

~

Over the next several weeks we practiced every Monday. Our play intensified, and so did the pain in my hip and back. One day, I stopped play rather abruptly.

"Hey, Angela, I need to rest a bit. Why not practice your serve? Then we'll do some serve and volley set patterns. Sound okay to you?"

"I'll take a break, too." We walked over to the two chairs by the sideline and toweled off. "I've been thinking, Lucie. As you know, Jack has given me some time off these last several months to play professional tournaments in northern California, Nevada, and Arizona."

"Of course. You won each of them," I said with a smile.

She glanced down at her racquet. "I've been dreaming of playing the pro circuit full-time. I'd like to enter some European tournaments."

"Really." *That was my dream once.*

Angela looked up and turned to me. "And I'd like you to be my coach."

"Seriously?"

"Seriously. I've observed you instructing players of all levels. You're patient and analytical. You're always helpful to me when you solve a weakness in my game. Your corrections are spot on."

"Thanks! You do have great talent. We know each other well, and I know how to be tough on you when you get soft."

She laughed. "So, whatcha think?"

"If you're serious, you'd have to reduce your teaching lessons, and I'd have to modify my teaching schedule, too. Obviously, Jack would have to give us his blessing. Maybe he could find a sponsor who'd pay for your racquets and some travel and coaching expenses," I said.

"Okay, we can work out the details, but would you like to be my coach? That's what I'm asking you."

"I'd love to."

The next day, we had a long talk with Jack about Angela pursuing the pro tour with me as her primary coach. He agreed, with the understanding that he would receive a small percentage of her earnings. Luke and Michael would take on most of Angela's students, which they were thrilled to do since it enhanced their respective incomes. I would continue giving private lessons exclusively to intermediate students. Jack promised to find a hitting partner for Angela because it was clear that my body simply couldn't keep up with the rigorous workouts.

A week later, Jack found a local sponsor to pay for Angela's racquets and travel expenses with one proviso: that Angela's tennis dress sport the company's logo on her shoulder. A legal contract had been drawn up which indicated that I, as her primary coach, would receive a small percentage of Angela's winning purse and Jack a smaller percentage. The contract also delineated a few other details. Things were now set.

The goal was to qualify for the 1977 French Open in Paris, which started at the end of May, in five months. Angela held a high enough ranking here in the United States, and if she won the prestigious clay-court tournament—the Fontainebleau Classic in France, held the first week of May—Angela would earn the right to enter the French Open.

Luke and Michael were supportive of us and agreed to get Angela in the best tournament shape possible. For months the two men ran her ragged around the court, varied the pace of the ball to throw off her rhythm, and served particularly hard to her. I focused on match-play strategies.

Our team effort paid off. She was playing beautifully. To top it off, Jack surprised me by insisting that I join Angela in Fontainebleau. I was thrilled.

We were going to France.

Chapter 29

Angela and I were headed for France in two-and-a-half weeks. We continued her preparations with Michael and Luke focusing on Angela's return of serve, cross-court backhand, and the serve-volley set piece, while I concentrated on match-play drills. With every practice, it was hard to contain our excitement. She was ready.

On my day off, I was rereading mom's letter from last week, in which she described their new home in the coastal village of Cotuit on Cape Cod, Massachusetts. They had moved there just two months ago, and they were meeting people through Mom's volunteer work at their church's outreach program and with Dad's new-found tennis group at the municipal courts. I had planned to visit them at Christmastime. In the background, Samuel Barber's *Adagio for Strings* was playing on National Public Radio. I'd first listened to this glorious piece in Aunt Lucie's living room when Mom and I visited her several years ago.

The phone rang and jolted me out of my reverie. It was Mom. "It's your father . . ."

"What about him, Mom?"

"He . . . your father . . . he . . . died. A few hours ago. He's . . . he's in Heaven now."

I choked out, "Daddy? Daddy's gone? How . . . how did it happen?"

"He was playing doubles with his men's group. He slid to reach for an oncoming volley and hit his head on the net's steel post."

"Oh, God. Was he . . . .in a lot . . ."

"No, sweetie. The coroner said he died instantly." The silence stretched from Massachusetts to California.

I couldn't help thinking how Dad always raced to retrieve a ball—any ball—to keep play going. He never gave up.

"Can you come soon, Lucie?"

"Of course. I'll call you later, Mom."

Fear seared my heart. *What would I do without him?*

I phoned Jack to tell him of the news, and I asked for some time off. Then I booked a flight to Boston for the next day. My dear Angela drove me to the airport.

I found myself alone in their new home. Mom left a note on the kitchen counter explaining that she was at a church meeting with the minister, making plans for Dad's final resting place. She'd be back around noon.

In the stillness, I wandered through the house to see what was new and what was familiar. My chest tightened when I opened the hall closet and saw his tennis racquet. I closed the door fast, and made my way to the living room. I knelt beside the cherry end table, the very one Dad and I had worked on when I was a cranky ten-year-old. I took a deep breath hoping to draw in its scent, but it was sealed away forever. No Dad meant no advice, no soft touch on my shoulder to comfort me, no laughter, no tennis together. I tried to remember every detail of his face and especially his hands when he would be wood-working. Never again. All I could do was cry. Deep, guttural, soul-wrenching.

~

Later that afternoon, Mom asked me to start going through Dad's last box. She wasn't ready to do so herself. When I walked into my parents' bedroom, a shaft of sunlight sat upon the large box tucked away in the corner. It had rained all morning, but now the room brightened, perfect timing for the opening of the last box belonging to my father. I'm not sure I was ready for what I would find, yet my hunger for his presence gave me the strength to see what was inside.

I dragged the corrugated box marked "Family" to the center of my parents' bedroom, where the sunshine was brightest, and sat down on the carpeted floor. Stacked inside were large manila envelopes with my dad's barely legible scribbling: "Lucie's report cards," "crayon drawings," "tennis," "early photos," "college days," and "Brownies and Girl Scouts." At the bottom was a package, carefully wrapped in brown craft paper and tied with twine.

I tore away the layers and caught my breath when I saw a framed *New York Times* sepia-tinged photograph of my teenage father on a tennis court at the Westside Tennis Club in Forest Hills, New York, dated September 3, 1933. The photo showed him and another ball boy reaching out to comfort a player who had been struck in the eye by a tennis ball. The caption said it was my tennis heroine, Alice Marble. Even deep breaths could not calm my soul.

I was not surprised that Dad had helped. It was something he did throughout his entire life, always lending a helping hand to no matter who. I wondered why he never showed me this photograph before. And who was that other ball boy? What became of him?

I glanced at the "Brownies" envelope. For me, Brownies was synonymous with Joanne Kelsch, my best friend from elementary school. Joanne also had helping hands and had defended me through those early years when classmates laughed at the awkward way I walked. Photographs have a way of stopping you in your tracks.

At the very bottom of the large box was what looked like a book, wrapped in brown paper. When I gingerly undid the old masking tape, I found a thick eight-by-ten-inch sterling-silver framed photograph of Dad, maybe in his late twenties, with his arm around the shoulders of a man in some factory. There were aircraft parts and engineering drawings in the background. The photograph was signed, "Your friend, Tomas."

As I turned over the frame, something slid underneath the felt backing. I bit my lip and carefully removed the backing to find an envelope. Inside was a note. I recognized Dad's scribble.

After the war ended, Tomas Kelsch and I worked for Eagle Aviation in different departments. I left in 1953, and he remained a few years longer. Our two families came to live in the same town on Long Island. During the summers, Tomas and I would often play tennis together and afterward go for lunch at the local diner. In May 1962, Tomas confided in me that an investigation was underway about forged Eagle Aviation documents that approved the manufacturing of faulty fuel tanks. Tomas decided to come forward and give state's evidence because he could testify as to who in the company falsified the paperwork. He also admitted his role in the cover-up. In order to protect Tomas and his family, the government recommended a protection program, which would cause him and his family to move away. I promised Tomas I would never reveal what he had told me. Charles, May 1961.

I slid down to the floor in disbelief and wept for my father's counsel, his laughter, his heart. I had often wondered what happened to Joanne and her family. It was a part of my soul. I remember the night she slept over. Joanne said that she overheard the previous evening her parents talking about a move. I guess Dad's note now explained everything.

After several minutes, I lovingly rewrapped the framed photo, put the note back in its envelope and placed them back in the box. On a sudden urge, I opened the envelope marked, "Brownies and Girl Scouts" and picked up a three-by-five-inch faded color photo of me and Joanne smiling and holding hands in our Brownies uniforms. Joanne's brown beret slanted a bit over her right eye, though not obscuring that sweet, chubby smile of hers. That was the day the two of us made a pact that no matter what, we would always tell each other everything. I turned over the photo and saw, in her own printing, the Brownie oath: "I will do my best to be honest and fair."

I smiled, remembering when we swapped our Brownie gold pins. It symbolized our pledge to one another. I still had Joanne's pin, safe at the bottom of my cedar chest, back home in Palm Springs. I held the two photos to my chest, astonished at what I had discovered.

Mom climbed the steps to the second floor of their new home. We hadn't had much time together since Dad's passing. I rose from the floor and met her at the door. "Oh Mom." I took her in my arms and wouldn't let go.

Eyes moist, she said, "Lucie, dear, let's sit over on the window seat."

We sat on the thick cushion.

"Can I get something for you Mom—water? Coffee?"

"No not now, maybe later." She held my hand and remained silent.

Several minutes later, I said, "I was going through the last box of Dad's and came across something." I walked over to the pile of items I placed in the corner. "Have you seen this before?" I handed her the framed Westside Tennis Club photograph.

"Why, no, but that is your father." She pointed to the boy leaning toward Alice Marble.

"Yep, with that wavy hair of his," I said.

Her fingers ran small circles around the glass frame.

I took a long breath. My left leg twitched. "There's another photo, Mom, and a note from Dad."

"Let me see that, honey."

I handed her the silver framed photograph and note, then moved to the other side of the bedroom to give Mom some privacy. I listened to her mumbling, periodically repeating certain phrases: "state's evidence . . . faulty fuel tanks . . . forged documents . . . Protection Services . . ."

"Mom, how about that coffee?"

"Yes, only a half a cup though. I'll meet you shortly in the kitchen."

The kitchen looked out over Cotuit Bay with gentle dune-lined stretches of sand. I waited about fifteen minutes before I called out, "Coffee's ready."

"Coming." She came down the stairs and walked over to me. I handed Mom her favorite floral mug.

"You've got a beautiful view here," I said. "Very calming."

"Your father loved it, especially since he always awakened early in the morning to catch the rising sun," she shared wistfully. "I've finished reading everything. Have you read all of it?"

"I have. It's incredible. Lots to digest. I'm trying to understand it. Now we know the reason why Joanne's family left so abruptly. I'm happy to know," I shook my head in disbelief. "I wish he were here. I miss him."

"So do I honey; so do I." We hugged each other knowing that it was just the two of us now. "Let's talk later on. I'd like to lie down now."

"I want to talk more about this," I said.

"Lucie, I'm tired. Not now," she left the kitchen and walked straight to their bedroom.

My mind swirled like the wind outside. Despite the wind it was clear, sunny, and unusually warm for April in New England. A fine day to walk down by the beach.

I pushed against the wind, which forced me to walk intentionally so that I wouldn't lose my balance, a challenge throughout the years. I recalled the day when I came in second place in the town track race and Dad told me to "never look back."

Yet that's exactly what I was doing. How could I not? My father was gone. I had so many questions. But it hurt too much to look back. I felt out of kilter.

The wind was now at my back, making it easier to keep my balance as I walked back to the house. By the time I opened the side door, Mom was already in the kitchen preparing dinner.

"Hey, Mom. Can I help?"

"Yes, pour us some tawny port, would you? It's in the cabinet left of the armoire."

I poured each of us a glass of wine. We clinked each other's glasses and toasted Dad. I wanted something stronger, but only port could be found in the armoire. I felt heavy, grieving for Dad and tending to Mom. She'd lost the love of her life, her husband of thirty-seven years. We said very little during dinner and retired early. It had been a long day.

～

Yesterday's winds brought dark clouds today, cooler temperatures and drizzle. Walking on the beach or hiking in the desert always seemed to clarify my thoughts. Today I would have to try to settle my emotions without a walk.

Mom shuffled into the kitchen.

"I've made a pot of coffee. How are you feeling?" I asked.

She leaned against the pantry door. "Didn't sleep well. Everything has happened so quickly." Her lower lip trembled. "I forgot to tell your Father to have a good game. I always did that when he left the house to play tennis. How could I forget?"

"Come sit." I took her arm and steadied her to the table.

I put some bread in the toaster and found a jar of plum jam. My stomach was churning. *How do I bring it up?* I placed two slices of toast in front of Mom. "This plum jam has a sweet aroma."

She reached across the table and took a napkin from its holder to wipe a tear from her cheek. "Thank you, dear."

A few minutes passed before I collected myself enough to ask, "About Joanne's family. What aren't you telling me?"

"All I knew was that her family had to move away because of something serious that happened at Eagle Aviation. That was all your father told me."

"You could have told me."

"I'm sorry. I had to promise your father I wouldn't. To protect everyone. All I can say is that, while Joanne left too quickly to say good-bye, she did not abandon you."

"But why did you have to keep it a secret?"

"It was necessary. To protect all of us."

The rain wouldn't let up that day. In an odd way I longed to be back in the desert, that dry, vast and pathless place whose constant sunshine often soothed my disquiet and harnessed my energy. There was something comforting and elemental in the stillness of the desert; nothing but me, the sand, and the mountains. But no beautiful landscape would ease the sorrow Mom and I felt. I stayed with her for a week, then returned to Palm Springs to prepare for the tournaments in France beginning in two-and-a-half weeks.

Chapter 30

I felt drained when I entered my small office on the second floor of the tennis center's main building. A bouquet of sunflowers placed on the end table welcomed me back. The card attached to the vase read, "We're sorry for your father's passing and extend our deepest sympathies to you and your mother." Every staff member had signed it. I leaned the card against the glass vase and wandered around my office, straightening the books on the side shelf, picking up a small Cahuilla woven basket, and moving it to the other end of my desk. I stared out the window, unable to put words to my feelings. I was jolted out of my stupor when Angela walked in.

She came across the room to where I was standing and hugged me. "I'm so sorry. How are you?"

"Thanks." I stared out beyond the tennis courts to those steadfast mountains, as if they stood sentry to my soul.

"Should I come back another time?" she asked quietly.

"No. Let's sit down here on the couch looking out to the Santa Rosa mountains." I shared with Angela the details of Dad's death and some of the contents I'd found in the big box.

"That's incredible information about your long-lost friend. Her father and his connection to your dad."

"Sure is. I do wonder where she is, how she's doing, her life now." I stroked my frazzled hair.

"That's a lot to deal with. How's your mother?"

"Hard to say. We've had some sweet moments. She didn't want me to leave so soon, but I felt I needed to get back here. After all, the Fontainebleau tournament is in two weeks."

She knitted her brow. "You sure you're up to it?"

"To be frank, I'm not sure of anything right now."

Jack knocked on the door and entered my office.

I stood to greet him. "Good morning, Jack."

"Welcome back, Lucie. I'm terribly sorry about your father. Please give my condolences to your mother."

"Thanks. Angela and I were just talking about Fontainebleau. She should go, and I'll decide if I'll join her. Angela and I need to chat further."

"Very well. Angela, when you're finished here, please check in with me. I need to review your teaching schedule for this weekend." He smiled at both of us and closed the door behind him.

I looked over at Angela. "We've worked hard to get you ready for this tournament. We need to leave in five days so that you'll be over jet lag and have enough time to practice before your opening match."

"You've decided to go?" she asked with a lilt to her voice.

"I need to work, Ange, so I don't drown in self-pity. Dad would want us to do this." I collapsed back onto the couch and wept.

Her long embrace and gentle humming settled me.

"We're in this together, Ange. I said I was going to get you to the French Open, and I will not go back on my word."

Chapter 31

Angela took the first set of her semi-final match 7–5 at the Fontainebleau Classic, the run-up tournament to the French Open. She was leading in the second set 6–5. But she looked exhausted. Her footwork was sloppy. Her wrist was dropping when she volleyed. Her strong serve was weakening. Something was wrong. Did I not give her enough practice time? Was she caving to pressure? Did she not feel well?

Come on, Angela, buck up.

It was now match point, and I noticed Angela took a deliberate moment to compose herself before she served. She bounced the ball ten times, which she had never done before. Then, she looked over at me and served. It whistled through the air fast and hard. That was it—an ace!

"Game, set, and match to Angela Overby," the referee announced.

She ran up to the net smiling. When she extended her hand to her opponent, boos started. Why? Who was booing? The crowd of about 500 were clapping. The booing continued with a few outbursts of, "Go back to Algeria! We don't want you here."

I left my seat immediately and waited for Angela to leave the court. After putting my arms around her shoulders, we walked straight to the women's locker room.

Angela chucked her racquet bag against the locker, a very different response from her endless patience years ago at the junior development program, when Karen whispered to the other girls, "She doesn't belong here."

"I've had it. I *do* belong here. Makes me sick."

I picked up Angela's tennis bag and placed it on the long, smooth bench. "Of course you don't deserve this. What can I do for you?"

"Get a cab, and let's get the hell out of here."

Five minutes later, the tournament director ushered us into a cab, apologizing for the incident and reminding Angela that the finals began promptly at two o'clock the next day.

We nodded, said our good-byes and jumped into the cab headed to the Chez Bonheur Inn where we were staying, a fifteen-minute drive from the tournament grounds.

Clay pots of red and purple petunias framed the front entrance. Willow trees ran along the perimeter of the inn's garden. Once inside, we moseyed toward a round table of wicker baskets filled with fresh vegetables, plump apples, and peaches. Before I could snag a few peaches, the concierge approached and handed me a note.

"Pour vous, Mademoiselle."

"Merci bien, madame," I said and turned toward Angela with a quizzical look.

Dear Mademoiselle,
I am the Sports Editor for *The Fontainebleau Monde* newspaper. We would like to interview Angela Overby tomorrow after her match. Would that be possible? If so, I will send Stephan Deschamps to the Chez Bonheur Inn. Kindly leave your response with the Concierge.
Thank you,
Pierre Florin

"What's it say?" she asked. I read the note to her. "Are you going to say yes?"

"They want to interview you, not me," I answered. "Would you like to?"

"Sure. I'd like to know how the tournament can allow 'Go back to Algeria' outbursts. Remember what I said to you when we hiked Joshua Tree? "

"Remind me," I smiled.

"You have to look below the desert's surface for its true character. That goes for me too—for all of us! Like each plant tells its own story, my story is told on the tennis court. Period."

Her eyes had a determination I had never seen before.

The next day, the women's final grew tense as the third set unfolded. Angela's opponent, a French native named Chantal Laurent, won the first set 6–3. Angela took the second 6–4. They were both playing well, even though the applauding French fans gave Chantal a distinct advantage. The late afternoon sun gave way to shadows streaking across the tennis court, which made it difficult for the players to see clearly and heightened the drama of the final third set. Angela was happy because, win or lose, she had qualified for the *crème de la crème* clay court tournament, the French Open. When a player is happy, she plays better.

She attacked the ball, taking it on the rise, so the ball bounced only six to eight inches off the court before meeting it with her beautiful, flowing strokes. Coaches and players alike know that if you hit the ball early and make your opponent run corner to corner, deep behind the baseline, you're in control of the match. It seemed as though Angela was doing whatever she pleased. She moved Chantal side-to-side with precise strokes and came to the net at will. When she decided not to come in,

Angela would bring Chantal to the net with short balls and pass her easily down the line.

Angela was in the lead with the third set score now at 5–6, 30–30. Chantal served. Angela shortened a long baseline rally with a drop shot, cut with sharp backspin, which landed just over the net and won the point. On match point, Chantal's first serve found the net. Angela moved two quick steps closer to the net and took the second serve on the rise, hitting a sliced backhand return deep to Chantal's forehand. Chantal ripped the forehand down the line, but Angela responded with a beautiful stretching volley which landed over the net—just like Dad used to do.

"Game, set, and match to Angela Overby!" the referee announced.

The applause was muted, and today a few slurs had moved into our court. Chantal extended her arm first and shook Angela's hand at the net. Angela smiled in return and said something to Chantal, though I couldn't hear.

I ran to the exit and threw my arms around her. She'd played smart and with a joyful air about herself, a feeling I once had when I played well and won a match. My joy was now for another person instead of myself, but I was happy to learn that it felt equally profound.

~

Reporter Stephan Deschamps arrived late at Chez Bonheur Inn. He had a pack of cigarettes in his shirt pocket and a pencil behind his left ear, and looked like he'd enjoyed one too many chocolate eclairs. After polite introductions, we strolled behind the two-story, limestone building, admiring the lavender beds that edged the courtyard.

"Let's sit down over by the poplar trees," I said. A waiter seated the three of us and asked what beverages we preferred.

"Three glasses of your finest champagne, and make it quick

as we are celebrating a victory," Monsieur Deschamps boasted.

The waiter soon returned with sparkling glasses and a bottle of *Mumm champagne*. Monsieur Deschamps didn't bother to thank the waiter, but rather took the bottle out of his hand and poured the bubbly into one glass for himself.

Good God, how rude.

Angela shook her head in disbelief. "You forgot why you are here, monsieur."

"Oh, yes, of course. Let me pour you each a glass. A toast. Congratulations, Mademoiselle Overby on your win. You surprised us all."

"Why 'surprised'?" I asked. "She clearly outplayed Chantal."

"Yes, mademoiselle's serve and volley caught Chantal off guard many times. Chantal's steady play and quickness around the court has won her many matches in the past. That is why the spectators expected her to win, especially against a Black person." He gulped another glass of bubbly.

"What did you just say, Stephan," I said. Angela reached out and put her hand on my arm.

"Sorry if that offends, but there are very few Black players in France. Or in Europe, for that matter."

"What's this about Algeria? People yelling for Angela to go back there. Why all this prejudice?"

He leaned forward. "A bit of French history, mademoiselle. Algeria was a colony of France for one hundred years. The French government seized control of the country's mineral resources and its marine ports. France promised to modernize the Algerian economy, which it did. But the French government never shared the economic wealth. As a result, protests spread throughout the country. By 1962, Algeria won its independence from France. There was terrible bloodshed on both sides. Even today, fifteen years later, there's friction between the French and Black people. Some were angry that a Black woman won."

He loosened his tie.

I'd mirrored his lean forward. Angela spoke before I opened my big mouth.

"Monsieur Deschamps, I'm used to those comments. I don't take them personally. Why not write a story about my tennis playing and what I want to accomplish?"

He refilled his glass. "No need to get angry, Mademoiselle."

She stiffened her back. "I qualified to play in the Fontaine-bleau tournament, won it, and now I'm qualified to enter The French Open. And believe me—no one handed me those wins because of the color of my skin." Angela took a sip of champagne, staring right at him.

He grabbed his pencil from behind his ear, opened his reporter's notebook and looked up. "Let's start from the very beginning. Where you are from and where you learned to play tennis."

"I'm from New York City. I learned tennis first on the Harlem public courts and later at the select Junior Development program. I'm also a teaching pro at the Palm Springs Tennis Center in California."

"Very impressive," he nodded.

Stephan continued to ask basic questions about her training and technique. To me, his interview was uninspired. His mind seemed to drift in and out like the tide. Soon enough, he began to slur his words.

"I have a deadline . . . to meet." He rose from the table and shook our hands. "Congratulations again, Mademoiselle Overby. All the best at the French Open." He emptied his third glass of champagne and got up from the table. "Good day, mesdemoiselles."

"Drive carefully," we said in unison.

After he was gone, Angela asked, "So, what do you think, Coach?"

I half-smiled and shook my head. "Monsieur Florin said that Stephan was a top sportswriter. I hope he's right."

Chapter 32

The following morning, Angela and I seated ourselves at Chez Bonheur's side terrace with the sun draped over our shoulders. Relaxed, we were enjoying a late breakfast when the Concierge hurried to us and handed me a note.

"Pour vous, mademoiselle."

"Merci, madame." It was another note from Pierre Florin. Reading the note, I blurted out, "I don't believe it! Stephan never filed the story! He wrecked his car while driving back to the office and broke his right shoulder. But Monsieur Florin is sending J. Aubert around noontime. I'm thrilled, Ange! I've read his articles in *USA Tennis* and *European Tennis* magazines. They're fantastic! He covers other sports, too, but seems to focus on tennis."

"Great! We got lucky," Angela said.

"Sure did."

While we waited for the journalist, I motioned to the waiter nearby for another cup of coffee, and Angela ordered some more tea. The restaurant was crowded, and I noticed a woman standing near the side entrance seeming to eye our table. She was wearing a stylish hat. I squinted in her direction, but the sharp sunlight hit a crack in the right lens of my sunglasses, making it difficult to focus.

"Damn, I've chipped my sunglasses somehow," I said.

"Maybe when you were in the locker room picking up my tennis bag?"

"Could be. I'm going to my room to get another pair. Be right back."

After several minutes, I returned. The woman I saw earlier was now sitting at our table chatting with Angela.

"Lucie, may I introduce you to J. Aubert from *Paris Monde*."

I glanced over at Angela and caught her eye.

Angela nodded. "She was apologizing for the newspaper's failure to get Stephan's story out on time."

I heard the words but couldn't register them. I took off my sunglasses to get another look at the woman. When she took off her hat, she smiled, a tiny dimple played at the corner of her mouth.

I paused. "Good God. It can't be . . . *Joanne?*"

"Yes. It's me, Luce. I didn't know you were Angela's coach. She just told me." My ol' friend rose from her chair and drew me into her arms. We hugged for the longest time.

I whispered, "So, you're J. Aubert?"

"Yes. I took my mother's maiden name."

"Oh, Jo, I can't believe it's you."

"Let's sit."

"Why the initial?" I smiled. The first word since the shock of seeing Joanne.

"Figured I had a better chance at succeeding in a man's world of sports journalism if I used my initial in the byline."

"Smart girl. I've read many of your articles. They're excellent. I thought they were written by a man."

"Hah! Thank you. So, how are you?" she asked.

"Shocked, but fine," I answered with a smile. "As you can see, I'm coaching now. Angela and I both work at the Palm Springs Tennis Center."

"After all you went through with your hip and legs in elementary school. And you became a tennis pro? Unbelievable and impressive."

"It's been quite a ride."

"Tell me, how are your parents?"

"Dad . . . Dad died a month ago," I stammered.

"Oh, no." She touched my forearm. "I'm so sorry. Was he ill?"

"He died doing what he loved—playing tennis. He slid, hit the net post . . . and died instantly."

"How awful, Luce."

No one calls me that name but Jo.

"And your mom? How is she?"

"Hard to say."

Angela leaned toward me. "Let me leave you two alone. You have lots of catching up."

"No, Ange. The interview must proceed. I can leave and come back when you're finished," I said.

"Do stay. I'll have some questions for you as well. Please stay," Joanne said.

I never could refuse her.

"What's your favorite shot, Angela?"

"Definitely the slice backhand," she answered. "I like how it glides low over the net and drops lower when it hits the ground. It catches my opponent off guard and forces her up to the net."

"That slice backhand shot reminds me of the elegant style of Evonne Goolagong and Maria Bueno," Joanne remarked. She jotted a few things in her notepad. "Tell me, which stroke have you worked on recently?"

"The volley. I love taking a ball right out of the air with a backhand volley and charging the net."

"Like Martina Navratilova!" Joanne responded.

"Gosh, Jo. You know your tennis players," I said.

"It's part of my job. Besides, I really like the game. I took lessons for a while, but my eye-hand coordination isn't too good, so I took up swimming."

Listening to Joanne and Angela tugged at my heart; I realized all that Joanne and I had missed out on since we hadn't been together.

"Angela, what do you see as your biggest challenge?" Joanne asked.

Angela took a sip of her tea. "Well, I prefer staying behind the baseline, like forever. It has its drawbacks, but Lucie turned it into a positive."

"How so?"

"With the long rallies, she showed me how to change the tempo by hitting the ball early, and then making a surprise move to the net. It's been hard, but Lucie's been patient with me . . . well, most of the time!"

The three of us howled.

"So, girls what's it like—being a coach-player duo and working together in Palm Springs?" Joanne asked.

"We try to set boundaries between personal and professional. It took a while, but I feel there's a give and take to our friendship," I said.

"I agree. She's much better at listening to me now than she was earlier," Angela said.

"That's interesting," Joanne replied. "Has it helped you to be a better player?"

"I think so. Lucie, what do you think?"

"You give me too much credit, Angela," I answered with a laugh. "I do think it's important for coaches to listen to their players. We don't always have ready solutions to player problems until we ask the players."

Joanne turned to Angela. "Are you playing at the French Open?"

"My first Grand Slam event. Can't wait," Angela beamed.

"Do you have a place to stay?"

"Yes, at the Hotel Villa."

"Ooh, that's a fancy hotel."

"Angela's sponsor is picking up the tab," I explained. "They chose the hotel."

Joanne looked down at her watch. "Damn."

"Everything okay?" I asked.

"I didn't realize how late it is. Deadline's in an hour. Call when you get settled in Paris. We have so much to talk about. Here's my mother's Paris address in the 5th arrondissement and her phone number." She scribbled her contact info on the back of her business card and handed it to me.

"She lives here also?"

"Yes, we moved here in 1974. Long story. I'll explain when you're in Paris." She turned to Angela. "Good luck at the French Open."

"Thanks, Joanne."

Joanne kissed me on the cheek. "I'll be counting the days until your visit."

We embraced and she was gone. And once again, I was left with that empty feeling I got when someone I loved was absent from my life.

I sat quietly for a moment or two, then said to Angela, "Before we leave for Paris, I need to make a quick call to Aunt Lucie."

"Take your time. I'll be waiting near the Concierge."

I walked over to one of the hotel's available private phone booths to place the call.

"Allo," Aunt Lucie answered brightly.

"Hi, Aunt Lucie. It's Lucie. You sound great. How are you feeling?"

"Much, much better. The medication helps."

We talked about Angela's success at Fontainebleau and her qualifying for the French Open.

Aunt Lucie was thrilled. "You sound tired, dear."

I did not have the energy to tell her about Joanne. "I'm fine."

"I'm so sorry about your father. Your mother called me a few days after he passed."

Sweat drenched my bra as I held my emotions in check. "I'm glad she called you." My voice choked as I continued. "How are the yellow roses? Did they survive the cold winter you mentioned in your last letter?"

"Yes, but they still need a lot of care, like most things in life."

Ever the philosopher.

Chapter 33

It was a light, golden evening with just a trace of chill in the air. Angela and I boarded the short, forty-minute train ride to Paris. A soft shadow spread across the passing landscape with fields of colza flowers wrapping the earth in a bright, deep yellow I had never seen before, not even in Southern California. The train passed a farmhouse with a woman taking down the laundry from the clothesline, reminding me so much of my mother; she still dried the laundry outside on a sunny day.

I winced a few minutes later when, in the distance, horses dotted the countryside, some work horses and some thorough-breds. I hadn't been around a horse since the accident almost a decade ago.

Throughout the short train ride, Angela kept humming a beautiful rhythmic tune, plaintive in its tone. I wanted to ask her the name of the song, but I didn't want to disturb her; she seemed relaxed just staring out the window.

The mood changed, however, when the train entered the noisy, crowded station. This was Paris, after all; home to eight million people.

Before exiting the train, I asked Angela the name of the tune.

"'There is a Balm in Gilead.' It's a Negro spiritual. My mother taught it to me when I was young. It's always stayed with me.

My favorite verse says,

> Sometimes I feel discouraged
> And deep I feel the pain.
> In prayers the holy spirit
> Revives my soul again.

I'm thrilled I won the Fontainebleau, but it makes me angry what some spectators put me through. The prejudice gets to me, and when I get angry . . . well . . . I look to Scripture to quiet me."

"Like the 'indwelling spirit' your Mother likes to call it?"

"Exactly."

~

The French Open started in five days, enough time for two-hour morning practice sessions and a one-hour session in late afternoon. My goal was to keep Angela loose and focus on her two weaknesses: return of serve and her backhand, cross-courts shots.

The practice clay courts at the far end of the Bois de Boulogne Park suited us. Angela stroked the ball well; her timing was perfect on the service motion, and her volleys were sharp. We still needed to concentrate on two weaknesses, but all in all, I was pleased with what I observed. On the other hand, I was a little anxious to see Joanne, and while my first obligation was to Angela, I wanted to visit Joanne alone. So how should I bring up the topic with Angela?

Jack had arranged for one of Angela's sponsors to cover our French Open expenses, so we had reservations for separate rooms at the *Hotel Villa*. The sponsor chose this hotel; neither of us had ever stayed in such a refined place. Embroidered silk sofas were positioned in the lobby, and the paintings that graced the walls were from the likes of Manet, Seurat, Pissarro, and Van Gogh.

Around the corner from the hotel, a quiet café offered an American menu. English was spoken at most of the tables. We lingered for a while, drinking our aperitifs before we ordered dinner: porterhouse steak, mashed potatoes, and mixed vegetables. A hearty dinner for an athlete.

As we were winding down our dinner time, I asked, "Ange, I've been thinking. I've got some mixed feelings visiting Joanne and her mother. Would you mind if I see them alone first?"

"That's fine! I totally understand. Go." She laughed. "Now don't stay out too late, Missy."

I chuckled. "Thanks, Ange. You're a good friend. I'll give her a call after dinner to set up a time."

~

The next evening the cab driver dropped me in front of a beautiful four-story stone building with Paris's signature sloping mansard roof, overlooking the Seine.

Once past the doorman, taking the stairs gave me more time to settle my nerves. I took the marble stairs slowly. My mind flashed back to when Joanne steadied my gait as I negotiated the narrow desk rows in our fifth-grade classroom. A voice startled me as I reached the last step.

Joanne's mother greeted me outside her apartment door. "Ah, Lucie, let me have a look at you. Still that sweet face of yours. Please come inside."

We embraced as if it were only yesterday that we'd been together. She was a beautiful woman who still possessed the same warmth I remembered from childhood.

"Hi, Mrs. Kel—I mean Aubert." I hugged her again and felt that familiar chubby waistline I used to bury myself in after scraping my knees on the Long Beach boardwalk. "I can't believe, after all these years, we meet in France!"

"Let me have your jacket, dear." She hung my navy worsted blazer on the brass hook left of the front door. "Joanne told me about your father. I'm truly sorry."

I wasn't ready to hear those words. Hot tears ran down my face unchecked. She held me close and walked me into the living room.

"Have a seat here on the couch." We sat quietly before she asked, "Something to drink? Water, port?"

I tried to smile. "Both, please."

Joanne arrived soon after her mother had returned with my beverages. "Sorry I'm late. Work caught up with . . . Lucie, are you okay?" She scooted over next to me, slipped her arm around my waist, and held out a tissue. Her mother left the room to get Joanne a drink.

"Dad gone, finding you again—I'm a little emotional. But enough of that." I dried my eyes with the proffered tissue. "That was a wonderful article you wrote in the *Fontainebleau Monde*. Angela agrees that you're a great writer."

"Thanks. Stephen gave me what I needed to finish the piece. I just developed it more."

Mrs. Aubert came back from the kitchen and handed Joanne her port. "Dinner is about ready. Where would you like to eat, kitchen or dining room?"

The kitchen was small with a whimsical collection of market baskets hung on the wall next to a window. It looked out at centuries-old Parisian facades. "Kitchen's fine with me," I answered. "It'll be cozy, like down at your beach bungalow."

Over vichyssoise soup, we reminisced about our early years together, my tennis career, and Joanne's new job at the *Paris Monde*.

"I spent my spring semester in 1970 at the Sorbonne; that's where I improved my French and fell in love with the culture. I eventually became fluent, and I graduated from the University of San Diego with a double major in journalism and French in '73."

"You were always good with words, Jo. Good for you."

Mrs. Aubert agreed. Her face lit up when she spoke about her recent promotion to manager at the celebrated bookstore, Librairie Galignani, a haven for both English- and French-speaking readers on the rue de Rivoli. It was only two metro stops away from her apartment.

We continued our delicious dinner of *poulet rôti, haricots verts*, and *salade verte*. I needed another glass of Sancerre to muster the energy and courage to tell them what Mother and I knew about their disappearance so long ago.

"Mrs. Aubert, Jo, I need to tell you something I learned after my father died. It involves your father, Jo."

Her lips tightened and so did my stomach. "I haven't seen him in years."

"After Dad died, I came across a 1933 *New York Times* photograph taken at Westside Tennis Club in Forest Hills where your father and my Dad were ball boys. They were helping an injured player."

"Wow, I didn't know they had known each other that long," Joanne said.

"There's more." I took a deep breath hoping they wouldn't notice my apprehension. "Inside the back of the framed photograph was a note written by my father dated May 1961. It explained why you all left and the—"

Mrs. Aubert finished my sentence. "Witness protection. It was a difficult time for all of us. The secrecy, the isolation, the lies."

"Especially for me," Joanne said. "It ripped me up to leave you, my home, and my school like that."

"I can't imagine what you went through. Was it difficult to

adjust to living somewhere else? Did you have many friends? What was high school like for you?"

Joanne fell quiet and traced that scar on her right cheek; that gesture, a reminder of our time together when she fell off her bike and had to have stitches.

"Oh, how selfish of me to dredge up these things. I'm sorry, Jo," I said.

Her voice broke. "It hurt me a great deal when my father left me, left us, I mean."

"Have you ever tried to locate him?"

"I thought of it when I graduated from college, but I was too focused on becoming a journalist."

"Maybe someday." I peeked at my watch. "It's getting late. Angela and I have an early morning practice session."

"I'll see you out, Luce."

We walked over to the front door, and Joanne grabbed my jacket.

"Remember when I stayed over at your house? The night before my family disappeared?" she asked.

"Of course."

"You asked me why I was always so nice to you. Picking you up when you fell, telling off those vicious girls."

"You said it was because you liked me."

"I've been thinking a lot about that answer through the years. It was only a half-truth. I helped you for me. It made me feel good to help you because you never expected it. It must be like that for you, as a coach."

"I don't know. I never thought of it that way. Maybe so."

We hugged and promised to see each other once the tournament was over.

≈

The cabbie stopped in front of the entrance to the Hotel Villa. He stepped out of the car, and with his umbrella he shielded me from the rain until I reached the main door.

Once inside my cozy hotel room, I plopped on the edge of the bed and stared out the window thinking about what Joanne had said.

Chapter 34

Angela and I arrived early the next morning at the Bois de Boulogne Park courts, which were not far from the French Open tennis grounds. I began our drills by hitting backhand, cross-court shots. "Turn your shoulder to accelerate your swing. Carry the ball on your follow-through . . . You got it! Now again. Much better, Ange!" We closed out our thirty-minute routine with a mix of quick volleys, drop shots, and target serves.

Although we had vigorous practices, when it came to playing actual games, Angela needed someone who hit a hard ball and moved her around at will because I simply could not match Angela's strength or speed. I had contacted a local teaching pro, Albert, who agreed to play two sets with Angela, who was striking the ball well and moving effortlessly; she was ready for her first-round match.

After the sets with the pro, I called, "That's it for today." I smiled at the assistant and paid him for his time.

"You two ran me ragged." Angela grabbed a towel from her tennis bag and wiped the sweat dripping from her face. "I needed the extra push for match play."

Not too far from the tennis courts, we found a charcuterie and ordered a typical French picnic of cheese, baguette, fruit, and pâté. We came upon a bench a few blocks from the charcuterie and spread out our picnic. People rowed their small colorful boats at a leisurely pace on the man-made lake at one end of the park. All was peaceful until a peacock roamed around our bench, spreading its feathers, hoping for something to munch on.

"Shoo, shoo." Angela waved the bird away. "Never liked peacocks, too flamboyant."

My brain felt like it was full of peacocks, each vying for my attention—Dad, Mom, Joanne.

"You're deep in thought," Angela noted. "Want to share?"

"No, I need to give you my full attention."

"Okay then. Can we go over strategy for my match tomorrow?" Angela plucked a few crumbs from her lap and pushed them onto the ground.

"I studied your opponent earlier and took some notes," I said. "Her forehand's weak. She tends to over-hit it. When she hits the ball down the line, it often goes wide, and her cross-court forehand often ends up in the net. I'd hit to her forehand often, and when she hits you a short ball, rush the net. That seems to unnerve her. You're quick with your feet and hands."

"Sounds like a good plan. I must admit, I'm a bit nervous. After all, this is The French Open. Hope I don't choke."

"It's natural to feel nervous. You'll be fine, Ange. I'll be in the stands, sitting in the lower tier so I can cheer you on. Remember Alice. She never gave up."

The following day was strikingly beautiful, sunny and cloudless, much like Angela's performance. Her strokes were flawless as she won her first-round match. 7–5, 6–2. It was exhilarating to watch her play. Yet, I must admit a jealousy uprooted itself and nettled my nerves. That could have been me playing my first-round match at the French Open instead of Angela. It could have been me being interviewed at Fontainebleau.

"Never look back, Lucie." I could hear Dad's voice.

I loved being Angela's coach and was grateful for our friendship. This was her day, her tournament, period.

~

The hotel's Concierge directed me to one of the separate rooms where hotel guests could have private phone conversations. After several attempts, the collect call to Jack went through.

I couldn't contain my excitement about Angela's excellent performance. "Hi, Jack, it's Lucie. Angela won her first-round match."

"That's terrific. How did she play?"

"She played smart, her serve was flawless, and her groundstrokes were spot on."

"And her return of serve?"

"Well, not as strong as we'd like."

"Remind her to shorten her backswing. That way she won't hit the ball too far behind her and be late. Always been her weakness. Be sure to practice it with her every day. Is Angela there? I'd like to speak with her."

"Sure, she's right here. Bye, Jack." I left the tiny room to give them some privacy.

Angela appeared in the hotel lobby after several minutes speaking with Jack. I waved to her from my seat near the baby grand piano. She walked across the cream-colored marble floor, which made every step echo. Patrons took notice.

"It was nice speaking with Jack. He has a calming effect on me. You know, he's like a father-figure. He asked me questions about how I thought I played, talked about my return of serve, and reminded me to return the ball deep and up the middle to take my opponent's sidelines out of play."

"Anything else?"

"To shorten my backswing and keep my eye on the ball from the moment my opponent tosses it into the air to serve."

"Jack's right. So glad you spoke with him."

Angela remained standing. "I've been thinking. I hope you're not going to Joanne's tonight," she said. She seemed a bit perturbed.

"I said we wouldn't go there for a few days. Are you okay? Come sit," I said, sitting on the edge of an upholstered armchair.

Angela pulled up the lyre-back chair, fitting since we were sitting near the baby grand piano. She frowned. "You seem distracted."

My emotions were at war with one another. I looked down, studying my fingernails. "I am committed to your tennis success. I'm always thinking about your game and managing your practice sessions. You're right, though. I am a bit preoccupied. I thought you understood."

"I do. Guess I'm needy too. I won my first Grand Slam match! I'd like to go to a nice restaurant and celebrate. Is that too much to ask?"

"Of course not. Choose any restaurant you want."

"I asked the Concierge earlier today to suggest a restaurant. He recommended La Grande Cascade, which is in a quiet section of the Bois de Boulogne Park. He said it has a beautiful terrace for outside dining and the food is unbelievable. So that's my choice."

The entrance to La Grande Cascade immediately drew in its patrons with its mint-green iron canopy in the shape of a half-moon. The restaurant's grounds were so lush and green that I forgot I was in a big city. As the maître d' seated us in the middle of the patio, I felt a few stares from the patrons. We thanked him for seating us at such a lovely table and ordered two glasses of champagne.

"Tomorrow we'll work on your return of serve and then have Albert play two sets with you," I said. Let's plan an extra thirty minutes in the morning session and skip the afternoon session. It will give you more time to rest before your match on Wednesday morning. Okay?"

Her mouth turned down. "Is it a good strategy to take the afternoon off?"

"Absolutely. A hard two-and-a-half-hour morning session with no breaks mimics match play conditions. A relaxing afternoon with jogging and simple stretching makes perfect sense for you."

"You're the boss."

I grinned. "That I am."

While having dinner, we discussed strategy for Angela's upcoming second-round match. We also chatted about the latest Paris fashion, trousers for women, and a musical festival that was scheduled back home in the Coachella Valley. We left La Grande Cascade and strolled down the block to hail a cab. A group of young men hung out at the corner underneath a streetlamp. You couldn't miss them, but I hoped they'd miss us. They did not.

"Hey, mesdemoiselles, let's go dancing," one yelled.

"Holy crap." I grabbed Angela's arm.

The tall guy walked away from the glare of the light and strutted toward us.

"You," he shouted pointing at me, "ditch the darkie. Come dance with me."

We spun around and headed to the restaurant, but Angela fell. Their laughter was piercing.

"Damn, my ankle."

"Give me your arm." She stood up, a bit wobbly and limped back toward the restaurant. The doorman came out.

"What's all the noise?" He ran toward us, and the hooligans scattered.

"Mademoiselle, lean on me. Can you hop on your other foot? It's not far. Take off your heels."

"Go slowly, please," Angela said.

The next fifteen feet were touch and go, but fortunately there were no steps to the restaurant's entrance for Angela to negotiate. An attendant opened the front door and made way for us quickly, bringing a chair for Angela.

"Thank you both," I said.

"You were a godsend," Angela said to the doorman who'd saved us.

"Not at all. I'll escort you to our staff room and someone will care for you."

Within minutes, a first-aid attendant came in. He gave Angela a bag of ice for her ankle and propped her leg on a cushioned stool.

"Thank you very much. Could someone call a taxi for us?" I asked.

"Of course. In fifteen minutes?"

"That will be fine."

Angela and I chatted while we waited for the taxi.

"I despise that word 'darkie'," Angela said. "Hearing it fires my being. How do I see the indwelling spirit in that word? I don't know how my Mother keeps her faith."

"What a horrible word, Ange." I readjusted her ice bag and placed my sweater over her shoulders. "Any better?"

"It will be."

Chapter 35

Angela fortunately had an extra day off before her second-round match, which gave her an additional day to ice, rest, and elevate her ankle. The Hotel Villa nurse had given Angela an ice bag and some aspirin to reduce any pain and swelling. It turned out to be a minor sprain, but nothing is minor to an athlete whose movement can only aggravate an injury. By nighttime, she had started walking around her room, and I massaged her foot. She mentioned that she had little pain.

A good sign.

The next morning, the day of Angela's match, the hotel nurse spread a medicinal gel on Angela's ankle and wrapped it well. Luckily, her match was scheduled for three that afternoon, which allowed her to warm-up in the morning and test her ankle. A taxi took us to the tournament grounds, and we walked slowly to the courts. I hit with her and watched nervously how she moved—gingerly at first—then smoothly as the thirty minutes unfolded.

"Looking good, Ange. You've got your fluid strokes back." I smiled. "How do you feel?"

"Pretty good, actually."

We remained at the tournament facility until her match rather than going back and forth to the hotel. She showered, iced, and received a foot massage from one of the tournament's physiotherapists. He re-taped her ankle. She was as ready as she could be.

～

Angela fought hard against an agile and gifted athlete whose footwork and balance almost rivaled the great Chris Evert. Shot after shot, Angela's fleet-footed opponent followed the same basic footwork pattern: sprinting toward the ball, no matter where it was on the court, then slowing down, and just before reaching the ball, stopping to swing freely and win the point. It was a close match, but Angela lost, 6–4, 5–7, 6–4. She played well, but was simply outmaneuvered.

Joanne was in the stadium covering the day's matches for the *Paris Monde*. After the match, she met Angela and me near the entrance to the ladies' locker room.

"Gutsy match, Angela. You had some fantastic shots. I'd like to invite you both for dinner at Mom's apartment tonight."

"We'd love to," I said. "Angela?"

"Definitely. What time?"

"How's seven o'clock?" Joanne suggested.

"Sounds good to me. Lucie?" said Angela.

"Seven it is. Thanks, Jo."

That evening, we took a cab to Mrs. Aubert's apartment and wound through the medieval streets of Paris and across grand boulevards. Given the unusual balmy weather, we rolled down the windows to take in the fresh air. Lovers strolled along the tree-lined promenades of the seventeenth century Jardin du Luxembourg Park located near the Latin Quarter, a few blocks from Mrs. Aubert's apartment. *I wondered whether Henry would enjoy Paris since he loved traveling. We hoped to see each other soon.*

Angela and I arrived at the building on Rue de Sulpice where the doorman came forward to greet us with his easy smile.

"Bonsoir, mesdemoiselles. Enjoy your evening," he said.

We nodded and took the elevator. Joanne's mother met us as the elevator doors opened.

"Mrs. Aubert, I'd like to introduce you to Angela Overby."

"So very nice to meet you, Angela. Please come in and make yourselves comfortable in the living room."

The room gave way to a large bay window framed by two bronze, torchière floor lamps. Angela chose to sit on the burgundy-upholstered couch near the bay window. I stood waiting for Joanne who came out from the kitchen with four beautiful, crystal champagne glasses and served each of us individually.

"I'd like to make a toast," Joanne began. "First, to Angela for playing so well in her first Grand Slam. You have a great future ahead of you. Second, to friendship. Who would have imagined after all this time that Lucie and I would meet again? *Incroyable ! À votre santé !*"

"Cheers and *à votre santé.* Great article, Jo. You really captured Angela's spirit," I said.

Angela took a sip of the champagne and turned to Joanne. "I really liked your references to Alice Marble and Althea Gibson. Loved your quote, 'Prejudice shadows the truth.' Strikes a chord with me."

"Thanks." Joanne looked pensive. "The connection between Marble and Gibson makes for an interesting angle on social issues and women's sports. Guess your story struck a chord with me as well. Hopefully, it will with the readership."

After cocktails, we relaxed with a delicious dinner of *steak frites, carrottes,* and *mousse au chocolat* for dessert. Although stuffed, we left enough room for some cheeses, brandy, and stories about tennis and our families.

"Lucie mentioned that you have a great job at a famous book shop. How long have you worked there?" Angela asked Mrs. Aubert.

"For a few years now; ever since we moved to Paris in 1974," she replied. "I enjoy recommending books to customers and meeting interesting people, both locals and tourists. Lucie tells me your mother is a nurse in New York City. You must be very proud of her. She also mentioned that your father was a pilot in the Korean War."

"Yes, ma'am. I'm very proud of her. My father died when I was four. I have little memory of him except for the photographs my mother keeps around the house. Here, let me show you a photo I keep in my wallet."

Angela sprung from her chair and gave Mrs. Aubert the photograph, the very one Angela showed me years ago. Major Jackson Overby was dressed in his Air Force uniform—blue, dress jacket with a gold, star-shaped epaulet on each shoulder; light blue shirt; and herringbone-patterned tie. I'd always thought he was quite handsome with his square jaw and piercing brown eyes.

"Oh, my. What a distinguished-looking man." Mrs. Aubert said.

"Thank you. I think so too. I look at it a lot, to keep him close to me all the time."

"Keep it safe with you always," Joanne's mom advised.

Joanne's eyes teared as she listened to her mother and Angela. I wondered what Joanne was feeling. Envy, loneliness, anger, betrayal, love?

Her voice caught when she spoke. "Angela, may I see?"

"Of course." She handed Joanne the photograph.

"He *is* very distinguished looking. You must be proud to see him in uniform. I threw away all the photos of me and my father. Yours is a keeper," Joanne said.

I paused, not wanting to abruptly interrupt their conversation. "I'm afraid it's getting late and time for us to go."

"Yes, of course. Good luck to you, Angela, with your future tournaments," Mrs. Aubert said.

"Thank you. It was very nice meeting you."

"I'm glad you're back in our lives, dear Lucie." Mrs. Aubert cupped my face and kissed my forehead.

"Me, too," I whispered.

Joanne and I promised to stay in touch. We had spent too many years apart not to do so. We were different people now, but the love between us hadn't changed.

Chapter 36

After her successful run in France and our return to Palm Springs, the staff greeted Angela with a huge round of applause and a beautiful bouquet of her favorite desert flowers, the California Poppy and Golden Suncup, along with several congratulatory cards. Representatives from two local businesses were also on hand to offer Angela endorsement deals.

Angela stood tall and proud. With her signature tilt of her head before she spoke, she addressed the group.

"This means a great deal to me and to Lucie. Your support and patience while I've been away has meant the world to me." She hugged her flowers. "These are gorgeous. Thank you all for everything."

What a well-deserved homecoming. I was thrilled for her. I loved coaching Angela and our friendship, and I realized the stupidity of my jealous moments, borne out of a yearning for competitive play rather than any ill-will toward her. I looked forward to charting a new touring schedule that worked for both of us and for the Center.

≈

The following Monday, I visited Henry, my erstwhile boyfriend, in LA. It had been months since his visit to Palm Springs. He greeted me at the airport with a yellow rose, a hopeful sign that it would be a wonderful visit. His eyes held me as I tiptoed to kiss him.

"It's been a while," he said with a grin. "Almost forgot what it was like to kiss you."

"I'm here now, that's all that matters."

We dined outside at his favorite restaurant, the Fox Westwood Village. The waiter seated us at a small table beneath a string of colorful lights with a lovely backdrop of palm trees and sage bushes. In the corner, the pianist played Billy Joel's "Just the Way You Are." At the end of the meal, Henry sat back and smiled, his eyes taking in every inch of my face. He leaned in and kissed me. Our time apart fell away layer by layer as we talked about his new promotion and Angela's successes on the European tour. I was too full of physical emotion to tell him about Joanne; that could wait. He touched the inside of my wrist and ran his fingers gently the length of my arm before lifting his eyes to me again. "I've missed you. Let's go back to my place."

We hurried into his bright apartment overlooking the Pacific Ocean. His arms wrapped around me, he pushed the door shut with his foot, and gently led me toward the bedroom. Our voices fell to a whisper—as did our clothes.

The next morning, we walked to another of Henry's favorite restaurants for breakfast. We passed a park where two toddlers on swings yelled in delight while their parents pushed them gently from behind. The scene reminded me of the day years ago when Mom and I walked through the Jardin du Luxembourg Park in Paris and watched the children poking their bright sailboats with sticks, hoping to win the race to the other end of the pond.

Henry pointed to the children. "I'd like a couple of those someday. You?"

"Very much so." I turned toward him and traced the outline of his ear with the tip of my finger. He pulled my hand to his lips and kissed it.

We strolled along the boulevard for a while, pausing briefly to eye the pastries in the window before we entered the café. I was hungry and ordered a California omelet with extra avocados, an English muffin and coffee. Henry seemed rather quiet and ordered a bagel with cream cheese and an espresso. When we finished eating, he took a last sip of his coffee and raised a hand signaling to the waiter for the check. He nodded to Henry and returned shortly to our table with the check and suggested a pastry to take with us.

"Two crispy churros, please. All right with you?" He glanced at me, then back at the waiter.

"Never had one before, so why not?" I said with a shrug.

"We can eat them later today, for a snack." He smiled. "Let's head back to my place. It's getting windy and darker."

The initial excitement of being together waned after spending time in bed that afternoon. Henry made it clear that spending time apart was not good for the two of us, and the only way to be together was for me to quit coaching tennis. My heart raced.

"It's only a game," he said. "You don't get paid that much, either."

"Only a game?" I said hotly. "It's *so* much more than that. It requires discipline and creativity. I get paid for loving what I do."

"Oh, come on Lucie, really? You make hardly any money compared to what I make. You've said before that you were raised to serve others in need. How is teaching tennis serving others?"

"If you're referring to our conversation in college about my interest in the Peace Corps, you're right. I guess hungry people in Senegal don't need tennis lessons. They need clean water and access to food. Honestly, Henry, I don't know how my body would've held up in such a physical environment with poor medical care. I never did submit the application. I didn't want to risk getting injured, not again."

I searched Henry's eyes for some understanding, but none came. He said nothing. The silence mocked me.

Finally, he said, "I've made dinner reservations at a restaurant near UCLA. It's a short walk from my apartment. We can sit at the bar while we wait for our table."

"I wish you could understand my point of view. What do you want from me?" I said.

"For us to be together more often. For you to move to LA. You have a college degree. You can find something else to do, a different career."

I flinched. "You don't want to understand, do you?"

"I understand what you're saying. I just want you to move here. It'd be easier."

"For whom?" I asked.

He never answered.

It was clear he didn't want to talk about my tennis career. He viewed sports for women as a hobby, not a real career. That always bothered me, but in typical fashion, I'd kept it to myself. I didn't want an argument. I needed to stop keeping things inside and start working through them. But how? In tennis you hit through the ball to get the point. It was the same in life; you have to work through things, not around them.

The drive back to Palm Springs the following morning was quiet and surprisingly relaxing. We wound our way through the San Gorgonio Pass, that corridor between the San Jacinto and the San Gorgonio Mountain ranges, which provided a natural environment for desert plants, animals, and a strong current of air and water for the entire Coachella Valley. It was a bit scary when you first drove through the mountain pass, especially if the wind whipped up, but it calmed down once you reached the foothills. Henry was an excellent driver, so I had nothing to worry about except for the silence between us. I rolled down the window, letting the wind speak. Henry left early the next morning for LA and his "important" work.

Chapter 37

The day was beautiful with a slight breeze and a few scudding clouds. I finished two private lessons and one intermediate group lesson when Louisa, our lovely receptionist, stopped me on the way to my office.

"There's a message for you from a Donna Peterson. She's in town and staying at the La Quinta Hotel and wants you to call her. She said you two were doubles partners when you were juniors back East."

"That's right. Thanks, Louisa."

My fingers rushed to dial Donna. "I can't believe you're in town. How are you?"

Donna laughed. How I'd missed that.

"Fine."

"What are you doing in California?" I asked.

"I'm competing in the Level 1-A Challenge at the Desert Equestrian Classic in Thermal. I had no idea where you were living until I read it in the *Desert Chronicle*. It's fantastic that you're a teaching pro."

"Thanks. Are you still playing tennis?"

"Once a week. Equestrian competitions have been my life for the last ten years. I live in Tennessee. This is my first time in California."

"Good for you! I know how much you love horses."

"Can you have dinner with me tonight at the La Quinta Hotel? Say, six o'clock?"

"Can't wait."

~

Donna sat outside the beautiful Spanish mosaic tiles of the hotel's front door. She looked fabulous, slim and tan, with blonde highlights in her long hair.

I ran up and hugged her. "It's wonderful to see you."

"You, too. How are you? Your parents?" Donna asked.

I couldn't keep the quiver out of my voice. "Dad died a few months ago."

"Oh God, Lucie. I'm so sorry." She pointed to a bench. "Let's sit by the fountain over there."

We walked slowly and sat by the soothing cadence of flowing water.

"May I ask what happened?" she said quietly.

I explained in halting sentences. My left leg started twitching.

After I finished the story, she replied, "I remember the weekend Angela and I came to visit you and we played doubles with your father. Such a kind man. What a wicked backhand he had. How's your mother doing?"

"Okay. It's been rough."

"Lovely lady. Please give her my best," she said.

"Thank you. I will. Let's walk through these peaceful surroundings before dinner."

"Sure, you lead the way."

Our path gave way to a grouping of vibrant Golden Suncups and deep red Mariposa lilies. "God's miracles," I said. "And a little help from a skilled gardener, no doubt. At the end of this pathway are the Mexican Thread grasses."

"They wave with the breeze," Donna observed.

"Sometimes I wave back at them!"

We continued down a different path and stopped in front of a cluster of casitas with unusual barrel-shaped, red-tiled roofs.

"I've never seen anything like this architecture," Donna said. "The bright-blue doors and window trim against the white walls are striking."

"Catches you by surprise, doesn't it, given the sandy colors of the desert? I like the contrast. The Cahuilla Indians originally inhabited this land; they believed the color blue brought good luck and protection from evil spirits."

"You sound like a tour guide. You must really like the desert."

"I do, very much. Where do you live in Tennessee?"

"Outside of Chattanooga," she explained. "I own an equestrian center with two other people. I give private and group riding lessons to children and adults. I'm fortunate to fly my competition horse to distant events twice a year."

"That's fabulous."

"Lucie, what's it been like for you with your back and all?"

"Tough at times. Tried the pro circuit for a short period, but the service motion felt like a rod stuck in my spine. I couldn't arch my back at all."

"And your hip? I remember it gave you problems from the very beginning."

"After the accident, my body slowly broke down. It was painful to reach for a wide ball. I'd feel a snapping sensation in the hip joint. I couldn't rotate my hip properly. I seriously considered surgery, but there was so much risk and no guarantee that my back could withstand the grind of the tour."

"You know, I often think about that accident and what I could have done differently to avoid what happened," she shook her head. "I'm so sorry."

I stopped walking and turned to face her. "There's nothing you could have done, Donna. Pie just got spooked by the deer. Besides, I do have fond memories of our time together—and of Pie, that gentle giant," I smiled.

"Well, we did have fun together. So, how do your orthopedic issues affect your job now?"

"I need to be careful. I limit the number of hours on the court and teach mainly beginners and intermediates, but occasionally advanced players. It's not too rough on the ol' body. With one exception: I coach Angela. She's turned pro."

She smiled in disbelief. "Really! You and Angela?"

"Yes! She'll be back in a few days after her exhibition match in San Francisco."

"What a shame, sorry I'll miss her."

"She'd feel the same. Hey, any chance I can watch you ride tomorrow? It's my day off."

"That would be great," she answered with a big smile.

∿

At ten, I met Donna at the middle stall as we had arranged. The warm wind blew dirt on my clean sneakers.

"Morning, Lucie. This is my horse, Cody."

Sweat spit off Cody's powerful body, his tail flowing carelessly in the breeze. I was still anxious around horses, but with Donna beside me I felt comfortable touching Cody's forehead. With a sigh, he lowered his head.

"He wouldn't do that unless he liked you. That's a good sign."

I took a deep breath. It had been so long since I'd been near a horse.

A smooth voice came over the loudspeaker: "Riders, please remember to have your bits checked, and check in with the warm-up steward when you arrive."

"That's my cue, Lucie. When we're finished, meet me at the far end of the arena." She pointed to the purplish-hued mountains I often hiked.

"Good luck," I smiled and walked to the small arena. It was crowded, but I found a good seat.

Cody's first few jumps were rhythmic, and I loved their arc from start to finish. They were a team, and so well-balanced together. It reminded me of the way Donna and I had played doubles together as juniors.

On the final jump, Cody did not land well and came out limping. Donna trotted a bit farther toward the rail but stopped and jumped off. She crouched low to take a look. She ran both her hands down Cody's foreleg, wrapping her fingers and palms around every inch of the front left leg.

I walked over to the rail. Donna's face told me it wasn't only Cody who was suffering.

"The joint below the knee is swollen and hot. I'll meet you in the stable after the medics have examined him."

"Can I do anything?"

"No, but thanks anyway. See you in a bit."

I ambled to the stable and leaned against a wooden post, watching other riders in the adjacent paddock. I admired the beauty, precision, and athleticism of show jumping. Awed with the unspoken trust between rider and horse, their shared intimacy. I winced thinking of Pie and our accident and wondered how he was.

Thirty minutes passed before Donna shuffled over. She pulled her hair into a ponytail while explaining that Cody had been given an injection of Butazolidin to take care of the soft tissue damage.

"Did you say Butazolidin?"

"Yes."

"Good God! That's one of the drugs they gave me when I broke my back."

"Yikes! It's no longer given to humans. Too many bad side effects. How long did you take that stuff?"

I thought for a second and replied, "On and off for almost two years. Thank God, they finally took it off the market. It's horrible on the stomach. Will Cody be okay? Is there anything they can do for him?"

"They're icing him for the next forty-eight hours. They'll bandage the area after each icing. It's not too serious, but serious enough that I had to withdraw from the competition. I'll stay with him this afternoon, and possibly throughout the evening.

"Is there anything I can do for you before I leave?"

"I'll be okay here with the on-site vet and the barn manager. There's a café where I can get a bite to eat. Thanks, anyway. I'll call you tomorrow. I know this is a very rough time for you. I really appreciate you coming out."

"You're good therapy for me."

～

The following morning, Donna called me at home.

"Morning, Lucie. Cody has taken a turn for the worse. Any chance you can come to the equestrian center today?"

"Sure, I'll come by this morning. But I'll need to leave by noon for my afternoon lessons." I hung up and dialed my boss.

"Hi Jack, it's Lucie. My old doubles partner, Donna Peterson, is here competing in the Desert Equestrian Classic. Her horse went lame. She asked if I could come and give her some support. Is it okay if I come in late today? All my lessons are in the afternoon.

"Yes, go."

"Thanks, Jack."

～

Each of the two barns at Thermal used the shade of the trees and a pattern of cloth sails to control the temperature. The stillness of today's dry heat stifled one's senses. Outside Cody's stall,

Donna sat hunched over, hair in a messy bun. Her head sagged in her hands.

"Hey." I touched her shoulder. "Brought you some lemonade."

She looked up.

Oh boy, trouble in those eyes. I poured her a cup. "Take a sip. Might make you feel better."

"Not much can make me feel better, but I am thirsty. Thanks."

"How he's doing?"

"The swelling hasn't gone down. And he's bobbing his head too much."

"Meaning?"

"He's in some pain. His head bobbing moves up, not down, which means his front leg is bothering him. That's where the joint swelling is. He's also shifting his weight from one leg to the other way too often. We'll have to wait it out."

I scooted next to her. We said very little. The silence between us spoke to the understanding we always enjoyed as doubles partners. We knew when to speak and when to listen.

Twenty minutes later, the veterinarian nodded to Donna and entered Cody's stall. I remained on the bench while Donna rose and stretched her neck and back.

She motioned to me. "Come and watch."

I stood behind Donna, tilting my head to observe the vet. He spoke softly to Cody, stroking the soft spot between his ears before beginning his examination. With both hands, he cupped Cody's upper left leg and tenderly ran his hands down all the way to the hoof. Crouching, he held Cody's left leg in a flexed position, then released it. The vet pressed the injured joint several times and smiled after doing so.

He turned to Donna. "Cody didn't flinch, and the joint is no longer hot—a good sign. Bathe him in cool water with a soft brush. Tie him to the hitching rail to keep him stable while you spray him. If he continues to improve, I'll take him out for a walk to evaluate his gait. I'll be back in two hours. Feed him a little, too," he said as he left the barn.

$\sim$

I enjoyed watching Donna spray Cody, who delighted in licking the droplets of water. After she toweled off the excess water, she took a brush and stroked him gently.

"Lucie, say hi to Cody. Speak softly, in a soothing tone. He needs us."

"Hey, Cody. It's Lucie. Hope you're feeling better. Donna and I used to play tennis together. She was the steadiest player I've ever known, lots of balance in her game. I bet she's like that in your saddle." I shrugged my shoulders toward Donna and we both smiled.

Donna patted his neck and filled his oats bucket before unlatching the stall's door handle. "We'll be back soon, Cody. Going to get something to eat." She re-latched the handle, took my arm, and we walked side by side into the afternoon sunshine. Donna shielded her eyes from the harsh brightness. She looked relieved to see a difference in Cody.

$\sim$

"Let's take a look," the vet said. "Bring him out to the east paddock and walk him in a straight line, then in a slow circle around the perimeter."

"Got it." Donna took a slow, deep breath and led Cody into the daylight.

They walked around the paddock several times before she mounted Cody. He trotted, gaining confidence and strength with every step. I was perched on an adjacent fence, noticing the beautiful trust between rider and horse. I thought of Pie and how terrified I was of his size. But Pie was my protector that day, standing guard until the ambulance arrived. I've never forgotten him.

"Hey, Donna, think I'll take a short walk."

"Okay, we'll be finished in about fifteen minutes."

I walked around the outer edges of the grounds and came upon tall, desert grasses that lined a path leading to a small paddock. I was stunned at what I saw next—a little boy atop a pony holding the reins with one arm. His right forearm below the elbow was gone, merely a stump. His father was right beside him, handling a different rein. All was quiet. I watched from afar.

"Walk on, son. You're doing great." They walked to the end of the post-and-rail fence and when they started to turn back, the boy slipped in the saddle. His father quickly held him up.

"I'm scared Daddy."

"It's okay; I'm right here. Let's stop for a moment. Sit nice and tall." The father stroked the boy's shoulders. "Listen to your horse. He'll tell you when to begin."

The horse's gentle tail swished, and then he snorted, signaling it was time. The boy kicked the horse with his heels. "Giddy-up," he said. He struggled with his balance at first, but then, by the second walk around the paddock, the boy rode perfectly.

"I did it, Daddy, I did it."

"You sure did. Way to go, son."

The father lifted up his son off the saddle and rubbed the top of his head. Together, they left the paddock's far gate, horse in tow. The boy grinned as if he had conquered the world.

He had.

The next morning, I couldn't stop thinking about the little boy. How brave he was, and how loving his father. I wondered whether the equestrian center had a program for people with disabilities. Our tennis center sure didn't. The phone rang and jolted my thinking.

"Hey, Lucie. Wanted to give you an update. Cody's eyes are alert, and his muscles are responsive to prodding. The bandages are off, and there's only a little swelling." I heard the smile in her voice.

"That's good news."

"The vet is coming at ten-thirty. If all goes well, Cody will be ready to travel back to Tennessee in three or four days. The vet needs to certify Cody before he can fly. Can we plan to spend more time together?"

"Would love to! Tomorrow is better for me. My schedule is packed today. Come by the tennis center around 4:30 for a tour and meet the staff. Oh, by the way, Angela called me. She's arriving tomorrow evening around six o'clock."

"How great! Can't wait to see her. See you tomorrow."

Donna and I waited in the airport's airy courtyard, excited to surprise Angela. Since the plane had been delayed because of strong, northwesterly winds, we measured our wait by counting the number of tall palm trees outlining the courtyard. It seemed like only yesterday, not ten years ago, when the three of us battled for the top tennis ranking. Remarkable that 2,500 miles away from where it all started in New York City, we were going to celebrate a reunion in Palm Springs.

What history Donna and I had, starting at the NYC junior development program. Our lives had taken different paths, though we shared an early bond forged through tennis and the accident. For Angela and me, it was different. I was her coach and her friend. We had set boundaries for Angela's tennis career to flourish, yet not at the expense of our friendship.

Angela approached us with her long, sprightly stride. She dropped her bags and opened her arms when she recognized who was standing next to me. "Donna?"

"It's me! I arrived a few days ago." She squeezed her tightly before Angela leaned back and shot a glance over at me.

"She was competing in the horse show out in Thermal," I said.

"But how did she know you lived here?"

Donna laughed. "I found her in a local newspaper article and tracked her down." She picked up Angela's bags and we headed for the car.

Chapter 38

Despite a sharp pain that had recently settled in my hip, I suggested the three of us head to the cinnamon-tinged Santa Rosa mountains for a short hike the following day. Angela and I often hiked in the area as a way to keep her fit and relaxed after a tournament. As we drove toward the mountains, I wondered whether Donna would appreciate Coachella Valley's natural beauty.

"Should we get a guide?" I asked.

"I liked it when we had one at Joshua Tree Park," Angela said. "But not a long time today. Okay with you, Donna?"

She looked around. "There's nothing out here. Feels like a wilderness."

Angela laughed. "Look a little closer and you'll see," she told Donna.

We trekked the upper slope of the mountain range and found a guide at the outpost.

Our guide first pointed to a cactus plant with chocolate-brown stems and furry golden arms. It's cuddly appearance resembled a teddy-bear, hence the name, the Teddy-Bear Cholla. "The plant grows in clustered formations in this desert sand," the guide said.

Donna leaned in. "They're like little villages of teddy bears!"

Angela smiled. "They do look like that, don't they."

"Walk with me up that hill and behind the rocks," our guide said. "You're in for a treat."

"How far?" Donna asked.

The guide pointed. "Just beyond that group of boulders."

We followed the guide and hiked passed winding dunes of sand before we came upon the rocks. "See those thin, arching branches and brilliant red, tube-shaped blossoms?" The guide said. "That's the Chuparosa plant. It's the hummingbird's favorite. According to Indian lore," she explained, "when someone comes upon a hummingbird, it's a sign of healing and hope; the spirit of a loved one has come to visit. Photographers come up here and settle behind those rocks and wait for when a hummingbird sips the nectar."

We lingered in the quiet beauty and hoped for a visit from a hummingbird. After a few moments, one swept in and hovered in mid-air then kissed the blossom and flew away. I stood still, and caught my breath. *Hi, Dad.*

"Are you okay?" Angela inched closer to me.

I nodded "Yes."

We ventured back to the end of the trail.

"So, Donna what do you think of the desert now?" Angela asked.

She hesitated. "I was hasty in my judgment. In Tennessee, we have rolling green hills. A stark contrast to here. I'm not used to the stillness. It's soothing, actually."

"Glad you feel the quiet. The desert offers more than meets the eye," Angela said.

"So true. I'm beginning to realize that," Donna replied. "Sure wish I could spend more time here, but I need to get back to Cody and prepare for our flight back home."

Listening to Donna and Angela's exchange reminded me of the conversation Angela and I had when we hiked Joshua Tree National Park many years ago; something about judging on appearances alone. About the illusion of the desert as barren, but how it supports life, has a beauty all its own, and a resilient nature born to survive and thrive.

Chapter 39

From mid-June to early December of '79, Angela and I travelled to tournaments in Denver, Boston, New Orleans, Phoenix, and San Diego. The professional tour and extensive travel were exhausting, but also exciting as Angela built a successful career as a well-respected player. Lots of sitting in planes and trains had stiffened my back, prompting me to pop a muscle relaxer every once in a while. Sometimes too often.

Mother decided in September to be with Aunt Lucie through Christmas. Since her health had not improved, Mom wanted to meet with Aunt Lucie's doctors, do chores around the house, and cook some French recipes. She said the visit to Normandy "would help her heal" since Dad's passing in April.

Angela finished the season in victorious fashion, winning several of the tournaments, including San Diego. What a relief to be back home.

One late afternoon while I walked from the outer court to Jack's office, hints of purple set on the Pinto mountains announcing the coming sunset. It was a week before Christmas.

I knocked on his door. "You wanted to see me, Jack."

"Yes. Have a seat," he said as he waved his arm toward the chairs. I sat and he continued. "We've had four years together.

You're well respected by your clientele and the staff. The membership has grown."

I nodded.

"And you've been a successful coach to Angela."

I have no idea why I'm here.

He stood up from behind his desk. "It's time I promoted you to Head Pro."

My heart leapt. "What an honor, Jack!"

"You've earned it. You'll oversee the junior program and the assistant pros and continue with your private lessons."

I leaned back in my chair to take it all in. "What about my coaching responsibilities with Angela?"

"That won't change. Your coaching of Angela has brought prestige to the center, and when she's available, people will pay a premium to take lessons from her as well as from you."

"I guess that's true."

"We'll figure out the scheduling. You'll need to cut back on your travel with Angela given your new responsibilities. I want you to start the first of February."

"Thank you, Jack," I shook his hand. I left his office with my heart still leaping with joy. What a way to begin 1980!

Later that evening, I placed a call to France. I woke up Mom and Aunt Lucie at seven o'clock in the morning to tell them the happy news and how grateful I was. Aunt Lucie was feeling better; she said their daily walks in the fresh air did wonders, and Mother's voice sounded calm. We had a lovely conversation and ended by wishing each other a Merry Christmas and good tidings for the New Year.

Chapter 40

Each new year, Jack required annual physicals of the teaching pros. Last year, I learned that my hip and back were showing signs of arthritis; no surprise there. To minimize its progression, I strengthened my core abdominal muscles and swam twice a week. I was eager to know if the arthritis had advanced. This year my doctor said the arthritis was stable and that my heart tests also looked good.

"What a relief!" I exclaimed as I hopped down from the examining table.

"But there's something else." He pulled up a chair. I stayed put. "Other tests . . . I'm sorry to tell you this. Tests indicate that you will be unable to bear children."

"What?" I wrapped my arms around my waist. "Why would you say that?"

"There's just too much scarring, possibly due to the riding accident." He kept feeding me information. Detail after detail nailed the lid on the possibility of my ever becoming a mother.

"Please stop. Please. I've heard enough. I'll get a second opinion."

"Lucie, it's clear. We've done extensive testing. I am so sorry." He quietly left the room.

I collapsed from emptiness, too weak to move or untie the hospital gown. After a knock at the door, a nurse entered. "May

I get something for you before you leave, some water perhaps?"

They didn't have enough water to fill the void.

I pushed up from the cold metal examining table and dressed, fumbling in my search for each button on my blouse, one button at a time. When I reached my car, I realized I had left my sweater in the examining room; I couldn't face going back in there. A nice drive to La Quinta fifteen miles away would relax me. I found myself stopping at a cluster of rugged rock formations. Beyond, rising abruptly from the desert floor, stood the Santa Rosa Mountain range.

I parked my VW and walked around a bit. Little vegetation and hardly any blossoms; mostly dirt and brittle branches lined the path. It hadn't rained all winter, nor last fall for that matter. I was thirsty, like the barren landscape, and needed help. I sat on a flat rock across from a lone bush and shrunk down in size. My breathing labored when I tried to take a deep breath.

How can it be that I cannot have children? How do I ignore this desire inside of me? How do I quiet the silent war within me?

Eventually, I stood up from the hard rock and drove home. Still thirsty, I poured myself a vodka. My body had betrayed me once again, and all I wanted to do was disappear within myself. Nothing could hurt me there, but I wanted to work through this hurt and not bury it. I was raw.

So, in my night-long lament, I wrote Joanne a letter.

I had my annual physical today. I found out I cannot bear children. It may be related to the horseback-riding accident. The doctor says there's too much scarring. Something has been ripped from me, Joanne—the soft skin of a child; the sigh of a child's voice and their first giggle; the joy of bringing a life into the world and nourishing its soul.

What am I to do? I'm at a loss. All I seem to do is cry. How could this be happening? Everything, everyone I touch leaves me, even my unborn children. I am as barren as the desert.

Wish you were here, Jo.

The following Monday I drove to Los Angeles to seek a second opinion. The physician performed additional tests, but the results were the same. I would be unable to bear children of my own.

Angela and I were having drinks at a local restaurant a few blocks from the Canyon Tribal Park entrance. The patio opened to view of the canyon's jagged rocks and clusters of the golden barrel cactus.

"Are you absolutely certain? I'm really sorry," Angela whispered.

"I've known for a few days. That's why I went to LA. For a second opinion. The doctor confirmed the results."

She put her comforting hand on my arm.

"I didn't tell Henry while I was in LA. I couldn't bear to have him see me looking so bereft."

"You know he's not my favorite person," Angela said.

"I know. Our relationship's mainly physical. Tennis brought us together. Ironic, huh? He thinks my tennis career is not the right one for a woman."

She shook her head. "So, what's your plan?" Angela asked.

"I'll call him later in the week, then drive to LA and tell him."

Henry told me to park my car near the pier's entrance and meet him there, as the parking spaces outside his apartment were all taken. The pier was crowded, but I found my way to him.

"Hi. I brought a picnic basket full of your favorites; spicy chicken salad, patatas bravas, chips, and sangria."

"Thanks. Take your sandals off and we'll go for a walk on the beach and find a place to picnic."

We walked farther along the water's edge before Henry said, "We haven't seen each other in a while." His eyes narrowed.

I had no response and shuffled my feet through the cold water. Then I took his hand and said weakly, "We've both been busy."

Henry always ran his fingers through his wavy hair when he had something on his mind. I cringed inside.

He lowered his head and pulled away from me. We walked several minutes without a word spoken. I might as well have been walking on my own.

"Let's sit here." He spread out the blue-and-orange plaid blanket.

I took the food from the basket, opening the various containers.

"I'm glad you came. You know, you're not around that often . . . because of your tennis schedule."

"I know. But we were together a few weeks ago and we've talked on the phone." I offered him a cup of sangria.

"Not now." His forefinger made circles in the sand for the longest time. "I've met someone here in LA."

I felt a cinching in my breast. "You've met someone? How long ago?"

"About a month ago."

"Are you sleeping with her?"

He ignored my question. "I don't think I can do this any-more."

"Can't do what anymore?" I asked, holding my knees to my chest.

"Your career and schedule." He looked out toward the withdrawing horizon.

"Well, there it is. My career—and my independence."

He was taken aback by my directness. "Maybe you're right," he replied. "You're never around. And—yeah. I do think my career is more important than yours."

I felt my voice rising. "You've never really been interested in what I do for a living, nor have you wanted to talk things out, to come to an understanding."

Silence. Nothing. Just indeterminable silence. I waited for some kind of a response.

He sighed. "I'm sorry."

I turned to him, softened my lips, and kissed him gently. Then with a swift caress, I stood and left. "Goodbye, Henry."

He remained seated as I walked alone to my car.

~

The next day Angela knocked on my office door. I turned from the window. "Come in and close the door, please."

"I got a message from Louisa to stop by your office. I came right after lessons. What's up?"

"Henry and I broke up."

"Really? What was his reaction about your diagnosis?"

"I saw no need to tell him."

She joined me at the window. "You're kidding."

"Nope."

Her eyes brightened. "Good for you."

I nodded. "Thanks for always being there for me."

"You bet."

~

Another letter arrived from Joanne a few days later. The first part was chatty. She reported that her mother still loved her job at the bookshop, that the weather had been drizzly and cold, and that she would be covering a skiing event in Grenoble, France.

The second part of her letter lifted my spirits. "Remember what I told you back in elementary school: Nothing is going to keep Lucie Sampson down!"

Chapter 41

On February 1, 1980—my first day as Head Pro—Jack, Angela, and I met in his office to review the touring schedule for the rest of the year. The plan was that Angela would travel alone to tournaments in Las Vegas, Seattle, and San Francisco, while I would continue to give private lessons and develop the junior program. One of the other pros would take Angela's lessons in her absence.

The international portion of the schedule included my traveling with Angela for the Flanders Open in Antwerp, Belgium, and the Prague Iron Classic in Czechoslovakia in June. Jack was opposed to Prague. He stood up.

"Too risky. It's behind the Iron Curtain. I'm not keen on the idea."

"But the European Federation of Tennis has assured players and their coaches that elaborate safety measures are already in place for the tournament," I said. "And three other coaches I know have already entered their players for Prague."

"I want to play the tournament, Jack," Angela said. "We'll be careful. There are no other important tournaments in Europe after the Prague Iron Classic. We'd have to wait till the following year."

"A close friend of mine lives in Paris and writes for the prestigious *Paris Monde*," I said. "She's their top sports journalist and speaks German, French, and English. I'll check with her about what's going on over there. Plus, I trust the Federation and the coaches' judgment. They have an excellent reputation."

"All right, then. Add Prague. But keep me apprised often."

∽

Mail piled up on the credenza, just inside the front hallway of my apartment. My fingers flipped through the magazines and bills, but stopped at the letter postmarked April 3, 1980, Paris. I ripped open the envelope from Joanne.

> Life behind the Iron Curtain is becoming unbearable for its citizens. Poland, Czechoslovakia, Hungary, Yugoslavia, Romania, Bulgaria, Albania, and East Germany live under communist state control. Food lines extend a mile long, free press is non-existent, churches and synagogues are shuttered.
>
> My contact at the French embassy in Prague is the Chief Attaché. He told me this: "Even on sunny days when I take a walk to the town square, darkness appears with guards watching our every move."
>
> Lucie, I know you might be thinking of entering Angela in the Prague Iron Classic. It's not a good idea. Remember when Martina Navratilova won Wimbledon in'78, beating Chris Evert? It was a big deal, but the Czechoslovakian state government declared a media blackout about her victory. They hated that she defected to the US in '75. In case none of this gets through that stubborn head of yours, I'll say this is in stronger language: DO NOT COME. It's absolutely too risky.
>
> I will tell you, however, that since I am now the senior sportswriter, my editor is sending me to both the Antwerp and Prague tournaments.

I walked to the living room, plopped on the couch and re-read Joanne's letter, slowly. Then I tore it in two and tossed the letter onto the carpet. The next day, Mom called to chat. From the sound of her voice, she hadn't been expecting the news I shared about the Flanders Open and the Prague Iron Classic. Then I added, "Joanne might join us. Her editor assigned her to cover both tournaments."

"Oh, Lucie, please don't go. It could be dangerous. Can't you just stay at home?"

"These are two key tournaments for Angela, with big endorsements. The Federation is taking player safety very seriously."

"Don't be so naïve," she replied.

"Joanne's editor is a close friend to the Ambassador to Czechoslovakia, headquartered in Prague, should we run into any problems."

"I wish you had a man traveling with you."

Somehow it was comforting that Mom would be here, in the States, worrying about me. Tethering her to me. I was determined to go, but Joanne's letter had rattled me. "I promise we'll be careful and alert. Don't worry."

"Easy for you to say," she said firmly.

I couldn't tell whether she was angry, disappointed, or fearful.

"I'll pay Aunt Lucie a visit once the tournaments are completed.

"All right. I wish you wouldn't go. But I know I can't stop you—"

"I'll call you when Angela and I arrive in Antwerp. Once we're back in Palm Springs, why don't you come out for a visit; say, in October? I think you might like it here. You can garden year-round, although the summers are a bit warm. But I've gotten used to the air conditioning, and you would too. Imagine not having to wear a heavy coat in winter?"

"I've never thought about it, but what a good idea. And Cape Cod somehow always reminds me of your father. Being near you would make things easier for me too," she mused, her voice softer.

"Great! Who ever thought you might consider living in California?"

~

We arrived in Antwerp in late June. I hired a local male pro to warm up Angela at a well-known tennis facility twenty miles south of Antwerp, in the town of Laeken, the home of the Royal Family of Belgium. Practicing away from the city of Antwerp gave Angela some much-needed privacy. Travel, media interviews, and the mental pressures of playing the professional tour had increasingly overwhelmed her.

Sports were a part of everyday life in Belgium—especially soccer and cycling, though tennis was a close third. At the Flanders Classic, the spectators numbered close to 3,000. Like the sport of tennis, Antwerp was becoming increasingly international due to its thriving diamond business and growing travel industry.

My strategy of keeping Angela away from the press and having quiet evenings worked. Her fluid game gave her wins in all her matches except the semi-finals. For the most part, her game was solid. She still had difficulty getting low enough on her volleys, which resulted in points lost. But her much-improved service motion now had the elegant reach to its form that so many spectators admired.

Angela and I stayed at the Old Town Antwerp Hotel, not far from the tournament grounds. It was four blocks from the central station, where we would take the train to Prague for the next tournament.

As promised, I phoned Jack to give an update on Angela's matches. Our delightful receptionist, Louisa, answered the phone and said she would relay my message to Jack that Angela played well, but lost in the semi-finals, 6–4, 7–5. She wished us luck for the rest of our trip. I also phoned mom to update her on Angela's good news.

∽

Angela and I sat by a tinted window at the hotel's café, enjoying Belgian beers while waiting for Joanne, whose editor gave her permission to accompany us to the tournaments. She entered the hotel lobby just as the bells of the sixteenth-century Cathedral of our Lady—which soared above the cobblestone street across the way—tolled six times.

Joanne was armed with a backpack and camera bag as she moved toward us, looking so much like a foreign correspondent. Over a beer, Joanne told us how utterly frustrated she had become in trying to obtain a visa for Czechoslovakia.

"The visa and press credential process at the Czechoslovakian embassy in Paris was very difficult," she explained. "Officials worry that foreign reporters will expose their readers to stories about wrongdoings and abuses of power. According to the STB, all negative stories are untrue. Anything critical of the communist regime is heresy. But I flashed my credentials and told them I was only a sport reporter for the *Paris Monde*, covering the Prague Iron Classic. They love sports in Czechoslovakia."

"What's the STB?" I asked.

She finished her beer. "The plainclothes, state secret police. After waiting for three hours on a hard, wooden bench outside the Czechoslovakian official's door, they handed me my visa, passport, and press card. They trifled with me; I hated it."

"What an ordeal for you," Angela said, shaking her head. "Lucie and I had to drive to LA to get our visas and passports, but didn't have to endure what you did. Bureaucrats asked us lots of questions, including why we wanted to go to Czechoslovakia. Our wait was just an hour."

"I can only imagine how difficult it must have been, Jo," I said.

Angela sat across from Joanne. "It'll be interesting to read what you write about the Prague tourney. You're a great writer. I remember the article you wrote for the *Fontainebleau Monde*—really gutsy and brave. Very few people bother to address the bias against Black tennis players. What was the phrase you used? 'Prejudice shadows the truth'? Love that quote."

"Thanks, Angela," she replied with a huge smile. "Nice to know you remember that article."

We settled into a typical Flemish dinner, devouring mussels, pommes frites, asparagus, and an assortment of Belgian chocolates before we boarded the night train to Prague. We knew it would be a long and tedious trip given the border crossing checkpoints.

As we shuffled our way through the crowded aisle to find our ticketed compartment, Joanne whispered to me that she had made some preliminary inquiries about where her father might be living. "Nothing's come up, yet."

Chapter 42

Our sleeper compartment was cramped and narrow, and the inescapable smell of diesel fuel mixed with chemical-laden toilets made sleeping difficult. When the train's gentle movement lulled us to sleep, a quick, jerking motion would wake us, starting the whole process all over again.

After six hours on board, darkness finally gave way to daylight. The train from Antwerp slowly came to a stop at the Czech border, about five miles east of the small Bavarian town Mitterteich. Hearing shouts outside, I left the compartment to see what I was hearing. I leaned out the aisle window and through the morning mist could not believe my eyes. With machine guns slung over their shoulders, guards inspected the underbelly of the train with Alsatian dogs sniffing all around. I quickly returned to the compartment and woke up Joanne and Angela.

"Jesus, girls. Guards with guns are swarming the area with dogs."

"Oh crap," Joanne mumbled. "They're the Border Patrol looking for Bulgarians, East Germans, Hungarians, Czechoslovakians, and God knows who, checking for contraband and fake passports. Anything suspicious, they confiscate."

Within minutes, a stern-eyed female guard jerked the door to our compartment wide open. She tightened her holster, and barked, "Get up! Passports and visas!"

Another guard immediately came in with mirrors to check under the seats and above the luggage racks. The compartment became a mess of blankets, pillows, and magazines strewn all over the place. No sooner had we extended our passports than the guard's eyes darted to the rack above Joanne and demanded to see what was sticking out of her backpack.

In German, Joanne explained that the gunmetal-colored steel was the legs to her tripod. Insisting they were parts to a portable machine gun, the guard reached up, grabbed the backpack, and snatched the tripod along with Joanne's passport.

"Sit. Stay!" She marched out.

Joanne looked right at me, her face pinched. "In my letter I told you about the fear, the surveillance, the lost freedoms, the grim living conditions. This is life behind the Iron Curtain."

"I remember what you wrote."

"Right before I left Paris, my boss showed me pictures of East Germans trying to escape," she continued. "One image struck me: A young mother clutching her child as she trudged through an opening in the barbed wire, while the father struggled to pick up the child's dropped stuffed animal. Heartbreaking."

I looked out the window. "Barbed wire is everywhere. What about those guards lined up outside wearing long leather coats? They're everywhere. Good God. Is history repeating itself?"

"Chill girls. Someone might hear you," Angela whispered.

It was the first thing she'd said since the guards left us. She started to hum that melody, the spiritual hymn.

"Pretty hard to do. I'm scared," my left leg kept twitching.

"I'm scared too. That's why I'm humming," Angela said quietly.

"Angela's right. Let's try to stay calm." Joanne drew in a deep breath. "Who'd have of thought my tripod legs looked like parts of a machine gun? I sure didn't."

The compartment door suddenly slid open. A different guard entered, stating in broken English that Joanne must get off the train and be escorted immediately to the border official up the road.

"No way, Joanne," I stammered. "Stay on the train with us."

"You, passport." The guard pointed right at me.

My hand trembled as I reached for my passport and travel papers. I inhaled a shallow breath and then struggled for another.

"Passport!" He grabbed my passport and left.

"Damn, now what?" I needed to stay calm.

"Lucie, go with Joanne. This is an important tournament to me. If they detain the three of us, I'll miss my first match tomorrow and be defaulted."

"No way. I can't let you go alone."

"Why not? We've been traveling to European tournaments before. I'll be fine."

"I can't. What if something happens to you?"

"Same question. What if something happens to you or Joanne?"

"What a mess we're in. Jo, what should we do?" I said.

"Best to cooperate and follow the guards. They don't care about us; only if we live behind the Iron Curtain, if we're West Germans, have contraband, or—hah!—are spies. Besides, we each have American passports."

"You still have your American passport?" I cut in.

"I was born and raised in the US. Why wouldn't I have it?" She knitted her eyebrows. "I also have a French passport because Mom is French. I have dual citizenship."

The guard returned. "Okay. You! Come with me." She pointed at Joanne.

I stood up. "But she's done nothing wrong," I said.

"The Board Director must inspect the item."

"But it's only a tripod for God's sake," I blurted.

"That's it. You, too, come with me," she ordered. "Another train will be here later. Bring your suitcases. Come now."

Angela hugged each of us. "I'll wait for you in the Rungelt Hotel lobby at nine tomorrow morning. That is, if you make the next train. If not, I'll get to the tournament grounds on my own and see you there, whenever you arrive." She tried to smile.

The guard slammed the door shut.

～

Tall pines fringed the path along the railway tracks, making for a dark walk to God-knows-where. I was edgy and anxious, uncertain of what would unfold. Joanne walked next to me, and the guard two steps behind. I turned around and watched as the train seemed smaller with each step forward. Other people walked ahead of us, also escorted by guards, whose cigarette smoke made it difficult for us to breathe freely.

We said very little, unsure what the guard would do if we spoke. Occasionally, we smiled at each other, trying to reassure one another that all would be fine. Joanne pointed up ahead to an ominous-looking high tower with a soldier peering through his binoculars. As we got closer, however, we saw that it was cardboard cutouts of guards placed in the high towers that were staring down at us.

Good God, what has the world come to?

"There, on the left is the cabin where the director will inspect the item. Wait here," our guard instructed.

Though it was only mid-morning, the sun was hot and the humidity so high that steam rose from the train tracks and sweat began trickling beneath my clothes. Joanne's short bangs were drenched, and her right index finger kept touching her scar. Up and down, up and down her cheek.

Fifteen minutes later, we approached the cabin—actually a wood shack—with black, orange, and yellow diagonal lines painted across it. We waited for the shack sentry to let us in. Finally, he stepped forward and grabbed my arm. The steely grip digging into my elbow caused a fear I had never known. It left me wondering what was in store for the two of us. We waited and waited for the sentry to open the door, his fingers digging deeper into my arm until he managed to open it and let us in (including the guard who had escorted us from the border crossing) to the Border Director's shack. He handed Joanne's tripod, camera bag, and our passports and visas to the director while we stood at attention. He nodded to the sentry.

The door closed behind us.

The guard stayed with us. Nothing was said and nothing was in the room except the director's metal chair and desk, one pen, a large black notebook, a rubber stamp with an ink pad, an ash tray, and a gray phone. One window allowed for a slight breeze; otherwise, it was oppressive.

"Guard, check their suitcases and purses," the director snapped.

The guard examined our personal belongings. We had no contraband, no newly purchased clothes from Western Europe, no weapons or liquor or cigarettes or fresh produce. I hoped we'd be okay.

The Director then lit a cigarette and disassembled Joanne's tripod, which took him forever. First the movable central column, which opens the legs; then he removed the rubber feet to look inside the hollow legs. He unscrewed the ball head and each cap, pushed up and down the center pole, and inspected all three locks to the tripod legs. He took a slow drag from his cigarette and flicked the ashes onto the floor, seeming to enjoy himself. He found nothing illegal in Joanne's tripod or camera bag.

At this point, my left leg started its infernal twitching and my back ached to the point that I knelt to the floor to relieve the pressure. I looked up, sweat dripping down on the floor.

From his desk the Director looked down, straight at me. *"Aufstehen,"* he said and sneered.

I turned to Joanne. "What?"

"Get up," she whispered. She helped me to stand up straight. *Good God, just like in elementary school.*

After we stood for another twenty minutes, the director let us go. He stamped our passports, returned our belongings to the guard and barked, *"Gehen.* Now go." He got up from his desk, stretched his back and walked over to the window.

I looked over at Joanne and followed exactly what she did. We were led out of the stifling shack into the glaring sunshine. The guard walked us back to the railway platform and said to wait here for the next train. Fortunately, the station's scattered benches were in the shade, giving us some relief from the steamy weather. In silence, we ate the sandwiches we'd brought all the way from Antwerp. The ordeal aged me. Gradually, we began talking about our careers and our fathers.

"I still miss Dad terribly," I said, "and he's only been gone for a year and a half. I can't imagine what it's like for you."

"I have mixed emotions," Joanne admitted. "I'm desperate to hug him, to speak with him. I do have sweet memories. At the same time, I want nothing to do with him. It's disquieting. Hate and love."

I simply listened. She also confided that she found it difficult to get close to men or trust them because she feared they would leave her as her father had done. Sure, she'd had boyfriends, she said, but never seemed to settle with one. Her job as the senior sports journalist made it difficult for her to maintain a relationship given all the traveling required. Joanne was hopeful, though, that she'd soon settle down. I could relate.

The next train finally arrived. The intimidating guards once again appeared from the pine forest, ready to perform their menacing routine. Exhausted and still anxious, we had to wait until the guards were finished before we could board the train to Prague.

~

The train lumbered through one distant town after another. When it took a soft corner, I could see in the distance the pale plume of smoke twisting behind the engine like a snake. I kept looking out into the night sky and wondered about Angela. Had she made it to the hotel? None of this would have happened if I hadn't mouthed off. God, I hoped she was safe.

Joanne and I slept most of the way. The train ride to Prague was uneventful, save for a few tense moments when the train conductor asked for our tickets, passports, and visas. The last hour of our journey we talked, as good friends do.

"Jo, I never told you how much it meant to me that you were my friend, my protector, when those pitiful girls made life hell for me. My physical challenges made no difference to you."

"Why should they? We had lots of fun together. You were sweet, clever, and funny. They were idiots. Cruel."

I pursed my lips. "Oh, Jo, I have missed you."

"You have no idea how much I missed you. But here we are, behind the Iron Curtain, of all places!"

"Yeah, about earlier. I'm sorry I lost my temper."

"You did lose your cool. But everything will be okay. Well, at least the drama will make for a good article," she chuckled.

"Remember all those skits you wrote?" I said with a grin. "We acted out most of them at your beach bungalow. I guess that was the beginning of your writing career!"

She shrugged. "Guess so."

The train rolled in at midnight. No taxis were at the station. We heard a cable car from around the corner with its high-pitched squeaking. When it stopped at the sign, Joanne asked the conductor, "Is this the right cable car to get to the Hotel Rungelt on Stepanska Street?"

He nodded yes.

Joanne stepped aboard, but I tripped as only one bare light bulb illuminated the dark car. She helped me up and grabbed my suitcase before the trolley pulled away. After a ten-minute ride, the trolley squealed to a halt right in front of the hotel, less than a mile from where Angela would be playing at the Prague Tennis Centre on Štvanice Island.

The street was empty. Joanne and I looked at each other and hoped for the best as we entered the hotel. The dimly lit foyer and dark brown velveteen curtains heightened our anxiety. We looked around at the sparse lobby and bar, which was closed.

Damn, could have used a drink.

The ravages of time and neglect under the communist regime had taken their toll on the hotel. The copper railings of the marble staircase were chipped and dulled. A once-elegant hotel had been elbowed between two ugly, cement, rectangular-shaped apartment buildings.

Joanne's eyes met the receptionist's gaze. She explained to him that we had been detained at the border for hours and had to take a later train. He nodded, checked our passports and visas, made us sign the registration forms in triplicate, and handed Joanne a key to a room on the first floor. We asked if Angela had checked in. "Yes." That was all. Thank God she had arrived.

Our accommodations included a private bath; a lumpy, upholstered chair; an ornate, walnut writing table; and two twin beds at opposite ends of the room, giving each of us a little privacy. Weary, we fell asleep immediately.

Chapter 43

We were hoping to sleep in, but the next morning, soft and diffused light awakened us early; the bedroom curtains were too sheer to keep the sunshine out. Our room had a view of Štvanice Island, a rather nondescript-looking piece of land, surrounded by the Vltava River. According to the stained brochure left on the writing table, the country had a long and rich tradition of the sporting life, and in times past had been the sight of numerous hunt chases. Skating and ice hockey were also very popular, as was tennis. I wondered whether Martina Navratilova had ever played tennis on Štvanice Island.

At nine sharp, Joanne and I left our room and walked to the lobby. We found Angela sitting by a window, dressed in tennis whites and her favorite cotton jacket with purple piping. Her back was turned away from us. So as not to startle her, I announced from afar, "Hey, Angela."

She turned and smiled. "Hey girls, so good to see you. What a relief! What time did you get in? How was your journey? Did you sleep well?" Her staccato voice expressed a nervousness all too familiar to me when Angela played in a tournament.

I hugged her tenderly. "We arrived around midnight. Quite an ordeal, but all is well, and the border director returned Joanne's camera and tripod."

"Thank God you're both here."

"How are you?" I asked.

"Yeah. A little nervous and relieved you're both here. Last night when I arrived at the hotel by taxi, the receptionist just stared at me when I entered, you know the usual looks I still get." She paused. "When I gave him my reservation confirmation, he shook his head, no. I stood firm and waited."

"Then what?" I asked.

"He shuffled some papers for the longest time, then pulled out a brown ledger and ran a slow finger down the page. Eventually he spotted my reservation. He grabbed the key for my room from the key rack and handed it to me."

"Thank God you're all right, Angela," Joanne said.

"Let's have some breakfast, girls," Angela announced. "I'm starving. I'll warn you; I've already had a cup of coffee. It's thick. *Really* thick."

~

Angela and I smiled nervously at the two uniformed security guards who opened the steel door to the tennis arena. We had arrived at eleven, plenty of time to warm up with one of the federation's hitting partners, before her scheduled match at one o'clock. Angela's hitting partner was tall, with a powerful forehand and a slice backhand that would prepare her well. The partner's serves varied from spin to slice to flat. The variation forced Angela to focus on his ball toss, signaling the type of serve to expect.

From the sideline, I watched Angela return his serves; I wanted to be sure she was keeping her eye on the ball and stepping in at the right moment—not necessarily for extra power, but for placement.

Angela looked ready. Before her first-round match, Angela reviewed the game plan she and I had strategized together on the train from Antwerp to the Czechoslovakian border: to be intentional with her shot-making and to vary her serve. She followed this plan and won all of her early-round matches. Next up, the semi-finals.

~

Joanne viewed the semis from the top row of the grandstands while I took my favorite spot—second row, at the very end. From there, I could get a better sense of the momentum and energy of Angela's hitting.

These days, my favorite stroke of Angela's was her serve, and it was flawless that afternoon. Everything about Angela's service motion was smooth, uncomplicated, and balanced. Her groundstrokes were deliberate and graceful. She won easily—6–2, 6–2—yet something was different about her. There was seriousness to Angela's demeanor that I couldn't quite grasp. I figured the border ordeal had unnerved her. She had endured bigotry over the years, but she always had a way to lift you up. Sure, she was testy at times on the court, but never at the expense of someone else.

The next day Angela won a close final—7–5, 7–5. Her younger opponent possessed a crafty, defensive-offensive game that had Angela constantly running wide and short, but Angela waited for the right moment to attack the net. She unfurled a gorgeous backhand that landed just over the net, unreachable for her opponent, and winning the point and the match. The stroke reminded me of Dad's backhand slice shots.

People stood up to applaud after that stroke of beauty. In fact, the spectators applauded both players throughout the match. I extended my arms and shouted, "You did it!" At the end of the match, Angela and her opponent ran up to the net to shake hands, with Angela extending her arm first and whispering something to her opponent, as was her custom.

Moments later, the two headed for the awards ceremony with the press circling near the podium to photograph them. Angela was beaming. After she and her opponent received their trophies from the tournament director, Angela waved to me to come forward.

"Here comes my coach, Lucie Sampson. She shaped me into the player I am today. I couldn't have done it without her."

A reporter scurried toward me. "Miss Sampson, what's it like coaching Miss Overby?"

"She's worked very hard and is very deserving," I said. "Like all professional athletes, Angela has had her ups and downs. As you know, this sport of tennis is all about resilience, skill, and heart. It's what defines you, and it defines who Angela is."

"Thank you all," Angela said. We left the podium area with Angela holding her head high.

"Great tournament." I hugged her and handed her a water bottle and her white jacket.

"Thanks! I wasn't sure I'd close out the match. Great feeling that I did it. My opponent was quick and had me worried."

"Had me worried too," I smiled. "Let's sit over by the canopy." We sat for a while after most of the spectators had gone. Journalists busied themselves snagging one more interview with tournament officials and ardent fans. Only Joanne was left in the top row, finishing her articles amid the commotion.

Angela became quiet, and that seriousness I noticed yesterday reappeared. "Lucie, I woke up this morning with a calm confidence. What I'm trying to say is this: I knew that, win or lose, this would be my last professional tournament."

"What!" I exclaimed.

"I'm exhausted and tired of the constant traveling. I want to return home and continue giving tennis lessons. Enjoy life a little bit more. I want to perfect my golf game, sing in the church choir, and find the love of my life."

Wow, I didn't see this coming. Where's my head been?

I cupped Angela's hand. "I noticed something different about you when you were warming up. Almost a sadness in your eyes. Sure this is what you want? Have I pushed you too hard? You still have many great years ahead of you."

"Sometimes you pushed me too far, but if you hadn't, I wouldn't have been as successful. I couldn't miss this important tournament because I'd already decided it would be my last one. Not playing in Czechoslovakia would have meant delaying my decision. That wouldn't do." She put on her jacket and took a long sip of water.

My back was stiffening. I stood for a moment.

"I wanted to tell you before, but this needed to be my decision entirely and at a time when I was absolutely certain."

"I respect that. Didn't you want to at least discuss it with me?" I sat down to take it all in.

"You'd probably try to talk me out of it."

"True." My lips parted in an ambivalent smile. "We've had a great run, and I love our friendship."

"Me, too. Please don't try and convince me to play another tournament. I'm done with the pro tour."

"You can't blame me if I tried, can you?"

"No. You can be very convincing. Let's go and celebrate."

"Hey, Jo, hurry up and finish!" I yelled. "We want to go celebrate."

"Give me fifteen or twenty minutes. Just reworking the last paragraph. Congratulations, Angela!"

Our cab driver spoke some English and recommended the restaurant, Café Slavia, on the banks of the Vltava, opposite the national theatre. We asked him to take the scenic route because most of the beautiful medieval castles, cathedrals, and city bridges had remained untouched by twentieth-century wars. He drove through narrow alleyways and across winding cobblestone streets until we reached a series of Romanesque, arched bridges over the Vltava River. Within fifteen minutes, we arrived at the Café Slavia.

The driver had a pale, thin and kind face. He warned us to be careful of the STB, the plainclothes secret police who might be watching.

Oh, just great.

Joanne thanked this gentle man, and the three of us entered some more unfamiliar surroundings.

The restaurant, distinguished by its strong art-deco feel with bold geometric designs, was filled with people sitting close together. A few huddled by one of the two windows, close to the back exit. Hushed voices could be heard throughout. The waiter led us to a table by the front window that gave way to a view of a medieval castle. From our vantage point, we could see the sunlight reflected on the nearby river, which brightened our spirits.

We ordered a bottle of champagne whose label bore a name we had never heard of. We tried again and again to order items from the menu, but each time the waiter would adjust his collar and utter, "Sorry, not available."

This became laughable after the third time, until a diner at the next table leaned over and whispered in German, "The state owns the restaurant and has eliminated most traditional recipes. Fresh produce is rarely available. Enjoy the goulash and cabbage." He looked down and went back to eating. Joanne thanked him in German, and ordered exactly what he'd suggested.

The champagne was almost undrinkable. We celebrated Angela's victories with beer and, an hour later, stuffed but happy, we got up from the stiff, bentwood chairs and returned to our hotel.

Joanne phoned her editor in Paris to obtain final dispatch instructions. They were simple. Joanne was to arrive at the French embassy at nine o'clock the following morning. The chief attaché would greet her at the main entrance. She would give him a manila envelope containing her articles, and he would hand over three airline tickets her editor had promised he would obtain from the ambassador (a close, personal friend). The chief attaché would then send Joanne's articles via telefacsimile to the *Paris Monde*.

Thunder rolled across the darkening sky as the cabbie drove us to the French embassy. The windshield wipers couldn't keep up with the driving rain, making it difficult for him to see where he was going.

"Luce, what time is it?"

"8:55."

"We've got five minutes," Joanne rushed her words.

Lightning flashed. The cabbie slammed on the brakes.

"Keep going!" I said.

We barely arrived at the embassy in time. Joanne stepped out of the cab, hunched over to protect the envelope and ran, head-down, up the steps. A fresh flash of lighting showed a shadowy figure at the top of the stairs holding an umbrella. Joanne handed her envelope over to him. The man opened his coat and pulled out something.

"Angela, I can't see through the slashing rain. What's going on?" I asked anxiously.

"Can't see either."

The car door swung open. Joanne slid to the back seat, soaking wet and handed me an envelope. "Here're the tickets," she said breathlessly.

"Are you okay?" I asked.

Angela handed Joanne a towel from her tennis bag.

"I will be," Joanne replied.

"To the Prague airport," I said to the cab driver.

By the time we boarded the plane to Paris an hour later, all was clear and calm, except our nerves. Joanne was still shaking; Angela was humming "There is a Balm in Gilead," and I was rubbing a knot coiled in my stomach. Despite the fact that Angela had played beautifully and won the tournament, I felt disquieted. Was it the precarious nature of our trip to Czechoslovakia? Joanne had warned me not to travel behind the Iron Curtain, but I'd dismissed her concerns. Was I too cavalier and pig-headed? Or did I feel this unease because of Angela's decision to retire? Actually, I was rather relieved that she was retiring from the pro tour. The travel was taking its toll on my body, and something else had been on my mind for quite some time—something I needed to pursue.

Chapter Forty-Four

Before returning to the United States, I drove from Paris to Cany-Barville and spent two days visiting Aunt Lucie. She was now in her mid-eighties, and I looked forward to visiting this gentle soul with a terrific sense of humor.

"Bonjour, ma petite. Bienvenue." Aunt Lucie kissed me on both cheeks when she opened the door.

I held her close. "It's good to be here. How are you feeling?" I asked. She looked a little thin.

"I have good days and bad days—mostly good. And how are your back and hip?"

"Good and bad days—mostly good." We both laughed.

"Where is Father Lucien?" I asked. "I enjoyed meeting him when Mom and I visited you in 1970."

"He was here yesterday. We had a nice visit, as always."

Aunt Lucie led me inside to her living room. Most everything was the same as before: finely sewn white lace curtains; comfy chairs; beamed ceilings; and brightly colored woven rugs. She had settled in the small bedroom on the first floor, adjacent to the kitchen. The room's bay window looked out to her beloved garden, which had diminished over the years. Fewer people attended to the flower beds of pansies and yellow roses. Much of the grass had been replaced with pebbles, making for easier upkeep, but the towering beech trees surrounding the house stood strong, as if protecting her.

"You know, I haven't been for a walk since the other day. Shall we?" she asked.

"Grand idea. But before we do, I have something for you. From the desert."

I helped her open the box and when she peeked inside, her eyes widened. She caressed the individual weaves of a Cahuilla basket. As a dressmaker she understood the loving effort that went into such a piece.

"It is *beautifully* made. I love it. Thank you, ma petite. Please, place it on the end table by the fireplace. Now, there's something I want to show you outside. Hand me my sweater hanging on the hook over there, please. My cane, too, by the door. Thank you."

Hanging next to the door was a sixteen-by-twelve-inch framed print. "Aunt Lucie, I've never seen this before. Is this painting new? I love the stars at night and how the light radiates on the water."

"That's Van Gogh's *Starry Night Over the Rhône*. It is my favorite. Most people know his famous *Starry Night*, but I like this one better. The signed print used to be in my second-floor bedroom, but I wanted it down here with me. I feel calm when I look at it. Can you see the two people strolling along the riverbank? Look closely."

I craned my neck. "Yes, I see them now."

"Art has a way of revealing something about ourselves," she said.

"After my riding accident, I had a stack of art and poetry books on my nightstand. Dad even had to build me a bigger stand. Throughout that year of rehabilitation, those books, along with the writings of Martin Luther King, offered me solace and inspiration."

"I'm so glad to hear that." She pointed to the front door. "Now let's go outside."

I took my great aunt's arm as she pushed herself up from the chair. *She's still such a sturdy soul.*

It was a cloudy, early July day, with no wind to contend with, as we headed down the lane. Every step made a crunch on the gravel beneath our feet. I chatted nonstop about how Joanne and I had rediscovered one another after twenty years, and I explained the ordeal Joanne, Angela, and I had recently withstood behind the Iron Curtain.

"Good God!" Aunt Lucie exclaimed. "How courageous of you all . . . and a little stupid, as well. It's a big force behind those barriers. So many obstacles we place on one another, and for what, ma petite? Power."

I began to slouch as we continued our walk. "Aunt Lucie, there's something else I want to tell you."

"Come. Let's sit over by the bench. What's on your mind?"

"At the border crossing into Czechoslovakia, I lost my temper with the guards. I knew there might be some danger, but I ignored it. They confiscated Joanne's camera equipment, thinking the tripod was a portable machine gun. I thought that was ridiculous, became angry, and mouthed off to them. Long story short, they rushed Joanne and me off the train and to the border director who interrogated us. We were eventually released and waited four hours for the next train to Prague. I was terrified; so was Joanne."

She put her hands on my shoulder and lifted my chin. "Do you think this would have happened if you hadn't lost your temper?"

"Probably not."

"Do you lose your temper often?"

"Sometimes. Mainly when I was younger. When my leg braces hurt and I couldn't sleep. Sometimes when playing tennis; I'd throw my racquet. Or when I think someone's been wronged. Like with Angela and Joanne. Guess I wanted to help them, protect them in some way."

"And did it help?"

"Well, I stood up for Joanne. But in the end, it just made matters worse."

"Ma petite. Your heart is in the right place. Sometimes you must use your head instead." She stood. "Let's continue our walk."

I nodded.

"See those two apple trees, one on either side of the gate?" she asked. "They are very special."

"Why?" I asked.

"Just last year, on the thirty-fifth anniversary of the Normandy invasion, a small group of German and French students from the Université de Sorbonne drove from Paris to the Cany-Barville's mayor's office. They wanted officially to express appreciation to me and my friends when we visited students during the Christmas holiday."

"Yes, I remember you telling Mom and me. You organized your lady friends, and you all brought homemade soups and desserts for the students. You did it for twenty-five years, no?"

"Yes. That's right."

She went on to explain that the student group arrived at her home to plant two apple trees in honor of the women. The mayor also brought a twelve-by-fifteen-inch cast bronze plaque in tribute to their generosity of spirit. He said the plaque would be placed in the town center next to the World War II stone memorial.

"It was a complete surprise, and very heart warming," she said. "The other ladies were not at my home at the time. But a few days later, I invited those who were still alive for tea. We ate Madeleine cookies, some local cheeses, and drank Calvados to celebrate our friendship and the students."

"What a beautiful story."

"I enjoyed being with them. We must always try to understand each other as individuals, to look for the light in each heart, especially now with so many suffering in Eastern Europe."

We walked the narrow and curvy lane back to her home. I slipped my arm into Aunt Lucie's to steady her. She leaned on her cane so much that she began to shuffle.

"After your mother's long stay with me, I realized I would need people to look after me. So, I have rented the second-floor bedroom to a middle-aged schoolteacher who also does the grocery shopping. An old friend's daughter, who is a nurse, comes by once a week to check on me and see my latest embroidery. The gardener comes twice a month. Father Lucien, my dearest friend, visits me every other day.

"I'm glad you have people looking after you." I patted her forearm.

"We all need to take good care of one another, wherever we are in life."

The next morning, Aunt Lucie and I attended Sunday Mass at Father Lucien's church. I was unfamiliar with the service, though that didn't matter. I was happy and humbled being with Aunt Lucie and in the presence of God.

Chapter 45

I booked a flight home with a window seat and stared out into the void, thinking of Joanne, Aunt Lucie, Mom and Dad. I thought lovingly of the days I'd go down to the basement in our Long Island house where Dad would show me how to use his favorite tool, the No. 4 hand plane. His workshop became my refuge when kids would call me 'It' or when my hip hurt too much.

Once, when I was about ten or eleven years old and feeling moody and cranky, I clomped down the basement stairs and asked my father what he was building. He took my hand and revealed a five-inch replica of his No. 4 hand plane—made from cherry wood, of course.

"It's for you," he said.

I ran my fingers across the plane, its edges smooth to the touch. Dad always said that the No. 4 hand plane had great balance and was the tool most often used to smooth out a piece of wood to prepare it for finishing.

"It's the prep work that determines the outcome," he said.

The No. 4 sits on my desk in Palm Springs, reminding me of the way he always smoothed things out for me and prepared me for the prep work in my own life.

〜

Before I headed back to my office the day after my return, I strolled through the gardens, pondering my next steps. Images of that little boy who'd lost part of his right arm riding a pony kept floating around in my head.

"Hi, Lucie. Welcome back," Omar, our head gardener, said.

"Thank you. Good to be back."

"Would you like to take a look at the new plantings?"

"Sure."

Omar pointed to a new tree. "This here is a Mexican Blue palm. The fan-shaped fronds will spread out nice."

"I love the bluish tint. Adds a nice dimension to the other green palms," I said.

Louisa came around the corner walking quickly.

"Lucie, there's a call for you. It's Dr. Sean Wilson from the children's orthopedic hospital. What should I tell him?"

"I'll take the call now. Excuse me, Omar."

I took the call from Louisa's phone. "Hi, Sean."

"Hi, Lucie. Two of my teenaged patients have made good progress from their injuries. They're eager to get back on the tennis court. Could you give them a tour of the tennis center?"

"Of course! I'll check with Jack, but I'm sure he'll approve. When were you thinking of coming over?"

"Would Saturday morning be convenient?"

"Yes. I'll be in touch."

Saturday mornings were always busy at the tennis center, even during hot July. This Saturday was no exception. It was a good sign. Lots of activity with kids and adults playing singles and doubles would hopefully encourage the two patients on their paths to full recovery.

Angela joined Jack and me in greeting Sean and his two patients: Alex, fourteen, and Clare, fifteen. Alex wore a shoulder sling and Clare used crutches since her left knee was wrapped in a heavily strapped brace. Each was recovering from surgery and highly motivated to play again. They had been playing tennis for two years.

"Hi, Alex and Clare, great to meet you both," Jack said. "This is Lucie Sampson, our Head Pro, and Angela Overby, who recently returned from a successful professional European tour. She's also a teaching pro at the center. They will give you a tour around the place."

"Watch your step and enjoy yourselves. I'll be in the club-house making some calls," Sean said.

Angela and I walked slowly around the facility with our guests. We stopped periodically at one of the four small patios situated throughout the grounds, giving the kids some rest and shade.

"In West Virginia, we played on red clay, not green," Clare said. "What's the difference?"

"Green clay is a bit harder and faster, but you still can slide like on red clay," I said.

"Cool, maybe I can play here soon."

"Once Dr. Wilson clears you, I'd been happy to hit with you."

Her eyes brightened. "Thanks, that would be great!"

"How about me?" Alex asked.

"Sure thing. Maybe we can even rope Angela into playing some doubles."

Angela laughed. "Anything to beat Lucie!"

As we returned to our starting point, Clare said, "Thanks for the tour."

"Anytime," I said. "Good luck with your rehab. You too, Alex."

He nodded and replied, "Thanks. Can't wait for that doubles match!"

"Ange, can you take them back to the front entrance? I want to talk to Sean before he leaves."

She winked. "Is that all?"

"Hah!"

I jogged to the clubhouse and saw Sean reading on the couch in the corner. "Hey, Sean."

His pensive look melted into a smile as soft as the morning light. "How'd it go with Clare and Alex?"

I took a long breath. "Just fine. They seem like good kids."

"They are. They could really use your help."

"I started out my career wanting to help others, but I don't know; maybe my ambition got in my way."

"Or maybe it just wasn't the right time."

"Maybe so. I'd be interested to know how best to help kids like Alex and Clare. Any suggestions?"

"Perhaps we could talk over a drink later? Say, six o'clock at the Hampton Grille? It's just a half a mile from the Center."

I felt a gentle breeze. "That would be lovely."

∼

The classical guitar permeating the bar cracked open my heart a little as I anticipated Sean's arrival. He came from behind and touched the small of my back. "Good evening. I see you ordered." He sat down and asked the barkeep for a beer on tap. "Nice place, isn't it?"

"Yes. Very airy with all the glass walls and potted palms."

He fiddled with his glass. "I come here sometimes when I've had a long day and listen to classical guitar."

My emotions rose to the surface as I listened to the urgent strumming relax into a hesitant, romantic plucking. I took a sip to collect myself. "I've heard of surgeons who play classical music in their operating rooms. Do you?" I smiled.

He looked at me. "I don't, but a friend of mine is a neuro-surgeon back in Chicago. He plays piano music while operating. They're usually very long surgeries."

"Are you from there?"

"No, I'm from Ohio. And you?"

"From Long Island, New York. We're both far away from home," I said with a smile.

"True, but this is my home now. I like it here. What brought you to the Coachella Valley?"

"To be a full-time teaching pro at the tennis center. May I ask you something?"

"Sure," he replied.

"I visited the Desert Equestrian Center a few months ago, before Angela and I left for the European tour. I noticed a little boy missing half of his right arm. He was riding a horse with his father handling the reins. Might you know him?"

"Yes. Sweet boy. Why do you ask?"

I heard a beep from his jacket.

"Sorry, it's my hospital pager." He took it out of his jacket pocket, looked down, and shook his head. "Damn, I've got to go." He looked up at me. "A patient of mine. We'll do this again, yes?"

I smiled. "I'd like that."

"Great. Enjoy your drink." He touched my forearm then paid the bartender.

"Good luck." I stopped fighting the music, melted into my chair, and let the strumming have its way with me.

〜

At the end of the week, Sean came by on his way home from the hospital and found me on Court Four where I gave all my private lessons. It was one of the end courts, which allowed for fewer distractions and more privacy.

"Thought I'd stop in to let you know that I've cleared Clare and Alex to hit some tennis balls," he said. "They're eager to do so. You made quite the impression on them during the tour."

"Nah. It was Angela's star power, no doubt."

"Player or coach, passion is passion, and kids always have a way of picking up on it. Are you in?"

"I'd love to. Have them call the front desk to schedule a time."

"Start slow. First week, two fifteen-minute lessons. Second week, two thirty-minute lessons. Week three, maybe a forty-five-minute lesson. We'll see how it goes."

"Very well. Thanks, Sean."

～

Four days later, Clare arrived on time, sporting a less cumbersome knee brace than the one she wore when I first met her. She kept fiddling with her ponytail and admitted to being nervous.

"I get that," I smiled. "After our bodies break down, it's hard to trust them again."

"Did your body ever break on you?"

"More times than you have fingers and toes to count on. We'll hit nice and easy. But first, let me see you swing the racquet. Like this." I demonstrated how to "carry the ball."

"Okay," I continued. "Do some swings, nice and easy. Will your knee bend enough to get into the ready position?" She winced, but settled into the bent-knee stance. She was a tough cookie.

From the half court, we hit back and forth for several minutes.

"I saw you grimace. Is everything okay?"

"A little scared, moving into the ball."

"I'll bet your knee's stronger than you think. It's easier if you step into the ball. Like this." I demonstrated, then I jogged over to her side of the court to correct her swing. "It's important to transfer your weight forward to complete the stroke. That's why you need to bend that knee a little to step into the ball and shift your weight from the back foot to the front foot."

"Bend knee. Step in. Hit through the ball. Is that right?"

"Exactly." I jogged back to my side of the court to resume hitting a few more forehands. "Let's hit some backhands now."

"Sure."

"Same routine as before: racquet back early, rotate shoulders and hip sideways, step into the ball, and 'carry the ball' across the net. Got it?"

"What does 'carry the ball' mean?"

"It's a phrase my coach used to say. It means keeping the ball on the racquet strings as long as possible instead of just swatting at the ball. You always want to control the ball when you're hitting it. Often, I repeat the phrase to myself during the follow-through. It really helps."

"'Carry the ball.' Got it," Clare said.

"That's it. Let's stop now. I don't want to push you too much. You're moving nicely."

We ambled back to the clubhouse, chit-chatting about school, physical therapy, and West Virginia. "Don't forget to ice your knee."

"I won't. Thanks."

～

At two-thirty, Alex arrived, happy to be on the court. He moved effortlessly, but had difficulty stroking through the ball. Not a surprise, given his shoulder surgery nine weeks ago. As a result, his backswing and follow-through were short and jerky. Like the session with Clare, we started at half-court with the forehand, then the backhand, and went through swing and footwork progressions—simple steps to build smoother movements. The "carry the ball" mantra really served its purpose for Alex. The last few minutes, we hit from the baseline; started slowly, then alternated between backhands and forehands. I noticed a funny hitch to his backswing that caused him to overhit.

"Let's call it a day, Alex. Your footwork is excellent. Your swing motion needs a smooth rhythm to it. That will come as your shoulder heals. Really enjoyed hitting with you."

He shook my hand. "Thanks a lot. Any chance we could hit again?"

"You bet. Call the front desk. Maybe next weekend. Take it easy with your shoulder."

"I'm going to practice every day, so I can play like I did last year," Alex said.

"Hang on there, Alex. You need to build in rest days to heal."

I just said the same thing Mom used to say, which I hated.

"Okay, I'll try."

~

Clare arrived ready to play two days later. She handed me a note from Alex, explaining that Dr. Wilson had told him to wait a while before returning to the courts.

Yep—rest.

"Please give him my best. Are you ready to hit some?"

"Can't wait to!"

After a smooth forehand and backhand exchange, Clare netted a wide shot to her forehand. She threw her racquet to the ground.

"Do you feel better throwing your racquet?" I asked. "Does it improve your game?" I was channeling what Coach Martin had asked me years ago.

"I don't know; guess not." She lowered her head. "I feel off balance. I get angry when I hit a lousy shot. That's all."

I walked closer to the net. "You're making progress, Clare. It's just on a different scale than what your healthy body was used to. Be patient. Let's try it again. Remember to get your racquet back early, step into the ball, and carry it through."

We hit back and forth for several more minutes. Then I hustled to the net thinking I would break Clare's rhythm. Instead, she passed me with a terrific down-the-line backhand.

"Wow!" I beamed. "Great shot! Let's take a break. Come

sit on the bench."

She sat beside me and wiped her brow.

I looked at her and said, "One thing I've learned, especially on days when you're frustrated, is to always end on a high note." I poured her some water from the thermos that each canopy patio provided for coaches and players. "Where you from in West Virginia?"

"Beckley. We lived there until I was eight. My father got transferred here seven years ago."

I wiped my brow. "Ever heard of a town called White Sulphur Springs?"

"Sure, it's pretty up there. Our family went to the Greenbrier Hotel there to celebrate my father's new job in California. Why do you ask?"

"My doubles partner invited me to visit her relative's place there. They owned horses and we rode along the trails. On the second day, a deer spooked my horse. I was thrown off and broke my back."

"I thought people died when they broke their backs." She shot me a quick look. "Sorry." She took a long sip of water.

"I guess my healing was a bit of a miracle, but it didn't happen because a fairy waved her wand. It took lots and lots of rehab, hard work, and persistence. And pain, to be honest. But now, here I am doing what I love."

"What can heal a broken back?"

"Like you, I was in the hospital for a while. Then I had to relearn things like posture, gait, and balance—and that was just to move through life, not play top-level tennis. That took even more work, which was hard because I didn't have much patience back then."

"You were like me?"

"More than you know. So next time you come, be prepared to show me how much patience and sportsmanship you have.

Got it?"

"Got it, coach."

As she left, with her head held high, my heart pounded with joy at the work I did. I was very lucky.

Chapter 46

After my morning private lessons were over, I caught up with Jack. He was sitting under one of the canopies, looking rather relaxed, and sipping some lemonade.

Ooh, carpe diem, Lucie. Just ask him.

"Got a minute, Jack?" I asked as I approached him.

He looked down at his watch. "Ten minutes until my next lesson. Have a seat, Lucie."

I did so. "Since Angela has retired from the pro tour, my schedule is a little more open and flexible."

"Yes, that's true. Disappointing about her retirement, but certainly her choice to make. Now, what's on your mind?"

"I've been thinking about organizing a fundraising event to benefit the new children's orthopedic clinic. Possibly in October or November. That would give us four months or so to prepare."

"What do you envision?"

"A mixed doubles, round-robin format. I know eight excellent tennis players who'd be interested in playing for a great cause. I mentioned it to Angela and she's in. We'd need sponsors, naturally, and publicity to promote the event."

He adjusted his ball cap, then nodded. "I like the idea. It would also showcase the tennis center and create goodwill in the community. Formulate a plan and have it to me by next week."

"Will do. Thanks, Jack." I couldn't wait to get started.

~

Clare and I had another lesson the next day, lasting a little longer than Dr. Wilson had recommended. Her strokes were crisp and decisive, and her footwork smooth. "Let's call it a day, Clare. We don't want to overdo it."

I poured her some water. "Drink up. You're hitting the ball well. I can see your joy as you swing."

"I feel pretty good."

"How about next lesson we tackle your volley?"

"Okay. Thanks, Lucie." She gathered her things and turned to leave. "Oh, hi Dr. Wilson. I didn't know you were here," she giggled.

"I was watching from the other end," he said. "Didn't want to distract you. How's your knee feel?"

"Pretty good. Lucie said I played well today. I'm not chasing down every shot. I'm taking it easy."

"Good girl, Clare. All good things come in time. Be patient," he patted her on the shoulder.

"Bye, doc."

"Patience. Always a tough thing for an athlete," I said.

"Well, you understand your students. You've got a gift, Lucie."

"That's quite a compliment. Thank you."

"I've been thinking. Would you like to help that little boy you saw on horseback? His name is Christopher."

"I would love to," I beamed. "When?"

"Not sure yet. In a few months. In the meantime, maybe I should take another lesson from you."

"My fees are double if I take you on." We both laughed. "I'm glad you stopped by because I was going to call you. I have a proposal."

"Do you now?" His smile was slow and easy.

"I do." My heart quickened.

"Do tell."

"I'd like to plan a fundraising event to benefit the children's orthopedic clinic and hold it at the tennis center. It would be a mixed doubles round-robin with top players, including Angela. All the ticket proceeds and donations would go directly to the clinic."

"I like that idea. When were you thinking of having it?"

"In October or November."

"Have you spoken to Jack about this?"

"Yes. He's on board. I'm working on a plan for him as we speak."

"Good. I know some people who'd be very interested. I've got to get back to the hospital now. Interviewing candidates for assistant director of the clinic. Thanks, Lucie. We'll talk soon."

I beamed again as he left the court.

～

Throughout the next three months, Jack, Louisa and I worked on the details of the charity event, First Serve, to be held the first Sunday in November. Along with the other teaching pros, Jack and I continued to give group and private tennis lessons. Periodically, Angela and I would play doubles or mixed doubles with guests from the LA area.

In early October, Mom came for a long visit. She jumped at the idea of spending time at the tennis center.

"I thought you'd like to see our garden," I told her. We strolled along as I pointed out the different agave succulents. "Those to the right are smooth to the touch, no sharp edges. We don't want kids pricking their fingers! Over there in the middle, we have lots of the Golden Barrel cactus."

She shielded her eyes from the sun and walked closer to get a good look. "I like how the landscaper grouped them together," Mom said. She always had a gardener's eye.

I suggested she observe one of my tennis lessons. While she hadn't played tennis since Dad died, Mom still enjoyed watching the sport. She sat far enough away under the pergola so Clare wouldn't notice someone else watching her.

Clare arrived wearing a simpler knee brace, which gave her a noticeable spring to her step. It had been two weeks since our last lesson.

"Hi, Lucie. Glad to be back."

"Great! Thought we'd try for forty-five minutes. Dr. Wilson okayed it. Think your knee can handle a longer session?"

"Yeah, my knee feels really good today."

"All right, then. We'll start from the baseline. Get in your ready position."

Clare's movement had improved to the point where she could manage low balls that required her to really bend her knees. We hit nonstop for ten minutes—and with no thrown racquets.

"Lookin' good, Clare, nice rhythm and balance," I hollered to her. "Now, when I hit you a short ball, follow it up to the net and stay there for some volleys."

"Got it."

I hit her some soft line drives to boost her confidence hitting the volley. Timing was different when hitting from the net as opposed to the baseline. At the net, balls fired back at you—anticipation is key. At one point, she missed an easy backhand volley and chucked her racquet into the net.

Boy, do I remember that feeling!

"Pick it up. I'll clear you for one thrown racquet today. Next one, you're out. Let's take a quick water break."

Clare stomped her foot and made her way to the bench. We sat just long enough for me to tell her what she needed to hear. "Clare, if you want to improve your game, remember three words: balance, anticipation and patience."

She nodded, took a sip of water, and jogged to the baseline to practice her serve.

"You have a beautiful arch to your back when you hit the serve," I said. "It reminds me of photographs of a great player. She was a Californian and won Wimbledon. Her name was Alice Marble."

"Who?"

"She's an interesting person who had some health problems. She'd always say, 'Never give up.' I bet the public library has info on Alice Marble. Check her out sometime."

"Okay."

"Now, back to your serve. I'd like you to hit the ball earlier by stretching up at the height of the ball. If you wait until the ball is already coming down, it ends up in the net. Takes practice. Try it a few times before we finish our session."

She gave it a try. "It feels weird."

"That's okay," I said, reassuring her. "Remember to reach up to hit the ball and hit it sooner." A few minutes later, I called, "Okay kiddo, we're done for today."

Before she left, I reached into my pocket. "Clare, I'd like to give you two tickets to the charity event as my guest. It's to raise money for the new children's orthopedic clinic."

Her eyes brightened. "Thanks. I'll be there for sure! What's that famous tennis player's last name again?"

"Marble. You know, like the marbles you played with as a kid." I smiled.

She laughed. "Got it; Alice Marble." She toweled off and left the court.

I met Mom at the far end of the court. She looked comfortable in her plaid Bermuda shorts and sleeveless pink blouse. She rose from her chair. "You certainly know how to push your student and encourage her at the same time. That's a gift!"

That stopped me in my tracks. "Thanks! It's always a challenge to find the right balance with students. Each one is different."

"So true."

"I've got some paperwork to take care of before we leave. Meet you in the reception area in, say, twenty minutes?"

～

I walked to my second-floor office, perused the binder I had created for the event, and made a few notations about ball and t-shirt inventory, then returned two phone calls. Before leaving, I gazed out the window at the sun resting on the foothills, stretching its last orange rays before evening beckoned the stars. It was peaceful here. It made a person quiet inside.

～

Mom and I enjoyed cocktails on the back patio of my apartment. The day had gone well despite the long hours I'd been putting in lately. First Serve needed to be a success. Any failure was on my shoulders—no pressure.

"You seem a little tense, dear. Everything all right?"

"I am a little stressed. I really want the charity event to go well, hopefully without a hitch."

"It will. I skimmed through the binder you made for the event when you brought it home one evening. You're organized and have lots of details you've delegated. Seems like you have a good staff to help."

"The staff is great. So is Jack, but I feel he's a bit anxious, too."

"It's his facility. Owners always have to worry about the bottom line. In the end, it's always about business."

"You make it sound so cut and dry. Jack loves tennis and the center's impact on the community."

"I'm sure he does. But bills must be paid. Your father knew that better than anyone. Those tennis lessons of yours and the tournament traveling costs were expensive. Bills mount up. It's why your father and I rarely took vacations."

"I see." I could barely swallow. I poured myself another Cape Codder and refilled Mom's glass of port. "These port glasses are tiny."

"That way I won't drink as much," she replied. "Is that your second or third Cape Codder?"

"Mom, whenever I drink a Cape Codder, I just get half a shot of vodka because I mostly like the taste of cranberry juice. When I drink slowly, I'm fine."

Mom ignored my response, but somehow, it seemed to register with her.

"It's getting windy. Let's go inside," I said as I got up from the lounge chair, tightened the straps on the furniture cushions, and closed the patio umbrella before heading inside. Mom grabbed our drinks.

The wind swept through the San Gorgonio Mountain pass and picked up speed. "Mom, look at the next-door neighbor's palm tree fronds. They're dancin' in the wind."

Chapter 47

The charity event was taking shape beautifully. The Chamber of Commerce of the Coachella Valley honored the tennis center by being its prime sponsor. Other sponsorships included KNCB News; Angela's tennis sponsor, Keep Playing, the sports equipment company; the Jasmine Hotel, where the guest players and Coach Martin were staying; and the *Desert Chronicle*, which agreed to cover the event. Angela volunteered to host Donna, who was thrilled to participate in the event. Jack also arranged for eight students from Palm Meadows High School to serve as ball boys.

First Serve would kick-off in ten days. I walked in the front door from a long day at work and announced, "Hey, Mom; I'm home!"

She met me in the hallway leading to the kitchen. "Here's a letter for you. From Paris. Special Delivery."

"Thanks. It's Joanne's handwriting. I'll read it in the living room."

I took off my jacket, plopped down on the couch, and ripped open the envelope, careful not to tear the letter inside.

"Dear Lucie," she wrote, "I have found my father."

"Good Lord, she's found him," I mumbled.

I now know what happened. At the *Paris Monde*, I have access to many databases, which quickened the process.

The *New York Times* photo and your Dad's note started my search to find him. I asked my editor for a one-month leave of absence, which he granted under the condition that I produce a feature story when I returned. Here are some of the details.

"Are you alright?" Mom's concerned voice interrupted my reading.

I held up an index finger, eager to finish. "Yes."

"Okay, dear." Her voice sounded less anxious.

First, I contacted the *New York Times* via email to confirm the photo of September 3, 1933. Even though not everyone is communicating by email, between news organizations, it's fairly common—which made my search a lot easier. I began my research with aviation because, when we were living in California, Dad took a job as an airplane mechanic at a small airport. On the weekends, he often took me to the airport to watch take-offs and landings; it was thrilling for me.

Since I knew he was in the Army Air Force during World War II, I contacted the National Personnel Records Center of the National Archives in St. Louis, Missouri, to confirm his military service record. I gave the staff member Dad's name, social security number, date of birth, etc. He responded by saying that 75 percent of the Army's records were lost due to the tragic fire on July 12, 1973.

Well, Lucie, my heart stopped. But he asked when Dad was discharged. I said 1944. He then explained the fire ruined the records of personnel discharged from September 25, 1947, to January 1, 1964. What a relief! Within two weeks, he sent me a letter confirming Dad's

service record along with a photo of him in his First
Lieutenant uniform: full jacket, shirt, necktie and silver
bar on each shoulder.

"Mom, she's found her father!" I yelled. "I don't know where
he is. Haven't got that far."

"That's remarkable!"

"Isn't it? Have a seat. I'll read the rest of the letter out loud,"
I motioned her to sit next to me on the couch.

I scoured aviation magazines from the 1970s to the present, but found no plausible leads. I was moved by the
tragic 1973 St. Louis fire the staffer told me about. So I
looked for articles relating to the fire.

One article's title caught my attention: "Restoration:
The July 12th Fire: Five Years Later." Several photographs accompanied the article. There was a close-up
photo of two men, one identified as a staff member at
the NPRC and the other man as a volunteer. I examined
the photo closely. The volunteer had a scar above his left
eye and a mustache just like I remember my Dad having.
He looked so much like Dad that I had to dig further.
I hired a private investigator. Our newspaper's investi-
gative department put me in touch with a reliable professional in the U.S. Luce, it turns out that Dad lives in
St. Louis, Missouri!

I stopped reading. My left leg started twitching, as it often
did when I was nervous. "Can you believe this news? She's
found him in St. Louis," my voice faltered as I turned to Mom.

"Oh, Lucie." She scooted closer, took my hand and gently
placed it on her lap.

I continued reading.

I have spoken to him on the phone. It's a beginning.

    Luce, I'll always be grateful to you for encouraging me to find him. Thank you also for the invitation to the charity event. Unfortunately, I can't get away from work since I've already taken a month's leave of absence to do this research.

Your friend always,

Jo

My tears fell on the letter, droplets of joy and sorrow. All I could think of was Dad, and to think that it was thanks to him that Joanne was able to find her father.

                         ~

The next day, I left work at four-thirty so Mom and I could go shopping at the opening of a new grocery store in La Quinta, about fifteen miles from Palm Springs. It was billed as the first organic store in the Coachella Valley, and to celebrate, live music and complimentary samples of its produce promised to make it a festive occasion.

    "Mom, I'm home. Ready to go shopping? Where are you?"

    "In the kitchen," Mom's voice faltered.

    I hurried down the central hallway to the kitchen and stopped in the doorway, shaking with nerves. Mom sat in the kitchen; her shoulders slouched.

Mother never slouches.

    Quietly, I approached and touched her shoulder. She met my hand, but said nothing.

    My left leg twitched. "Mom, what's going on?"

    "Father Lucien called." That was all she said.

    Silence kept quiet about what Mom was unable to say.

"Mom, please say something."

"Aunt Lucie had a stroke. She's gone."

I dropped to my knees and grabbed Mom's trembling shoulders, my own stomach tightening. I rose to sit next to Mom and held her.

"This is too much," Mom said. "Your father, and now Aunt Lucie."

Tears ran down my face as Mom spoke those unbearable words. A few minutes later, I asked, "What should we do?"

"Return to France."

"I'll call the travel agent. When do you want to leave?"

Mom remained stoic, her body still. "Day after tomorrow."

"I'll let Jack know. He'll re-arrange my teaching schedule. Would you like some port or some tea?" I asked.

"Tea, please."

I returned with the tea tray and placed it on the table. Mom's head was bowed, and tears fell onto her clasped hands. I left her sitting alone while I called my boss from the living room.

"I'm terribly sorry to hear about your aunt's passing, but First Serve is in six days. I need you here this week," he said.

"But Jack, they were extremely close to one another. I need to be with my mother. I've created a detailed notebook for the event. Contact names, phone numbers, safety protocols, equipment inventory, publicity. It's all there. I can go over the notebook with you and the staff tomorrow."

"You've taken too much time off as it is. It sets a bad example."

"Yes, when my father died. You're faulting me for that?" I could barely breathe. I felt heat in my throat.

"No, of course not. You took time off when Donna's horse was injured."

"But I made up the time, except for one lesson."

"It disrupts things around here. When my uncle died, I didn't fly across the country to Montreal to attend his funeral."

I had no idea how to respond to that statement. Jack had a good heart. Did he not trust me?

My voice cracked. "But this is my family, Jack."

A long silence ensued. "All right then, but be back two days before the event," Jack directed me. "I'll need to dock your pay. Others have to cover for you, again. Meet me in my office tomorrow at eight sharp to review your notebook. Give my condolences to your mother."

Chapter 48

Mom and I dragged ourselves out of the Paris airport after a fifteen-hour flight. I dreaded the two-hour drive to Cany-Barville because my back was sending me signals it was not happy. I needed to remain alert, as the winding two-lane road to Aunt Lucie's village was difficult to navigate.

Full-canopied trees spread for miles before we entered the driveway of the town's only inn. The scenery looked different from the last time I was here. It didn't matter how beautiful the area was in Normandy; Aunt Lucie was gone.

We checked in at the inn, changed our clothes, and ate a quick meal. Then we drove two miles to Father Lucien's parish church outside the village center.

The Romanesque arches of the small stone church curved over Father Lucien as we walked slowly toward him. His black cassock and white collar contrasted with the cluster of yellow pansies he wore on his lapel—Aunt Lucie's favorite flower.

He extended his arm and hugged Mom. "My condolences."

"Thank you, Father. You remember my daughter, Lucie."

"Yes, of course. Your aunt spoke of you often. My sympathies to you." He shook my hand and the kindness in his eyes made me tear up.

"Thank you. Aunt Lucie often mentioned how much she enjoyed your visits."

He nodded. "So did I. Let us step inside. The church is empty now." He led us to one of the back pews and bowed his head. "If you wouldn't mind a prayer?"

"Yes, of course," Mom whispered.

He closed his eyes. "Give us grace to carry forth and the light breath of your peace. Amen."

We remained quiet for several minutes before Father Lucien spoke. "You must be very tired from the trip. May I suggest we drive to her home tomorrow? As executor of her estate, I will read the will there."

"Yes, Father," Mom said. "It's been an exhausting day. Thank you for your care of Aunt Lucie. Good night."

~

After breakfast the following morning, we picked up Father Lucien at the parish house. I took the narrow lanes, bordered by hedgerows, that twisted and turned through the countryside. Fifteen-foot-high hedgerows in a tangle of trees, shrubs, and prickly brambles made for cautious driving. I never knew what I'd meet around the corner.

After we reached Aunt Lucie's home, Father Lucien opened the front door, and we stepped into the dark house. With the curtains closed, it felt like someone else's home, not Aunt Lucie's. The light was gone, but never her spirit.

Grief slipped out of Mom; she wept, and I stood there frozen for a moment, not knowing what to say. I took my mother's arm and helped her to sit in the nearby chair.

"Lucie, please, a glass of water for your mother," Father Lucien said.

"Yes, of course." I paused at the signed print Aunt Lucie loved so much, *A Starry Night on the Rhône*. I remembered admiring it when I last visited her. It was as if Aunt Lucie were there to comfort Mom and me. I could almost hear her say,

"Light will drive out the darkness in our souls."

I returned from the kitchen and knelt to give Mom the glass of water. "Take some sips. Here's a glass for you, Father." I stood, but my left knee buckled. I dropped the glass on the rug. The priest extended his arm to break my fall.

"Thank you, Father. I'm off-balance today." I retrieved a couple of kitchen towels and mopped up the spilled water.

Mom was quiet. Father Lucien brought up a chair for me. I lowered my head to the shoulder sleeve of his cassock. He waited a few minutes then suggested, "Shall I read the will?"

"Yes," Mom said.

To Isabelle Leredu Sampson, I leave the house, which is to be sold. The proceeds will be divided in the following manner: 70 percent to Isabelle, 15 percent to Father Lucien, and 15 percent to his parish, Paroisse de Cany. Isabelle will distribute the house furnishings as she sees fit, except for the print, *A Starry Night on the Rhône* by Vincent Van Gogh. It is bequeathed to Lucie Suzanne Sampson.

I nearly dropped my glass again. I righted myself and gripped it. The lump in my throat stopped my breath. Tears welled my eyes.

Mom rose and grabbed my hand. "Let's sit on the couch over by the window." We walked across the room and sat down.

Father Lucien nodded to Mother. "It's a beautiful sunny day. I'll go sit out in the garden for a while."

I snuck my hand through the crook in Mom's arm, and sat quietly for a long time, until Mom broke the silence.

"After my parents divorced," she began, "I lived with my father until he died. And from the age of eleven, lived with my father's parents. I spent all my summers with Aunt Lucie in France. She was like a mother to me. I will always miss her."

I rubbed Mom's arm. "I never knew you spent all those summers with her. No wonder you adored her."

We stood up and walked hand in hand out to the garden, where Father Lucien was relaxing in the sunshine.

"Father, we're going to drive to Aunt Lucie's favorite city, Rouen," I said. "It's less than an hour away. Would you like to join us?"

"Thank you, but I need to pay a visit to a parishioner who's a bit under the weather."

"Okay. When is the funeral?"

"Eleven o'clock tomorrow morning. See you at 10:45."

Within an hour we arrived in Rouen, situated on the river Seine and the capitol seat of the Normandy region. The river meandered snakelike through the medieval city and offered us an opportunity to walk along the cobbled banks.

"Did you and Aunt Lucie spend time strolling the riverbanks?" I asked.

"Oh, yes. We'd window shop or picnic, and occasionally we'd stop to admire the timbered buildings still slumped and crooked from centuries of settling," she said wistfully.

"I've never seen this type of building. Dad would love the wood construction and carvings. I do remember studying the Impressionist painters, Monet and Pissarro, in college." Monet's famous paintings captured the Rouen cathedral and its changeable moods. My voice faded. "Things come full circle, don't they Mom?"

She did not answer, but pointed across the river. "The cathedral is over there, in front of the hillside. See the tall spire?"

"Will we visit it?"

"Sorry, there's no time. Instead, I'd like to take you to L'Auberge de la Couronne, where Aunt Lucie took me for my sixteenth birthday. The restaurant was built in 1325 as an inn. It welcomed merchants and dignitaries near and far.

"That old?" I was amazed.

"Yes. Incredible, isn't it? The restaurant published a cookbook, which she gave me. Aunt Lucie taught me how to cook French cuisine. She always made me feel special."

I choked up. "I know what you mean. She always gave comfort."

"We'll have an early dinner and then head back. I don't like you driving in the dark for very long."

"Yes, Mother," I chuckled.

The waiter ushered us to a cozy table near a lead-paned window. The afternoon light filtered through, lending a golden glow to the room. Mom was in her element, speaking effortlessly in French with the waiter. I brimmed with pride listening to her speak with no affectation, just a lovely rhythmic accent to her voice. The waiter recommended the specialty of the house, Duck à l'Orange or the Dover Sole.

"Lucie, which would you prefer?"

"I'll be adventurous and try the duck. I'd also like a vodka cocktail."

Mom looked back at the waiter. "Monsieur, I'll have the Sole and begin with a Dubonnet. Merci."

The waiter suggested a Pinot Gris to accompany our main course. He brought a half-carafe of wine and delicately poured two glasses. I wanted so much to comfort my mother, but I felt ill-equipped to do so. Mom remained mostly quiet through the evening's meal, except when I asked the waiter for another half-carafe of wine.

Mom threw me a sharp look. "More wine?"

I raised my voice. "Because I want to."

"Or you need to?"

My shoulders stiffened. "Okay. I'll order just another glass. I feel like I'm a kid when you speak to me like that."

"Because you're acting like one. I'll drive."

"No, I'm fine," I said.

It was a half-hour before we left the restaurant and headed back to Cany-Barville. My mind drifted on the drive home, the delicious meal and drinks made me a bit sleepy. The final curve and hedgerows leading to the village square came up faster than I had remembered. I slammed on the brakes, side-swiped the hedge, and came to an abrupt stop. My head jerked forward and hit the steering wheel.

"Oh, God." I grabbed my head, my heartbeat racing at an alarming rate. "You all right, Mom?"

"Yes, I think so. And you?"

"Yes." I touched my forehead. A bump, that's all. "Sure you're all right?" I looked over at her.

Mom's jaw tightened. "My shoulder hit against the door at impact. I'll be okay."

"You're sure you're okay?"

"Yes."

"I'm sorry."

"Be grateful we're not hurt more. Can you drive rest of the way?"

"Yes, the inn's only a mile up the road from the church."

The night was chilly. When we entered the inn's foyer, the stone fireplace blazed, a warmth that didn't reach my heart. We walked to our room in cold silence.

"Father Lucien wants us at the church by ten forty-five for the service. And Lucie . . . "

I interrupted. "I know what you're going to say." I turned and stared at Mom.

"Do you?" she asked quietly. "What then?"

"That I could have seriously hurt us."

"I was going to say, 'I love you.' And yes, you're right. You could have."

Chapter 49

The bump on my forehead gave me an unrelenting headache, and Mom's face told me everything about the discomfort in her shoulder. We entered the church at 10:45 as Father Lucien had requested. The thirty-minute funeral service was in French, though Father Lucien spoke slowly enough so that I could understand most of it, especially when he said, "the darkest nights still find the day." It was a hopeful belief and a much needed one for me and my mother.

We all gathered one last time in the anteroom to enjoy the tea, coffee, and port. Father Lucien had thoughtfully laid out a table adorned with colorful pansies and yellow roses. Despite her grief, Mother greeted each guest: Aunt Lucie's gardener, the schoolteacher, the mayor, an old friend from up the road, and an appreciative customer of Aunt Lucie's who lived in Rouen. Mom took time to ask each of them questions about their individual lives.

My mouth was parched, so I slipped away to Father Lucien's table and poured two glasses of water from the pitcher. From across the room, I noticed Mom's lips would quiver, and moments later her eyes would brighten listening to their stories. She looked oddly serene, yet I wondered what she was feeling deep down.

I returned and handed her a glass. "Here, Mom, thought you might be thirsty."

"Thank you dear. I'd like you to meet Madame Ducasse, one of Aunt Lucie's clients from Rouen."

"Very nice to meet you, Madame. Rouen was Aunt Lucie's favorite city."

"Enchanté, Mademoiselle. Your aunt was a superb dress-maker with beautiful needle work and an exquisite eye for design. Years ago, she made this suit for me. It's still my favorite." Madame stepped back with a full sweep of her arm to show off the streamlined grey tweed suit.

"I love the burgundy trim," I said.

"Thank you. It was part of her signature style, along with three-quarter length sleeves. A lovely person, your aunt. You should be proud of her."

"I am. I appreciate you coming from such a distance to honor her."

Father Lucien thanked everyone for paying their respects, then led us in prayer and showed the guests out through the main sanctuary. Mom and I stayed behind for a moment to gather our thoughts. We still had a two-and-a-half-hour drive to the airport and also needed to reconcile with the rental agency for the damage to the car. Our flight home was at five-thirty, which left us four hours to complete everything.

The tall oak trees stood in noble salute as we drove away from the town of Cany-Barville. I winced at the thought of never returning and wondered what Mom was feeling; after all, Normandy was her second home.

"Mom, do you think we'll ever return to Normandy?"

She wiped away a tear. "Probably not."

After we drove along route D-131 for an hour in silence, I ventured to speak. "Want some music? Maybe there's a classical channel on the radio."

"No, too distracting. Just keep your eyes on the road, dear." She looked straight ahead and sighed.

The weary tarmac of the county road slowed us down; I picked up the speed. Time was too precious now. The faster I pushed the rental, the more Mom twitched in her seat.

"You alright? You keep squirming. My driving too fast for you?"

"That's not the problem. The shoulder strap on the seat belt digs into my shoulder. It's too tight."

"I'll turn off at the exit right before we take the main highway. Ten minutes, max."

"Very well."

Ten minutes had passed, and there was still no exit. My heart slammed against my rib cage.

"There's the exit, Lucie," she yelled and pointed to the right.

I braked hard and took the exit. "Sorry. The high hedgerow blocked my view. Are you okay?"

"Yes. Oh, look. Up the road are some shops. We can stop there."

I slowed down and found a parking place to adjust Mom's seatbelt. After I made several attempts at sliding the strap up and down to fit comfortably, I put my sweater behind her neck for extra support.

"Okay, Mom. Comfy?"

Finally, she looked at me and smiled. "Yes. Thank you."

~

A few miles farther, we entered the highway with cars whizzing by at ridiculous speeds. I was clocking eighty miles per hour and making good time. I could not miss the flight back home. Although the silence between us was unsettling, I needed to stay focused on the road as idiot drivers were weaving in and out of lanes. The slow lane suited me just fine.

Finally, we arrived at the crowded Charles de Gaulle airport at three o'clock. I hoped we had enough time to drop off the car, fill out paperwork, and pay for the damages. I parked in the return lane and helped Mom out of the car to the agency's tan, lifeless building. I pointed to a group of chairs near the window. "Mom, have a seat over there while I take care of this."

"Very well." We exchanged much needed smiles.

I was hoping we wouldn't run into France's notorious administrative red tape, but the nine-deep line gave a hint of what was in store. My back stiffened as the minutes dragged on. I looked down at my watch. Holy crap. It's gonna be tight.

"Next," the clerk hollered.

I hurried to the counter and briefly explained what happened.

"You should be more careful . . . you . . . Americans." He shook his head. "Start filling out these forms. I must inspect the car. Wait here, mademoiselle."

I was finishing the paperwork when he returned fifteen minutes later smelling of cigarettes. "There is many damages, mademoiselle." He squared his shoulders, fully in command. "Let me do the calculations. It will take a few minutes."

"Sir, we have a plane to catch."

"I'm going as fast as I can. My supervisor must approve your application. She is on break. She will be back in fifteen to twenty minutes. You should have come sooner, mademoiselle."

"We couldn't. We attended a funeral," I snapped.

He looked up and said nothing. The red tape bothered me more than my wretched headache. "I'll wait over there with my mother."

"We'll never make it, dear." Those were the worst possible words to hear. But she was right. It was closing in on four o'clock.

We still had to finish here, get to the airline terminal, and wade through the security line.

I sat down next to her. "I'm afraid so. I promised Jack I'd be back two days before the event. That's the only reason he gave me permission to miss work."

Chapter 50

We arrived in Palm Springs the day before First Serve. I couldn't help retracing the path that led us to the bureaucratic and expensive mess—my own stupidity and negligence. I dreaded entering Jack's office. My stomach tightened with guilt.

"You're a day late. You were supposed to be here yesterday to give us two days to get ready for First Serve. What happened?"

"I'm sorry, Jack. We missed our flight."

"Obviously." He pursed his lips. He remained standing behind his desk.

"I tried to call the tennis center twice before we left Paris, but I got a busy signal both times. We had a minor car accident, which delayed us."

"Oh, I see. Any injuries? How's your mother?"

"She's okay. A bruised shoulder."

"I'm sorry to hear that. Luke and Michael substituted for you again. It was Michael's day off. I think you need to smooth things over with him."

"I'll check in with everyone, including Michael." I swallowed hard. "Anything else, Jack?"

"Look. I need to be able to rely on my Head Pro at all times. You need to get back to work."

I nodded and closed the door just as Angela came up behind me and gave me a hug.

"Thought you were coming back yesterday."

"Do you have time to come to my office?" I stammered.

"Yes. Are you okay?"

"Let's take the shortcut up the stairs."

We ascended in silence and entered my sun-lit office.

"Have a seat on the couch," I said, unable to make eye contact.

"How's your mother?" Angela asked.

I kept fiddling with my watch. "Not sure."

"Why? What's going on?"

"Something I need to tell you." I half-turned toward Angela. "We had a little car accident. I . . . I had been drinking." I wrung my hands.

Angela stared into my eyes. "Tell me you weren't drunk."

"God, no. I'm not that stupid. Just some wine that made me drowsy."

"Was your mother hurt?"

"Yes."

"And . . . how is she?"

"A bruised shoulder. Mom and I were having dinner at a restaurant in the city of Rouen; I was full of emotion, and had . . . I had more than my share."

"Okay, then what?"

"I was about a mile from the town square, driving too fast, and I hit some hedgerows. Damaged the passenger side and two tires. Mom's shoulder is a little stiff. I bumped my forehead."

"You're sure your mother's okay?

"Yes."

"Are you okay?"

My left leg twitched. "Yes. I know I made a stupid, terrible mistake."

"People make stupid, careless decisions. I know I have. So, what are you going to do now?" I wasn't used to Angela's unsmiling tone.

"I need to make this right with my mother and myself."

"Girl, you do." She got up to leave, but not before she nodded a smile.

∾

I had put in a long day at the center, including a talk with Michael to clear the air between us and to pay for eight tennis lessons he and Luke gave in my absence. The car accident was ever present in my mind, tightening my chest.

Mom was in the back yard when I arrived home. The sky darkened while I watched her from the kitchen window, carefully trimming the branches of the Palo Alto tree. A silence echoed through the kitchen. Only the whistle of a distant train disrupted my soul.

She finished the trimming and came inside, right before the rain began.

"I've got the tea kettle going. Want some tea?" I asked.

"Yes, please. It'll take the chill out of my bones." She rubbed her arms to warm herself.

"Which kind would you like: chamomile, ginger, peppermint?"

"Peppermint tea is fine," Mom said.

"Have a seat, Mom. I've been thinking. Have you given any more thought about moving here?"

"First let's talk about—"

"The accident," I cut in.

"Yes, and more precisely—"

"Why must you always be so precise?"

She paused. "I suppose I learned that from Aunt Lucie. She taught me how to sew, how to be precise with each stitch. I like things that fit properly. Maybe it helps me understand what I'm doing. I was impatient with the hand-baste stitch, until I realized how important it was."

"I hated that stitch when you tried to teach me how to sew."

"I do remember your endless sighs. If you don't hand baste first to hold the fabric still, things fall apart. Do the prep work first and things fall into place."

"You know that woodworker's tool I have on my desk? The No. 4 wooden hand plane that Dad made for me when I was little? He said it was for the prep work—to smooth the wood and prepare it for finishing. Said it had great balance, too."

Her response was long in coming. "He loved his woodworking as I love my sewing."

"Guess I did the prep work to get back on the tennis court. Worked hard at my physical therapy, my tennis workouts, and my job at the tennis center."

"You did. You're resilient. Look how far you've come," she said with enthusiasm. "Look at the vision you have for the event."

"But sometimes I feel something's off. Like my life is too focused on me.

"Well, perhaps First Serve is what you've discovered about yourself."

"What do you mean?"

"First Serve will benefit children who truly need help, beyond just recovering from surgeries. They need inspiration to see what's possible, to give them hope, to put smiles on their faces."

Christopher flashed through my mind. "Guess that's why I named the charity event First Serve."

She nodded.

I reached over the table and held my mother's hand. "About the accident. I'm really sorry what I put you through. I apologize. It was reckless and selfish of me."

"Yes, it was, Lucie. You must be careful with the decisions you make." She rose from her chair and kissed my forehead. "Now, about moving out here . . . I like the idea very much; let's plan on it once the charity event is over."

Chapter 51

That evening's rain brought hints of lavender light the next morning, a good sign for the First Serve event, despite the tension between my boss and me. As I finished my coffee on the back porch, the sunrise colors began to change to warmer hues of red. If only I could linger to enjoy the unfolding sight—but it was already six forty-five.

The ringing of the phone startled me. I answered. "Hello."

"Morning, Lucie. It's Jack. I need to see you. Get here as soon as you can."

"I'll be there by 7:30. Everything okay?"

"No, not really." He hung up the phone.

Now what? The fast-twitch muscle fibers tightened in my left leg, shaking like never before. I grabbed the counter to keep from falling over. Not now. I can't lose control today. I took a deep breath and sat down to scribble a note to Mom saying something came up at the tennis center.

I headed straight for Jack's office by way of the side entrance to avoid meeting with anyone. I knocked on his open door.

"Come in. Sit down."

Winded, I said, "What's happened?"

"Have you seen this?" He slid a newspaper in front of me.

I stared at the headlines, slack jawed: "Your Local Tennis Pro: An Arrest and Drug Use."

"This is horrible. What newspaper is this?" I turned over the cover to read: *The LA Spotlight*. "What the hell is this, Jack?"

"Some gossip rag. Louisa stopped at a 7-Eleven for coffee this morning and saw the headlines waiting in line at the cashier register. It's a big headline, but a short article. Let me read it to you."

When he finished, I struggled to quiet my fury. I held it inside. I looked up sharply at him.

"This is not right, Jack. I was not locked up in jail for days. You know about my arrest; I was not charged. I have no record. And yes, I took drugs when I broke my back, but not now. You know that by the drug test you require us to take. And yes, sometimes I drink too much vodka. But that's all. Good God, how many people have read this? Will it affect the charity event? Who wrote this?" I was exhausted from talking so much.

"Karen Mitchell."

My voice pitched. "This is character assassination!"

"Keep your voice down. Most people don't read that paper anyway. But we must be prepared. If anyone asks you about the article, tell them to speak with me."

"Okay," I stood up, still shaking.

"Let's get on with it. We have things to do before people start arriving at eleven."

"I need to speak with Louisa. May I take the newspaper with me?"

"Yes, take the paper."

Tears slipped down my cheek as I left his office.

"Hi, Louisa."

"Good morning, Lucie." She rose from behind her desk and hugged me.

"About Karen's article . . . it's humiliating. It's inaccurate and full of falsehoods."

"What do you expect from a paper like the *LA Spotlight?*

They create whatever they like and call it journalism. Isn't it fitting that Karen is on staff there?"

We both laughed.

"Lucie, I know how committed you are to the tennis center. This will pass. What do you want me to say if someone asks about the article?"

"Tell them to speak with Jack. Thanks Louisa. I'm headed to my office if anyone needs me."

~

The weather was perfect for tennis—no wind, low humidity, sunny, and seventy-four degrees. I stood by the window, checking off items on my trusty clipboard and occasionally looking out onto the courtyard. All was quiet.

Finally, I could relax for a few moments before the spectators arrived. My tummy rumbled like it used to right before a match; nervous energy that every athlete feels. It was a good sign. I thought of Dad when I first watched him playing tennis; the sheer joy of lifting the racquet in my hand and swinging freely that first time he took me out onto the court. It lit a fire in me all those years ago, a fire that had led me to this very moment.

I sat down on the couch and closed my eyes, thankful that the headache from the accident was no longer a visitor.

A few shouts from outside startled my gratitude. I bolted from my seat to see what was going on. Someone was climbing the fence. I called Jack. No answer. I called Louisa, busy signal. I called her again.

"Louisa, do you know where Jack is?"

"Yes, he's at the far end court with Omar, patching up the net."

"Please get him. There's someone out front yelling. I'm on way down now."

"Will do. Be careful, Lucie."

I darted out of my office, but took the stairs carefully then ran straight to the main entrance. A woman with a ball cap covering much of her face stood inside the main gate yelling and waving something.

A cold shiver shot down my spine when I realized who it was—Karen Mitchell, my old nemesis. Old fears entered in.

I swallowed hard. "What the hell are you doing here?"

"This event has been publicized in LA and all over the southwest. I wanted people to know the real you. That's why I came."

"How'd you get in?"

"Climbed the fence; it's not that high. Don't you remember? I'm a much better athlete than you." Her eyes surveyed me from top to bottom. "Still pathetically puny."

I took a few steps closer.

"How'd you like my article?" She jammed it in my face.

I stepped back. "Get your facts straight. You have no idea what you're talking about. You made up crap."

She seethed. "It's all there in the article!"

"Full of lies. You're a liar; you always *have* been a liar. You need to leave."

Karen slapped my face hard. I recoiled. The sting throbbed.

"Leave!" I pointed to the exit.

"Who do you think you are? Think you own this place and can boss people around, huh?"

"Just go."

She thrust her hands into my chest. I gasped.

I shoved her as hard as I could against the fence. "Go!"

With that, she took a big backhand swipe at my face. I sidestepped her, and she fell to the ground.

Jack ran toward us with Louisa following not too far behind. "Are you okay, Lucie?"

"She slapped me across the face and slammed into my chest."

Karen dusted herself off and said nothing.

"How'd she get in?" Jack asked.

"She climbed over the fence."

"That's trespassing. Karen, come with me." Jack grabbed her arm and led her to his office. "Louisa, call the police and have them meet us in my office."

~

"What happened, Mr. Simmons?" the police officer asked.

"I'll let Lucie Sampson explain, since she was directly involved in the incident."

After I gave my description, he asked whether I wanted to file charges. I conferred with Jack; we agreed. "Yes, officer," I answered, "we do."

"How ridiculous! You're not serious, are you?" Karen shouted. She stood cold, like her heart.

The officer looked over at Jack.

"Trespassing, assault and battery, officer," Jack said.

The broad-shouldered officer walked right at her. "Karen Mitchell, turn around." He cuffed her and read Karen her rights.

She shot a glance at me with her angry eyes. Eyes that could never hurt me again.

Chapter 52

At noon, Jack stepped up to the podium. He welcomed the crowd and thanked the sponsors for their generous support of the new Coachella Valley Children's Orthopedic Clinic. He introduced me and asked that I say a few words.

My legs shook as I walked up the steps to the podium. Nervous sweat stung the red mark on my face. I scanned the grandstand, hoping to see Sean, and found him in the front row with Christopher. Sean's steady smile helped me center. I took a deep breath to slow my heartbeat.

"Welcome all," I began. "Thank you for coming. This event is near to my heart. I was born with a bad hip, which made it difficult for me to walk correctly. But with the support and guidance of doctors and physical therapists, I learned how to play competitive tennis. Many years later, I suffered a broken back in an accident. To the young people who are here today, please remember that even when life's challenges weigh you down, you can always begin again. I did, and with hard work I became a tennis coach. Know that there is always someone to help you along the way, to push you through your limitations and help you set your sites higher than you ever imagined. Believe that it is possible. Never give up and never look back!"

I continued: "Now, we have a real treat for you today, as incredibly talented tennis players will play a mixed doubles

333

format. First group is Team Advantage, with Angela Overby from La Quinta and Allen Siegel from San Diego. They will play against Team Volley, with Jonathan Toomey from Houston, Texas, and Judy Kiley from UCLA."

I pointed to the second group. "Next, we have Team Ace with Michael Cervantes from Palm Springs and Sharon Jepsen from Tucson, Arizona. They will play against Team Smash, Donna Peterson from Chattanooga, Tennessee, and Brian Thurston from Santa Barbara. Each team will play two out of three set matches. The winners of the two matches will play against one another in the finals."

Jack stepped forward. "Thank you, Lucie. There will be a thirty-minute break before the finals. During the break, please walk around the grounds, visit the Pro Shop, or get a bite to eat at our grill."

The temperature had topped at eighty degrees with a slight breeze coming from the east, keeping conditions comfortable. To shield themselves from the bright sunshine, most people donned baseball caps or white, wide-rim tennis hats.

I watched a few matches, chatted with the young patients during odd-game crossovers, and took some candid photographs of the players and spectators. I noticed that Sean was no longer present, but I walked over to Christopher and his father, anyway, and introduced myself.

"Hello, I'm Lucie Sampson, Head Pro here. Thank you for coming."

"Nice to meet you. Dr. Wilson has spoken highly of you. This is Christopher, my son."

I smiled. "Great tennis action, huh!" I took off my ball cap. "Here, Christopher. I'd like you to have my hat; it's brand new. It'll keep the sun out of your eyes."

He beamed when I handed it to him.

"What do you say, Christopher?" asked his dad.

"Thank you, Miss Sampson," Christopher answered in a soft voice.

"You bet. Enjoy the matches."

All four matches were extremely close, heightening the suspense and enjoyment for all. The finals would not disappoint.

~

"Team Advantage with Angela and her partner, Allen, will play against Team Ace with Donna and her partner, Brian, for the Finals," I announced. "At the end of the match, we'll be giving away T-shirts to everyone—the same ones the players and I are wearing. The finals will be two-out-of-three sets."

Hardly any mistakes were made throughout the match. It was as if the players were putting on a clinic—hitting sharp angles, whistling cross-court forehands one after another, and serving aces. The spectators kept clapping.

When Angela served, she would extend her body toward the sky, arch her back, and strike the ball just as it reached its peak, often impossible for her opponents to return. Angela's strokes and movement were a thing of beauty, always with a fluid, clean swing and nimble, effortless footwork. Like the grace of a gazelle in flight. I teared up watching Angela. Oh, how I missed coaching her.

I overheard one kid say, "She makes it look so easy."

Another adult said, "She's so light-footed."

And another parent even added, "Her smooth backhand reminds me of Evonne Goolagong."

They were all spot-on, and I was thrilled at the spectators' reactions to the match.

Both teams played their hearts out. It came as no surprise that the finals went to three sets with Angela and Allen winning 7–5, 4–6, 7–5.

After the four players exchanged handshakes, I stepped up to the podium. "What a match! Congratulations to Team Advantage. How about a big round of applause for *all* the teams for playing such terrific tennis!" The applause of the spectators was truly incredible.

I continued, "Jack and I would like to thank you for coming out today and supporting this important cause. First Serve could not have happened without our big-hearted sponsors. A huge thank you to all of them. I would also like to recognize our coaching staff: Michael; Luke; Angela; our Executive Assistant, Louisa Alvarez; and our incredible maintenance and gardening staff, Will, Luis, Marianna, Omar, and Miguel."

The crowd kept clapping in appreciation. It was a wonderful sight. I waited, then spoke again. "One last thing. Personally, I'd like to recognize someone who was always on my side, rooting for me when I first learned how to play this sport. He's taught me a great deal about tennis and life. My coach and mentor, Mr. Jim Martin. He's here somewhere in the stands." I searched the grandstand and found him. "There he is." I pointed. "In the second row. Please stand, Coach." He did, and smiled at me.

"Coach Martin told me years ago that 'in life as in tennis, first serve then follow through.' Good advice, don't you think? Thank you all again for coming."

Lots of kids lined up outside the center court to get Angela's autograph. She had a brilliant idea.

"Lucie, can we bring some of the T-shirts over here and I'll autograph them?"

"You bet."

Michael and Luke stood near me. "Can you run up and get them, please?" I asked. They took off.

They returned with the T-shirts just in time. The reporters and photographers from the *Desert Chronicle* and the KNCB local affiliate circled the area, taking group photos of the players and the kids receiving their T-shirts. I glanced up at the grandstand. Many people had made their way to the parking lot except for a few people here and there. One person stood in the top row, right-hand corner. I squinted, shielding my eyes from the late afternoon sun to get a better look. The woman waved.

It can't be.

The woman took each step carefully as she walked down, waving, and calling out, "Lucie!" I took measured steps toward her as if matching hers, and we met at the bottom of the grandstand.

A small smile played on my lips before I whispered, "You came."

Chapter 53

"Lucie!" Jack called over to me and signaled for me to join him at center court, where he was surrounded by the journalists and television crews.

"Sorry, Jo. I'll be right back," I told my dear friend.

"Go. I'll be right here."

I hurried to Jack.

"They want to interview you now," he said.

The interview felt like it would never end. Fortunately, they asked easy questions, and nothing was said about Karen. I thanked them for covering the festivities and shook the producer's hand. We exchanged business cards, and I gave him and his crew some T-shirts.

"Thanks again." I gave some final instructions. "Walk toward the garden on the right and you'll see the parking lot straight ahead."

Angela came over and pulled me aside. "Karen?" she whispered.

"Jack called the police. They handcuffed her in Jack's office before the crowd came."

"Cuffed her," her eyes bulged.

"For trespassing and assault and battery."

Angela howled.

"More fun for you than me." I rubbed my jaw. "But get this—Joanne's here!"

"Where?"

"Over by the stands. I'll meet you inside the reception area. I need to speak with her now."

"Can't wait to celebrate!"

"Me either."

∾

I bee-lined to Joanne. Her dimpled smile said it all. "Big hug, Luce. I was a little late, but saw most of the matches."

"Let's sit for a bit. How are you? When did you get in? Where are you staying? Sorry, one question at a time," I laughed.

"I got in late last night with Dad."

"Is he here now?"

"He's at the hotel. We're staying at the Ingleside Inn."

"Is everything okay?"

"For the most part. Mom knows I came to the U.S. to locate him and attend your event. Five days ago, I tracked him down in St. Louis, Missouri, where he's been living for almost twenty years." Her voice dropped. "Seeing him after so many years was . . . I couldn't speak at first. I just cried. Too many conflicting emotions. It was wonderful in the strangest way! To feel that connection again. I believe in my heart he felt the same."

"And your mom?"

"I hope she will be happy that my research has paid off. She knows how I suffered after he left. Time will tell."

"Come with me." I was so excited, I danced a little jig. "Let's go."

"Slow down, Luce."

"Come on," I insisted.

We scurried back to the clubhouse by way of the garden, enjoying the red bougainvillea that lined the walkway. We were about to enter the clubhouse when several people caught my eye through the window. The reflective late afternoon glare made it rather difficult to make out who was in the lobby, except for a bearded man. I stopped short.

"Joanne, does your father have a beard?"

"Yes, why do you ask?" She drew her hand over her scar.

"I think he's inside." I opened the door.

"Dad!" Joanne's lips quivered. She walked up to him, shaking her head. "I was going to pick you up at the hotel."

"I know, honey, but I needed to do this my way."

Everyone most dear to me was gathered in this one place: Mom, Angela, Donna, Coach Martin, and Joanne. Mom stood between Coach and Joanne's father. Angela and Donna were seated next to them. No introductions were necessary, except one.

I walked up to Joanne's father. "Hi, I'm Lucie; remember me?"

"Of course, Lucie."

I fidgeted with my watch. "It's nice to see you. You've met everyone, I imagine?" I shook his hand.

"We've all met. Your mother and I had a nice chat. I was hoping we could all go out to dinner. I have so much to explain to you and Isabelle. Does it sound all right with you?

"Have you asked my mother?"

"He has," Mom said. It's fine with me only if it's okay with you." Mom's eyes had an added warmth to them, reminding me of Aunt Lucie.

I turned toward the group and spread my arms. "How about if we all meet in an hour at the Ingleside Inn in Palm Springs where Joanne and her father are staying? Donna and Angela can come with Mom and me in one car. Joanne has a rental car and can take Coach. Sound okay with everyone?"

Donna and Angela strutted toward me.

"We'll join you for a drink to celebrate the event," Angela said. "Donna and I've been invited by our doubles partners to join them for dinner across town.

"Okay, sounds like fun. See you shortly," I said.

$\sim$

Ingleside was a quiet, secluded hotel with an outstanding restaurant, Melvyn's, where the legendary Frank Sinatra used to hang out. The restaurant was known for its fresh ingredients and creative cocktails. Once you drove into the property, the high hedges created a sense of privacy until you entered the courtyard with several Spanish Colonial Revival casitas dotting the perimeter.

Everyone met at Joanne's casita with its large sun terrace that overlooked the San Jacinto mountains. After all the guests arrived, two waiters appeared seemingly from nowhere—right out of central casting, dressed in the classic black trouser and matching vest, white shirt with black bowtie, and the obligatory white cloth draped over their left arms. With a flourish, they balanced their trays and poured the bubbly into fluted glasses without an errant drop and offered a glass to each guest.

Angela clinked her glass with her car keys and began speaking to the group: "Donna and I cannot stay very long, as our doubles partners have invited us to dinner across town. Before we leave, I'd like to say a few things. This is a very special evening for all of us, a reunion between friends, between daughter and father, between student and coach. What brought us together is tennis, which has given me my livelihood and my friendships."

Angela raised her glass, scanned the faces of our group and concluded, "I am grateful to you all, and most especially to Lucie, my teacher and friend."

We clinked each other's glasses and chatted with one another.

I walked over to Angela, took her aside, and as my voice cracked said, "You are gracious, Ange. I've always known that. Thank you for what you said." I kissed her cheek.

We both turned when Donna spoke. "I'd like to say a few words, too, before we leave. As you know, Lucie, Angela, and I go way back to when we were teenagers. Together, we fought our way to the top of the junior national circuit. Laughed and cried along the way. Then our lives unfolded in different directions. We faced what life threw at us, and threw back at it as well. Life doesn't always give us what we want, yet somehow gives us what we need. For that, I am grateful to my friends, Lucie and Angela." Donna raised her glass. "So, a toast to friendships."

"Beautifully said, Donna," I whispered to her.

~

Mom, Joanne, her father, Coach Martin and I were all gathered around the dinner table.

Coach broke the ice. "So, Tomas, tell us how you ended up living in St. Louis. What brought you there, a job?"

I shot a glance at Mom, who gave a slight shrug to her shoulder, and then looked over to Joanne, who was stone-faced.

Tomas took a long sip of wine, then wiped his mouth with a napkin before answering. "It's a long story."

"Oh, Dad, keep it short, please," Joanne chuckled.

"After my divorce from Joanne's mother in the late 1960s, I moved to St. Louis, Missouri. I have worked as an airplane mechanic for many years. I also volunteered in the summer of 1973 after a massive fire at the National Personnel Records Center. Fifteen million veteran service files were destroyed.

"Out of how many?" Coach asked in disbelief.

"About twenty-two million. Almost 75 percent of the records were lost."

"Heartbreaking, Tomas," Mom said.

"How'd you help out?" I asked.

"Volunteers directed food and water distribution for all the construction, medical, and government personnel."

Coach Martin shook his head. "What a terrible mess. How'd they salvage the remaining records?"

"After the records were pulled from the debris, they were dried with a NASA vacuum-drying chamber technology that extracted the water. Space was needed for the files to dry out. That's when the parking lot became a tent city. Dozens of tents and thousands of milk crates were used to dry what was left of the veterans' records."

"How long did the clean-up take?" Mom asked.

"Over a year."

"Did you volunteer the whole time?" I asked.

"Yes."

"That's quite a commitment, Tomas," Coach said."

I looked over at Joanne and couldn't help noticing a calm dignity about her. I also couldn't help thinking about Aunt Lucie and the volunteer work she did at Christmas time with the international students studying at the Sorbonne.

Tomas sipped his wine before he spoke again. "I hope that wasn't too long of an explanation."

"Not at all. I tip my glass to you, Tomas," Coach said.

We all followed suit.

Tomas nodded, then asked Coach Martin, "Jim are you still a teaching pro on Long Island?"

"Yes. We've expanded our programs and just completed construction on two all-weather courts. I've also hired a full-time assistant pro. We hold several tournaments from May to October."

"Do you still have the parent-child tournament?" I asked, remembering the days Dad and I played that tournament together.

"It's one of the club's favorites!"

Coach announced that he had an early flight the next morning. Everyone said their good-byes. I walked out with him to the hotel's main entrance. My lips quivered when I spoke. "You've always been by my side, Coach. You once told me, 'Whatever you do, do it with heart.' I'll always remember that, and I'll always be grateful to you." I hugged him.

"Thank you, Lucie." He turned around and stepped into the waiting taxi.

Chapter 54

The steep San Jacinto mountains were the backdrop for our breakfast the next morning at my apartment. Joanne, Tomas, Mom and I enjoyed a vegetarian omelet, local pink grapefruit, and Mom's homemade, buttery croissant. And, of course, café au lait.

Joanne coaxed her father. "Dad, it's time."

"Very well," he said with a nod. "My daughter was relentless in locating me. Never thought I'd see her again. There are a few things I need to explain. After I graduated from college, I signed up for officer training in the U.S. Army Air Force. After ten months, I was assigned to the 422nd Night Fighter Squadron and shipped out to the European campaign in early 1942. On one of our missions over Belgium our plane was hit, forcing a crash landing in a field surrounded by barns. The crash injured five of us and killed my navigator."

"Dad, I didn't know that," Joanne said softly.

"My buddies and I were rescued by farmers who risked their own safety to help us. My left eye was slightly burned in the crash, which affected my distance and depth perception, thus ending my pilot career."

"That's why you have that scar over your left eye," Joanne said.

He nodded. "I joined Eagle Aviation in 1944. My job was to review data sheets and maintenance logs for the fuel tank pressurization and drain valves. When I began to analyze sets of figures, they didn't coincide with my own calculations. I re-calculated, thinking I'd made a careless mistake, but I got the same result. Things didn't add up. One day I witnessed two employees changing tolerance levels allowed on key parts and falsifying tests on airplane engines. I confronted them." Joanne's father stopped abruptly and gulped his coffee.

"Then . . . I made a terrible, terrible mistake. The two men offered me a lot of money to say nothing, to look the other way. I knew I was being silenced, but needed the income to support my family. I took the money and never reported their actions. Instead, I quit Eagle Aviation and found another job. A year later, when I heard through the grapevine that the Federal government was investigating some irregularities, I came forward to give state's evidence of what I had documented and my role in the wrongdoing.

"Officials recognized the precarious position my family and I were in. They described a new program called the Witness Protection Services. This was 1961. It was in its infancy and designed to protect people like me who were in possible danger of being harmed by guilty parties who knew they would be sentenced for crimes they committed. The government representatives believed we were at risk and recommended a new place for us to live.

"Several days later, we moved cross-country to California and lived under the protection services. It was a difficult life for us. We couldn't get close to people for fear we'd expose ourselves. Eventually, the strain caused Joanne's mother and me to divorce. That's when I moved to St. Louis, still under witness protection. Twenty years was long enough. I believed it was safe to surface and hoped that someday our family would reunite." He leaned back in his chair and looked at me and then Joanne, and then he smiled.

Mother and I remained quiet.

Joanne sat there, her arms crossed, listening to her dad. Finally, she spoke and looked right at me. "It was the 1978 'Restoration' article in the St. Louis newspaper that set things in motion. When I located Dad in St. Louis, he told me most of what he just told you both. Pretty stunning, huh? That's my Dad. A hero in my book." She beamed.

"I'm no hero. But there is one hero in this story: Charles Sampson. He and I were good friends from our tennis ball-boy days, then at Eagle Aviation and, of course, raising our families in the same town. I had confided in Charles about my role in the wrongdoing and that I had come forward to give state's evidence. He remained steadfast and told no one. Lucie, your father was a brave man. He protected both families, and at the cost of your friendship with Joanne.

"Thank you for telling us," I said. "Wish Dad were here, seeing us all together."

Mom looked over at me. "He is in spirit."

Chapter 55

Joanne and her father flew to Paris the next morning. Donna stayed for another day to visit the Desert Equestrian Center and thank the staff who took such good care of her horse. After seeing Donna off at the Palm Springs airport, I returned to the quiet of my office.

Today was the day I would tell Jack about a new program for the tennis center. If he didn't go along with it . . . well, I'd do it on my own somewhere else. It meant that much to me.

I picked up the framed photo of Joanne's father and my dad helping the player, Alice Marble, and smiled remembering the hours he and I played tennis together, the life lessons he gave me, and the moments we spent in the basement at his woodworking bench with dust dancing in the sunlight.

I gathered my thoughts. Deep down, I knew that this little girl had risen because of the love and grace of so many wonderful people. I chuckled when I heard my father's voice: "Never look back, Lucie."

I whispered, "I'm not, Dad. Only measuring how far I've come."

A knock at my door made me jump. I turned to see who it was.

"Hi, Sean, come in. It's good to see you." I tried to ignore my quickened heartbeat.

"Hi." His gaze met mine, his voice warm and inviting.

I walked around the desk to greet him. "I missed speaking

with you at the event. I introduced myself to Christopher and his father," I said.

"I know. Christopher told me. He wore the hat you gave him at his appointment yesterday."

I let joy settle in.

"Sorry I had to leave early," Sean said. "Had an emergency at the hospital. I understand the event was a big success. You and the staff raised a lot of money and lifted the spirits of our young patients who attended."

"Thank you. I appreciate you coming here in person. I know how busy you are."

"So are you." He stepped closer. "But can you squeeze in dinner with me this Saturday?"

"I'd like that."

"Pick you up at six-thirty, Saturday night, your place?"

I chuckled at his raised eyebrows. Grabbed a notepad from my desk and scribbled my address. "Here ya go. See you Saturday."

He grinned. "Great. See you then."

$\sim$

It was time to call my boss. I took a slow, deep breath and dialed. "Hi, Jack. If you have any time this afternoon, I'd like to discuss something with you."

"Why not come down now? I have a lesson in thirty minutes."

"Be right down." I rushed to his office.

As I walked in, he said, "Have a seat, Lucie. Does this have to do with Karen?"

"No. I've been thinking about something for a while now. I'd like to specialize in teaching tennis to kids with disabilities and to set up a new program here at the center."

He leaned back in his chair. "Well, you do have a great way with kids."

"Thanks. I'd like to work with kids in physical therapy and those with handicaps."

"Do you mean invalids?"

"I don't see it that way. They just have serious limitations. Introducing a sport will help them see what's possible for their lives."

"That's a tall order."

"I'd have to make changes in the way I teach and to understand each individual need." My left leg started twitching.

"It'll take some re-structuring of our programs and staff assignments. Any ideas on how we're going to afford this?"

"We can increase our fees a bit, especially to out-of-towners who come for the weekend. They've got big bucks. We can also create a philanthropy foundation to support the venture and hold an annual fundraising event, like First Serve. Maybe insurance companies will consider the lessons as physical therapy. I believe it would be good for the center and surely for the community."

Jack took a sip of water. "I don't know. It's a tremendous amount of work. Recently, I read about Brad Parks and his work with the disabled. He started wheelchair tennis right here in California, but he's gotten some resistance from the tennis community." His eyes challenged me. "You think it's worth the effort?"

"With all my heart, Jack. We all need encouragement and understanding, especially those with physical challenges. We have a responsibility to one another. I'll contact Brad Parks and learn from him and meet with physicians at the children's hospital. I'm sure we can do this.

"Well, you certainly have passion and purpose. We'd have to start small. A lot of details need to be worked out before we go public, like a business plan and a budget." He shook his head and smiled. "Yeah, Lucie. Let's go ahead and give it a try."

I rose from my seat, beaming. "Thank you, Jack! You won't be disappointed."

I hurried back to my office, too excited to sit with the thought of how we could make a difference in children's lives. I gazed at the painting Aunt Lucie gave me, *Starry Night Over the Rhône*. She was right. The bright stars, reflected on the dark water, had a calming effect. Hope overflowed in my heart for the children who would someday join our venture. For me, it was a new beginning. Tennis, like all sports, teaches us to problem solve, to persevere, to care. To uplift the human spirit beyond the field of play.

I finally realized that tennis had become my purpose in life. It had been right in front of my eyes all this time. How did I discover it?

First, serve.

Author's Notes

The September 3, 1933, *New York Times* photograph mentioned in the novel hangs in the living room of my home. It inspired me to write *First Serve*, as it represents how sportsmanship extends beyond the field of play. In the photo, one of the players on the tennis court, American tennis champion Alice Marble, had injured her eye. She is bent over near the net and attended to by my father and his friend who were teenagers serving as ball boys at the Westside Tennis Club in Forest Hills, New York, where the U.S. Nationals were held until 1977.

~

Alice Marble had a notable tennis career in which she won Grand Slam championships in Singles, Doubles, and Mixed Doubles from 1936–1940 at Wimbledon and the U.S. National Championships (now known as the US Open). In 1950, she challenged the tennis establishment to allow Althea Gibson, a Black women's tennis champion, to play the U.S. Nationals. Marble wrote in the July 1, 1950, edition of *American Lawn Tennis*, "If tennis is a game for ladies and gentlemen, it's also time we acted a little more like gentlepeople and less like sanctimonious hypocrites." That summer Gibson received an invitation to the U.S. Nationals and won the tournament in 1957 and 1958.

~

The French Open (another of the four Grand Slam Championships) is held in Paris for two weeks beginning in late May and ending in early June. The other Grand Slam is the Australian Open.

~

On July 12, 1973, a heartbreaking fire did occur at the National Personnel Records Center in St. Louis, Missouri, which destroyed over 73 percent of official military personnel files. The loss can only be an estimate because the records were not indexed nor did any computer database exist at that time. The files for 80 percent of Army personnel discharged between November 1, 1912, to January 1, 1960, were destroyed. In addition, the records of 75 percent of Air Force personnel discharged between September 25, 1947, to January 1, 1964, with names alphabetically after "Hubbard, James E." were also destroyed.

~

Brad Parks advocated for athletes with disabilities after he became paralyzed from the waist down as a result of a skiing accident. During his rehabilitation in 1976, Parks was introduced to recreational therapist Jeff Minnebraker and to wheelchair tennis as part of his treatment. By the early 1980s, a wheelchair tennis tournament circuit had been created with Parks at the helm. Today, wheelchair tennis has grown into a professional tour and is an official event in the Summer Paralympics. For his vision and efforts, Brad Parks was inducted into the International Tennis Hall of Fame in 2010.

Acknowledgments

I am grateful to many people for believing in this story and guiding me along the way. I offer my heartfelt thanks to:

Kathy Weyer, who read many drafts of the novel and remained steadfast with encouraging words and constructive criticism.

Denice Hughes Lewis, for her fresh perspective and attention to detail.

Kathryn Craft, for her excellent suggestions.

Spencer Anderson, for his wisdom.

Eliana Tobias, for reviewing passages and pages, and telling it to me straight   but always with a warm smile and good humor.

Bruce Rodin, for his incisive pen, valued counsel, and reassuring comments.

Nancy Clark and Julie Fatherley, for their encouragement and insights.

The Palm Springs Writers Guild organization that jump started my dream to write a novel.

Meredith Miller Richards, former librarian at the International Tennis Hall of Fame and Katie Harnett, Researcher and Education Manager, for their enthusiastic assistance in accessing the archives related to Alice Marble and Althea Gibson.

The late Millie West, a pioneer in women's athletics at the College of William and Mary, for our delightful conversations about her admiration of Alice Marble and the history of Title IX.

Elizabeth Michael Faxon, Pilates professional extraordinaire, for her advice on rehabilitative exercises.

Tony Palafox, my beloved tennis coach, who taught me the magic of the game of tennis.

Lynn Jones Green, copy editor, for her careful diligence.

Mark E. Anderson, AquaZebra publisher and book designer, for his calm and steady manner throughout the publishing process.

To my family, for their enduring love. And especially, to my sister, Sandra, for her generous heart and devotion to this story. She's the best cheerleader anyone could ever ask for.

About The Author

Cynthia Suzanne Sauer was born and raised in Long Island, New York, and has worked for most of her life in the field of education. She enjoys teaching students from diverse backgrounds and is inspired by their willingness to seek their own voice.

Cynthia is a Fulbright Exchange Fellow and taught at the Antwerp International school in Belgium, teaching the International Baccalaureate and researching WWI and WWII landscape memorials. Using that experience, she created a documentary, Remembrance and Reconciliation, based on Carl Sandburg's poem, "Grass." She also contributed to the iBook, Bringing the Great War Home, produced by the University of North Carolina, Virginia Tech, and The American Battle Monuments commission.

Cynthia was a ranked junior on the tennis circuit, played in college, and was a teaching pro for a decade. She is a certified professional with the Professional Tennis Registry, the preeminent international tennis coaching organization, and a member of the United States Tennis Association. Her passion for the sport has led Cynthia to work in media services for the Connecticut Open, the Winston Salem Open, and the BNP Paribas Open in Indian Wells, California, where she now lives.

Cynthia holds degrees from the University of Tennessee and Columbia University. An avid hiker, bicyclist and photographer, she also serves as a volunteer for the Disabled American Veterans, and is a member of the Palm Springs Writers Guild.

Visit Cynthia at www.CynthiaSuzanneSauer.com.

www.ingramcontent.com/pod-product-compliance
Lightning Source LLC
Chambersburg PA
CBHW030632020726
47493CB00006B/1682